NED'S CIRCUS OF MARVELS

THE DARKENING KING

JUSTIN FISHER has been a designer, illustrator and animator for both film and television. He has designed title sequences for several Hollywood films, branded music TV channels and has worked extensively in advertising. But after many years of helping to tell other people's stories, he is now following a lifelong passion and writing his own. Justin lives with his wife and three young children in London. He has never worked in a circus but he can juggle. Sort of.

~NED'S~ CIRCUS OF MARVELS

THE DARKENING KING

JUSTIN FISHER

HarperCollins *Children's Books*

First published in Great Britain by
HarperCollins *Children's Books* 2018
HarperCollins *Children's Books* is a division of HarperCollins*Publishers* Ltd,
HarperCollins Publishers
1 London Bridge Street
London SE1 9GF

The HarperCollins website address is:
www.harpercollins.co.uk
1

ISBN 978–0–00–812458–8

Justin Fisher asserts the moral right to
be identified as the author of this work.

Typeset in Garamond/12pt by
Palimpsest Book Production Ltd, Falkirk, Stirlingshire
Printed and bound by CPI Group (UK) Ltd, Croydon CR0 4YY

MIX
Paper from
responsible sources
FSC C007454

This book is produced from independently certified FSC™ paper
to ensure responsible forest management.

For more information visit: www.harpercollins.co.uk/green

For C

Thank you again, and again and again.
For always and for everything

X

CONTENTS

PROLOGUE

The vast forests of the East Siberian taiga cover more than a million square miles, from impenetrable marshlands to unending carpets of ancient woodland teeming with bears, reindeer and other more secretive creatures not often seen by man. Of all of its villages, few are more forgotten or remote than Kazimir.

Captain Nikolai Volkov and his men had travelled all the way from Irkutsk. The city was home to the 24th Spetsnaz Brigade and the young captain had long been counted in their ranks as the man to "get things done". He was not in a good mood. The stories he'd heard were not untypical for such remote parts of the region. Superstitions and old wives' tales about "magic and monsters", silly stories to keep their children from straying into the woods and a complete waste of Volkov and his specialist task force's time. The cramped cabin of his DT-30 mobile base was at least warm, though its powerful diesel engine was interminably loud and smelt even worse than it sounded. Outside, the twenty-five-strong squad of men travelled on sledges behind harnessed reindeer. Each one carried GPRS tracking devices, night-vision goggles, grenade launchers, specialist automatic rifles and every other gadget and technological advancement that the mighty Russian Army provided. But their most valuable asset was the Siberian reindeer. Reindeer did not break down and a reindeer could travel through a forest's thickest region where a twenty-tonne troop carrier could not.

The villagers of Kazimir had greeted them with teary eyes. Salvation had finally come after months of begging. It was only when officials from the local district had ventured into the woods and subsequently disappeared that the high-ups from Irkutsk had ordered Volkov to the area.

"Go, Nikolai, put these poor villagers' minds at rest," they had said. "We know it's a bear, you know it's a bear, but the denizens of Kazimir need proof."

That had been days ago and here he was now, in the middle of a forest with the most highly trained pest control unit in the world.

"Magic and monsters," he muttered, as the DT-30's caterpillar tracks ground to an icy halt.

Bang, bang! came the pounding on the cabin's hatch. "Captain Volkov, the transport can go no further."

Volkov stepped out into an impossibly cold night. Even his gruelling training could not stop him from pausing to catch breath. It must have been -55°C at least. Surely not even a bear could withstand this cold? And anyway, didn't bears hibernate in the winter months? In front and behind the forest lay black; their DT-30 had taken them as far as its tracks would allow.

"A curse on this cold, a curse on Siberia and a curse on this blasted mission!"

"Your orders, captain?"

His number two, though covered in extreme snow gear, was easy enough to recognise for the simple fact that he was the size of a bull. Galkin was younger by almost a decade but in Volkov's opinion as able a leader as he was and Volkov was always glad of it.

"Take three men and scout the way forward; we'll follow with the supplies."

The bull saluted and paced on ahead.

Volkov never liked to walk through a forest at night. It made him feel as though the stars had been sucked out of the sky. After more than an hour, even the deep winter snow could no longer find its way through the taiga's wooded canopy. There were no stars above and no snow below, just the ice-cold embrace of a pitch-black wood. As they trudged through the frozen mud and pines, Volkov's gut started to twitch. His gut had never let him down. Like a dog sensing danger long before it arrives, Volkov's gut always told him when trouble was brewing and the reindeer clearly agreed. The beasts came to a complete standstill, honking in their throats nervously, their hooves skittish on the ground.

"What's got into them?" seethed the captain.

As a born and bred Siberian, no one knew more about reindeer than Volkov's handler, not even the actual reindeer.

"I wish I knew, captain. I've never seen them like this, never."

Volkov's gut began to rumble more steadily. A quick gesture of his hand and his column of men pulled down their night-vision goggles. Everything turned to electric green and the reindeer stopped. As Yenotov and the other handlers pushed and prodded their now immobile animals, something through the trees moved with a flicker of dark green over black. Volkov raised his weapon and those not tending to the herd followed suit. The targeting dot from his laser slowed by a tree and something behind it moved.

"Six o'clock."

"Eight."

"Eleven."

One by one his men called out movement in the trees, and seemingly from everywhere.

"Brace!" ordered Volkov.

The Spetsnaz dropped to one knee and prepared to fire.

All of a sudden, their supply column of reindeer broke free and fled from their handlers, all twelve animals with their heavy packs and Volkov's much-needed supplies bolting as a feathered storm flew at the squad, a flapping of a hundred wings, magpies, pigeons, sparrows and hawks, swallows, barn owls, finches and crows, filling the air in a living squall, then just as suddenly parting.

Nothing.

Volkov and his bemused men got back to their feet and were trying to understand what had just happened when the first scream called through the darkness ahead of them.

Without a word, his men fanned out wide, running as

best as they could through the undergrowth and straight to the sound of their screaming comrades. A little way forward something big was running towards them, crashing through branches with all the violent force of a crazed animal. It was Galkin, Volkov's number two.

His helmet and scarf had come away, lost somewhere in his flight, and his eyes rolled wildly in their sockets. The man was crazed with terror. Volkov had seen this before with new recruits, young soldiers that had no place with the Spetsnaz, but Galkin? The man was unbreakable, or at least had been until now.

"Galkin, calm yourself. What happened?"

"M-mmm—"

Volkov grabbed the man by the shoulders and shook him hard.

"What, man? What are you saying?"

"M-magic and... and m-monsters," Galkin finally managed.

Two of the squadron stayed with their sobbing second in command, as Volkov led the others forward. Some way through the forest the trees began to thin till they came to a vast clearing. At its centre firepits bellowed and a great iron structure jutted out of the ground like an angry tooth. To Volkov it looked very much like the beginnings of some fortress. The Spetsnaz had grade one clearance – they would know of such a thing, surely? Why had he not been informed? And what had happened to the sky? At first he thought he was looking at a mirror, or that the world had turned upside down. The air was black with smoke from the firepits, and the stars – every one of them had fallen to the ground. They lay along the clearing, too many to count. A great wondrous carpet of yellow and white in all its shimmering glory. Volkov and his men removed their goggles.

And the stars roared.

What had looked like heaven quickly became hell. The stars were not stars at all but the eyes of a great horde, monsters from old wives' tales suddenly made real. From the lick of orange light spewing out of the firepits, the Spetsnaz saw row upon row of hideous creatures, fanged, clawed, hoofed and winged, edging their way closer and preparing to strike.

Captain Nikolai Volkov let his rifle drop to the floor. As his end approached, he could think of only one thing to say. It fell from his lips with no particular recipient in mind and it was to be the last three words that he would ever speak.

"Magic and monsters."

CHAPTER 1

Godshill

Godshill on the Isle of Wight was as pretty a village as the Armstrongs could ever hope to find. Spring was finally rearing its head, bees buzzed along the thatched roofs of its ancient cottages, and a large medieval church at its centre could not have drawn a prettier picture. Ned and his little family had never found the time to go on holiday. He thought, as they walked down the road, how nice it might be to come back here one day, when they actually could. But here and now, like always, there was only the hunt, and the Armstrongs were in the unique position of being both predator and prey.

He'd lost count of the hotels and motels they'd stayed in. Never staying for more than a day at a time because of what they were searching for, and what – or rather who – was searching for them. As far as Ned could tell, *everyone* was looking for the Armstrongs, and on both sides of the Veil.

Backpacks, T-shirts, jeans and jumpers – holiday gear for the perfect "happy family". Only, the Armstrongs hadn't been truly happy for quite some time. "Happy" was for families that weren't on the world's most wanted list. "Happy" was for people who had the time to buy an ice cream and sit in the sun. And herein lay the problem – the Armstrongs and the world that they lived in had run out of time.

The Darkening King was on the brink of rising.

They now stood on a street corner outside Mavis's Ye Olde Tea Shoppe, est. 2012. It was the sort you find dotted about the villages of England, particularly ones frequented by tourists. What was not known was that Mavis's Tea Shoppe was in fact a safe house for the Hidden, especially those who had run out of places to hide. It was one of her rarer and more nocturnal patrons that the Armstrongs had arranged to come and see.

"Whiskers?" called out Ned's dad.

There was a muffled squeak from somewhere in Ned's backpack.

"Remember everyone on the other side knows about Ned and his mouse – that means you, furball. Not a squeak out of you till we get back to the caravan park, or you'll blow our cover."

The backpack remained deathly quiet.

"What's he doing?"

"Err, I think he's following orders, Dad."

"Right. Good. Now, son, wait here. Me and your mum need to check the place out first."

"Just a tick, darling, and don't talk to any strangers," added his mum.

Ned's eyes rolled and his parents opened the door to the welcoming *ding* of a bell. "Don't talk to strangers" was what you told a six-year-old – not someone who had saved the world. Twice. But it was always the same now, wherever they went. And the truth was – they had every right to worry. Ned's ring no longer listened to him when he tried to use his powers, and his mum and dad had become so protective that he was barely allowed to do anything any more, except sit and wait with his shadow and his wind-up mouse.

He slumped on to the steps of the tea shop. Across the street he saw an old man in a tweed jacket, huffing and puffing with a Zimmer frame to steady his balance. He was tall and spider-leg thin, with barely any remaining white hair and a long reddish nose that seemed to be attached to the rest of his face with a criss-cross pattern of wrinkles.

He was struggling across the road towards Mavis's and when he looked towards Ned he smiled between great rasping breaths. The poor old dear either thought that he knew Ned, or that Ned might be able to help him on his way, which of course Ned would. Stranger or not, the man needed help.

"Hello. Are you all right?" Ned asked.

Now almost on the other side, the old man grinned at Ned, revealing quite the most extraordinary set of teeth. They all pointed in different directions. Some were grey or brown, others chipped or missing, and one looked as though it would have been more at home in the mouth of a dog.

"I will be, young man, with a little assistance," he rasped.

But Ned couldn't take his eyes off the man's teeth.

"Might I bend your ear for a moment?"

As he spoke, a small device in Ned's pocket began to shake. It was the perometer that his great friend George had given him a few months earlier, when the Armstrongs had had to leave the Circus of Marvels and go on the run. The device could sense danger, and as it began to shake, Ned stumbled to his feet. The old man let go of his Zimmer frame, his bony fingers instead reaching into his jacket pocket. When they came out again he was holding a thin-bladed dagger, and his eyes shone black.

"Gor-balin!" spat Ned.

"Yes, boy! Been watching Mavis's for weeks, I have. End of the road for you, my friend."

Gor-balins were not uncommon amongst Darklings and were often sent on missions across the Veil's borders, due to their more human size and shape. But as the creature's glamour began to fade, Ned was reminded that that was where the similarities ended. The creature walked upright and easily now, the whites of his eyes turned black and his skin darkened to a wet, mottled grey. His nose grew more crooked, the tips of his ears longer, and his bony fingers now ended with claws.

"I wouldn't come any closer if I were you," stammered Ned.

"Why, what you gonna do about it?" jeered the gor-balin. "Not much, is what I heard…"

Ned raised his hand and focused on the band of metal at his finger – the same band of metal that had flattened a whole host of the creatures on the rooftops of St Clotilde's. But that had been a different time and a very different Ned. He thought of ice and the air around his finger shimmered with intent. As he pictured the atoms in his mind coming together and growing still, he could feel the ring's tendrils hum under the pores of his skin. And for a moment, just a fraction of a moment, he thought his powers had finally returned.

"Please," he whispered.

The air crackled with the brief sparking of atoms and then, just as it had a hundred times before, his ring grew quiet and the air stilled.

"I said, don't come any closer!" said Ned, trying to sound braver than he felt.

The dark hollows of the gob's eyes shone and his lips broke into a smile. He walked forward, slowly now, relishing every second as Ned backed away further down the alleyway that ran alongside Mavis's tea shop.

"So it's true... Not the boy you was then, are you? You ain't nothin' without your mum and dad."

The creature was right. But even now, powerless as he was, Ned wasn't alone, not quite.

"To be fair, I did try and warn you. Gorrn?" he breathed.

Ned's shadow – his slovenly familiar – did not make tea, or do the dishes. In fact, there were relatively few things the creature did well, except for fighting and biting.

"Arr," said the shadow, and the smug grin on the gor-balin's face was promptly removed as the darker recesses of the alley began to shift.

The shadow that was Gorrn raised himself up from the ground as a wall of toothy darkness, thickening and darkening as he stretched to fill the width of the alleyway between Ned and his assailant.

"Grak!" spat the gob.

And in a violent and silent second, Gorrn lunged, enveloping the Darkling in his folds before spitting him out like a mouthful of chewed food and into one of Mavis's green recycling bins.

A shaken Ned closed the lid on the unconscious assassin, quickly and quietly.

"Thanks, Gorrn."

His familiar oozed back to the ground before blending into thc shadows.

"You there, Whiskers?"

"Scree."

"I know Dad told you to be quiet and keep our cover, but next time someone comes at me with a knife can you assume the cover's been blown and, you know, do something useful?"

The Debussy Mark Twelve remained silent.

Ned's heart was pounding for more reasons than he could count. For one thing, Barbarossa's minions were dangerously close, and not for the first time. Had it not been for Gorrn, the assassin would have ended him then and there. But that wasn't what was really troubling him. What really scared him was that he still couldn't work his Engine, no matter how hard he tried. How was he ever going to defeat the Darkening King if he had no powers? Not to mention the fact that if his parents found out about his face-off in the alley, they'd wrap him in so much protective cotton wool that he'd end up suffocating. He'd tell them later, after the tea room and in his own good time. He hid the gob's Zimmer frame down the alleyway and out of sight, and paced back to the corner of Mavis's tea shop.

"Not a word about this, from either of you. Not till we get back, OK?"

"Arr."

"Scree."

"I thought I told you – no talking to the mouse, Ned!"

Ned looked up to see that his dad had come back out of Mavis's to get him.

"Sorry, Dad. I thought, erm… there was nobody about so…"

His dad cocked his head slightly.

"You OK, son? You look a bit ruffled."

Gorrn shifted guiltily along the ground by Ned's foot.

"I'm fine, Dad, just a bit nervous, you know? About who it is we're going to see."

"Well, keep your wits about you. Danger could be lurking anywhere."

"Yes, Dad, anywhere…"

CHAPTER 2

Afternoon Tea

Mavis's was in fact just as it should have been. Scones, cake, proper teapots with proper tea and lacy pink curtains to match the lacy pink tablecloths. It was also, much to Ned's surprise, completely empty apart from an extremely overdressed and bejewelled lady – presumably Mavis, thought Ned. No doubt her business was going well, though you wouldn't know it from the state of her empty premises. His dad walked up to the counter and spoke to her quietly, leaving Ned with his mum.

"Do you think he – *it* – will actually be there?" Ned asked his mum.

"I hope so, darling. I'm so tired of all the running and chasing. All the grinning and pretending we're on holiday."

"You know, we could lose the grinning? It's not like everyone's always happy when they're on holiday. We could pretend we've come down with some sort of tummy bug – you know, from all the exotic hotel food?"

His mum chuckled. "Oh, Ned, we're on the Isle of Wight, not Outer Mongolia. The food's good but hardly exotic."

"You're right, Mongolia was last week," smiled back Ned.

"Was it? Oh yes, that dreadful business with the cyclops. Do you know, I thought it was Spain for some reason."

"That was the week before."

Ned watched as his dad passed Mavis a brown envelope full of used notes. She peered in and nodded appreciatively, then returned the favour by passing something small over the counter and tipping her head towards a door at the rear of the shop in a way that said, "Over there but I didn't tell you."

The happy holidaymakers that were Ned and his family made their way down a cramped corridor, past a loo, towards the door at the back. They walked through and found themselves in a small windowless room with red velvet wallpaper and a pair of long-backed mahogany chairs arranged either side of a tall mirror.

Ned saw it and sighed. "Really?"

"Yes, really," said his dad.

"I thought we agreed, no more mirrors!"

Olivia Armstrong managed to look quite sheepish, which was not something the ex Mother Superior and Circus of Marvels agent was prone to do.

"Ned, we have avoided mirrors at every possible turn. We have travelled in the cargo holds of freighter ships, aeroplanes, a military troop carrier… even strapped to the bottom of a horse-drawn cart. This is completely unavoidable. Where we're going isn't on any map – it's in the mirror-verse."

Ned's few experiences of stepping through mirror-portals had not for the most part been pleasant.

"*In* it?!" he shrieked at a far higher pitch than he'd intended.

"Safest safe house in existence. Son, this is the closest we've come in months. The last three informants were murdered before we even got there and Spain… well, Spain was an unmitigated disaster."

His dad was not wrong. The "informant" they'd gone to meet had turned out to be an agent for the BBB, and had it not been for some quick thinking from Olivia, and Gorrn providing cover for a speedy getaway, the Armstrongs' mission would have come to an end. It had only been after the battle over At-lan that Ned and his family had discovered who the BBB actually were. A josser network of highly trained spies, seemingly with unending resources and a fascination with the Hidden in all their forms. Their goal? No one really knew. But the BBB were getting better, smarter and more cunning. Everywhere the Armstrongs turned the message was the same – they were after Ned and his family and would go to any lengths to find them.

"Yes, it was a disaster, Dad, and your sources could be wrong about this too. We don't know what's on the other side of that mirror."

"Nor what's behind us."

For a moment Ned thought about Barbarossa's assassin still lying unconscious in a wheelie bin outside. And there could be more on their way.

"Fine," managed Ned.

"Right," said his mum. "Let's go and find ourselves some trouble, eh?"

Given that trouble was regularly finding them, maybe turning the tables wasn't such a bad idea.

His dad held the sliver of glass that Mavis had given him, and the Armstrongs all joined hands. Then quietly and without fuss they proceeded to walk through the mirror.

That was the thing about trying to find a Demon – they always seemed to hide in the most awkward places.

CHAPTER 3

The Door

Ned had only travelled by mirror a handful of times. Even so, he still had to adjust his brain as he pressed his nose to the glass. His reflection appeared to wrap around him somehow, and the glass had give. It was cold – somewhere between ice and water. Not slush exactly; slush was wet. But not dry either. More like jelly, only without its stickiness.

His reflection warped and blurred and joined with another until, quite seamlessly—

Shluup.

Ned popped out on the other side as though nothing had happened.

"This is it, son," said his dad. "Mavis's *real* tea shop."

In front of them was a single carved door with images of fair-folk and Darklings all about its entrance. What was strange and very mildly terrifying was that it appeared to float on thin air, just above the red carpet they were standing on. Above and below was a starry sky with no moon to light it but what looked like the aurora borealis – a great dancing show of coloured light playing out around them.

"Wow," said Ned. "Where are we?"

"Well, son, technically Mavis's tea shop isn't anywhere. Those stars out there are actually mirrors, just like the one we stepped through. This is somewhere in between the reflections, between the light. Geographically speaking, 'here' doesn't really exist—"

"Now, Ned, I don't need to spell out the dangers," interrupted his mum.

"Yes, son, you've not been yourself for a while now, so if there's trouble in there, you leave it to me and your mum, OK?"

Ned bristled, but he knew he was right. Ned was like a tiger without claws – no more capable of defending himself than the boy he'd been before discovering the Hidden and his powers. His mum saw the look on his face.

"Terrence Armstrong, sometimes your mouth gets in the way of your brain! Ned, darling, you're finer than fine. It's just a phase. I'm sure plenty of Engineers before you went through just the same sort of thing, and anyway, I don't have any powers, do I? There's nothing strong bones, a highly developed set of reflexes and quick thinking can't get you out of!" said his mum, clearly trying to sound upbeat.

Ned knew she didn't really believe it, just as surely as he knew she was wrong, but he smiled as best he could.

"That said, stay close," urged his dad. "Now…"

They turned to the door. The entrance was completely silent, and Ned wondered whether the mirrored version of the tea shop was as empty as the one they had passed through to get there. A pink neon sign rearranged itself from a jumble of words till it read, MAVIS'S YE OLDE TEA SHOPPE, and then the sign changed again to: NO COFFEE DRINKERS ALLOWED.

Its oak door had the most lifelike carving at its front in detailed knots of intricately tooled wood. Ned had to blink – it looked very much like the Mavis they had seen back on the Isle of Wight, only "woody", and both younger and a little less full in the face.

"Who are you?" croaked the wood.

Ned gawped – there was little he hadn't seen behind the Veil, but this was definitely his first talking door.

Ned's mum paused for a second, quickly recalling the cover story they had decided on before setting out.

"Ahem," began Olivia in quite the regal tone, "I am the Lady de Laqua, with my warlock and nephew, Tarquin."

The carving's wooded eyes peered at them slowly, till the entire door started to shake, before breaking into creasy, knotted laughter.

"Ha ha ha! Come on, dear, no one ever tells me their real name here, but Tarquin?! Looks more like a Cecil to me."

Ned's mum scowled at Ned, as though he had somehow let them down by not looking "Tarquin-ish" enough.

"It matters not," said the door. "Everyone is welcome here, just as long as you have coin. You do have coin, don't you?"

"Yes – yes, we have coin," replied Ned's mum.

"ENTER!" croaked the door and flung itself wide.

CHAPTER 4

Boiling

They were met by a wall of colour, sound and heat. Mavis's Ye Olde Tea Shoppe was bursting at the seams with its tea-drinking patrons and, to Ned's amazement, there was not one but at least a dozen other Mavii all in the same heavy make-up and outfits as the one on the Isle of Wight. They moved through the crowd with all the skill and expertise of a lifetime pouring tea. Quick, amiable and with no time for nonsense.

"Doppelgängers," whispered his mum. "Don't stare."

"Well, that's one way to save on staff," breathed his dad, his nerves finally settling into the mission at hand.

At its very centre Ned saw the real Mavis, who was at least in looks completely identical to her counterparts working the room, except for one amazing and inescapable difference. The real Mavis was a giant. Ned could only get a proper look at her from the waist up, but she must have been at least thirty feet in height and her great warbling voice shrilled with banter and laughter in equal measure, seemingly having several conversations at the same time. Around her was a great circular bar area arranged on three floors and the heavily bejewelled Mavis had teapots for rings on brown-stained fingers, pouring her cups ten at a time and on every floor. Her great earrings swung like chandeliers and she was coated in at least a gallon of make-up. Great rollers the size of tractors were in her hair and her shimmering dress was in gaudy, sequinned reds. It appeared that only an original outfit would do for the original Mavis. No matter how loud the raucous tea room got, her voice carried over all of it.

"My darlings, yes, of course!" she boomed to a boisterous gathering on the top floor. "Have you tried my new range in health teas? A little antioxidant? It'll give you zip! We've Ener-tea, Strawber-tea and my absolute favourite, Zipi-tea. That's trademarked, by the way, so don't get any funny ideas."

For a moment Ned felt on familiar ground, as if he was at a party at the Circus of Marvels. All the fear, all the worry from running and hiding finally ebbed away as he took in the splendour and fanfare of a Hidden get-together, with its bunting and pretty lanterns floating in mid-air. Soft music was being played by a band of nymphs on the second floor and all around them the air seemed to bubble. It was only when Ned's eyes adjusted that he began to notice why, and he finally understood why it was so hot. Every wall had built-in glass kettles that were constantly boiling away, ready to create one of Mavis's multicoloured concoctions. Every tea imaginable, catering to every taste, was on show. The smell of herbs and spices was dizzying. Saffron and cardamom, lily and sage, rose water, bluebell and forget-me-not. And further along into the darker corners of the tea room were pickled egg, carcass and swamp bile. Because as Mavis had explained to them – "everyone was welcome at Mavis's", even Darklings.

Ned's mum put a heavy hand on his shoulder as they inched their way through the crowd. "Stay close," she whispered.

Ned had no intention of doing anything else. They were deep now in the Hidden's underbelly. From the dwarves to the dryads, each and every one was hiding from something. What astounded Ned was that they could share a room, let alone a table, with Darklings. Goblins, pirates and cut-throats, imps and a pair of nightmongers, who were creatures too foul to share a table with anyone. How it hadn't erupted into outright violence was beyond Ned, till he walked past a table where a blue-painted dwarven berserker was in a heated debate with a knot-skinned mud-goblin, its hair and teeth a mess of rooty browns.

"You owe me for that cup, Guldrid – now pay up!"

"Want payin', do ya?!"

The mud-gob threw his teacup at the dwarf, who barked in pain before smashing the table clear in half. No sooner had the sound of breaking china been heard than a giant arm came tearing through the room. The arm belonged to Mavis.

"NO FIGHTING IN MY TEA ROOM!" she bellowed.

The music, along with everything else in the room, suddenly stopped.

Realising what they'd done, the guilty parties pleaded in terror.

"Preease, we meant no 'arm," begged the mud-goblin.

"RULES IS RULES!" warbled Mavis, and in one great sweep she grabbed both dwarf and goblin and hurled them out of a third-storey window.

There was no ugly splat outside, just their horrified cries as the two brawlers were launched into the mirror-verse, destined to float there long after they both had starved.

"Blimey," whispered Ned.

"Shh," replied his mum.

"WHAT IS RULES?" boomed the giantess now, with none of the cheeriness she'd shown only a moment ago. Her great eyes peered at the crowd defiantly, demanding a reply.

"Rules is rules!" warbled the crowd, no doubt with more than a pinch of fear-induced bravado.

"THAT'S MORE LIKE IT. MUSIC!"

The band started up again and seconds later the incident was seemingly forgotten.

Ned's dad tapped one of the Mavii on the back. With all the commotion they were now running late for their appointment.

"Excuse me, madam?"

She turned with a blue-shadowed flutter.

"Yes, sir. Fancy a cuppa?"

"No, thank you."

The mini Mavis scowled.

"I mean, yes, shortly. But, you see, we're here to meet someone." He whispered a name into her ear and the waitress's face blanched.

"Are you sure?"

"The name's quite correct. We were told that he had something for us."

"No, I mean are you sure you *want* to meet him?"

Ned's parents both nodded.

"I see. You had better follow me then."

Past a throng of mercenaries and several other Mavii, their waitress took them to a dark corridor leading away from the main hall.

"This is the VIP area. If you need anything, feel free to scream."

She knocked on an unmarked door.

"Enterrr."

"I'll leave you to it. Remember, scream if you need me – one of us will hear."

The mini Mavis moved back down the corridor as fast as she could, making no secret of her desire to leave them to it. As soon as she was out of earshot there was an audible "Unt" from Ned's shadow. Ned's familiar and trusted bodyguard, bound to him as a servant to do his bidding at whatever cost, made his feelings quite clear. "Unt" meant a lot of things, but in most cases it meant "No". Gorrn would not be entering the room with them.

"Oh, fine," sighed Ned. "If you must stay out here, at least try to blend in."

The undulating mystery that was Gorrn did just that and merged with a shadow by the door.

A room full of tapestries and Persian rugs was waiting for them. At its centre was a low, round table surrounded by luxurious silk cushions. It was all very dimly lit except for a small sprite-light that was presently dancing on the table. The little creature looked quite unhappy about the VIP she was dancing for and it was only when the creature leant out of the shadows that Ned could see why.

Some Demons, even in their human form, are not pretty.

CHAPTER 5

The Demon in the Tea Room

As the Demon's face came out of the shadows, Ned caught his breath. He was wearing a red velvet suit with black collars. In one hand was a ceramic cup full to the brim with a tarry, burning liquid. It flamed gently as he sipped from its edge, but it was his face that made Ned wince.

The Demon's hair was immaculately groomed, slicked back with oil that smelt like coal. Its skin in contrast was as frail as old parchment and stretched across high cheekbones and a deeply lined brow. Black veins crept across its pores as though the creature carried some terrible disease, yet even in its weakened state it brimmed with quiet power, like some deposed king unseated from its throne but still sure of its rightful place.

"You are late," he breathed.

"There was some commotion in the bar," began Ned's dad.

The Demon responded with a smile that wasn't a smile.

"There is some commotion everywhere."

And the expression he wore was between sorrow and something else, some deep trouble that refused to reveal itself. The Armstrongs took their places at the table, Ned's mum making sure that her son was furthest away from the creature that they had come to meet. The little sprite-light was clearly happy to have less frightening visitors and proceeded to glow with more of a spark. To Ned's amazement, the perometer in his pocket was quite still but all the same he drew it out subtly and laid it on the floor under the table, its lid open. There was a rustling from his backpack, which he promptly thumped before sheepishly laying it to one side.

"Thank you for agreeing to meet us," began Ned's mum.

"Whether you thank Sur-jan later remains to be seen."

The soft-spoken Demon they were talking to had never met Olivia Armstrong, which she was about to make quite clear.

"Demon, you are at a disadvantage. You see, I have come across your kind before yet this is the first time that you have come across me. I have always walked away in good health — those in my wake have been less fortunate. Do not mistake me or my family for cowering jossers. We know well how to deal with your kind."

The hairs on Ned's neck began to prickle uncomfortably. Picking a fight with a Demon was considered suicide no matter what his mum claimed. Coupled with the long arm of Mavis and her tea-stained fingers, a scrap of any kind at the tea room would not bode well.

The Demon's eyes thinned and his cup rattled. Under the table the perometer's needle turned briefly to Sur-jan before settling languidly again.

"I know well the Armstrong name wo-man. It is not I that would trouble you, but what I have to say."

Terry Armstrong put his hand over his wife's and she started to un-brittle.

"Sur-jan, many of your kind have fled the Demon strongholds at great risk, choosing to live amongst the jossers rather than remaining with their kin. If what I believe is true, you are not our enemy."

The Demon's face shifted angrily and Ned finally understood. In his eyes he saw something unique. It was fear. An emotion that Demons were supposedly unable to feel, yet there it was and Sur-jan did not wear it well.

He sat at the table like a hot coal on ice, spitting and crackling, steaming and sparking with visible malcontent. All creatures, it seemed, no matter where they are from, become angry when frightened.

"I have risked much to be here. To be away from the earth in this nowhere-place. It has made me sick. But better to be sick than a slave."

"I don't understand – what are you saying?"

There was a rattling from under the table. Ned's perometer had come alive quite suddenly, but not, as he had at first feared, because of the Demon. The needle was pointing away from the creature and towards the door.

"The Darkening King – it is not welcome by those of us that remember."

And the more he spoke, the more the perometer's needle twitched. First one way and then another, in quick jerks of frantic movement.

"If you feel this way then help us! Tell us where he is, how to defeat him." Terry Armstrong was now more animated than Ned had seen him since they had started their mission, hope burning brightly in his eyes.

The needle spun now in all directions, faster and faster.

"Defeat him?"

"Dad?"

"Not now, son!" urged his father. "Go on, Sur-jan, what can you tell us?"

Down the corridor, Ned heard footsteps running at a pace and the needle was spinning so hard that the perometer started to rattle.

"DAD!"

"Ned, what's got into you?" said his mum, and then her eyes fell to the floor and the Tinker's device. "Oh, dear."

Ned snatched it from the floor and slammed it on to the table, narrowly missing a now terrified sprite whose light crackled then dimmed. A spin of the perometer's dial could mean any number of things. Barbarossa's men? The BBB? What was left of the Twelve and its pinstripes was still after them too.

The Demon remained quite calm, his head turned to one side, and he closed his eyes as if listening to something that Ned couldn't hear. Finally his skin began to glow a fiery red.

"Trouble is here – here for you."

Ned and family were up on their feet in an instant.

"What trouble? What do you mean?!"

"Find the old one – he will give you what you seek. Now go. NOW. While there is still time."

"The old…?" Ned began to ask, but a second later he was shoved out of the door by both Mum and Dad, with a fast-moving sprite at their heels, out into the corridor and back into the tea room, and that's when Mavis made herself heard.

"HOW DARE YOU? THIS IS *MY* TEA ROOM!"

CHAPTER 6

Grey-suits

Mavis's tea room was eerily absent of any noise. But noise was clearly coming. The Armstrongs watched from the edge of the corridor they had just been led through. It was like looking at a stick of dynamite, its fuse lit and burning, waiting to explode.

The entire bar was still. Each and every one of its hardened criminal tea drinkers caught in mid sip. The reason stood at what was left of the entrance to Mavis's Ye Olde Tea Shoppe. The carved door lay broken on the ground, its breakers two men in light grey suits standing to one side of the wreckage.

"I thought this place was supposed to be safe?!" whispered Ned's mum.

"It was till we got here!" spat Ned in far less of a whisper.

Two more grey-suits walked quietly and confidently into the room. One was built like a giant square brick, with the kind of face that never smiled. In front of him was a slighter man who Ned assumed was their leader. He had red-blond hair and despite their surroundings could not have looked more at ease. Something in Ned's chest pulled – he recognised this man! It was the very same man who'd fought Benissimo the last time Ned had seen him, at the circus, before At-lan and their battle in the sky.

"I assure you, you are in no danger. We mean you absolutely no harm. My name is Mr Fox and I am searching for two adults and a child. The child is an unremarkable-looking boy usually accompanied by a mouse."

"Unremarkable?!" fumed Ned. With his powers failing as they were, the intruder had hit a nerve.

"Shh!" ordered his mum.

As the fox-haired man spoke, "big" Mavis was removing the teapots from her fingers and flexing her mighty hands before curling them into fists. Knowing full well what was coming next, some of the patrons nearer the bar began to edge away.

"Don't want no trouble? Do you know how long it took for my gnomes to carve that door? How much I had to pay for the magic what was woven into its wood?"

"Madam, we will recover your expenses. Unfortunately the door was not willing to open."

"If you had half a brain you'd know why. You see, my tea room has been a safe house since before you was born. It's the one place between everywhere that doesn't get bothered by lawmen, or politicians, or taxmen, or anyone else. Once you step inside these walls my guarantee is that you are safe from all the nonsense out there – to enjoy my home-brewed wonders at your leisure. To that effect, there's only one law here: Mavis's law. And rule number one is: IF MY RUDDY DOOR DOESN'T WANT YOU IN, THEN YOU DON'T GET IN!"

And that was when the lit fuse blew.

Mavis's gigantic right arm tore across the ground-floor bar. The fox-haired grey-suit and his number two ducked but the two door breakers behind them were not so lucky. Her fist connected with them both and there was a sickening crunch of bone on bone. They were flung to the walls violently before slumping to the floor in unconscious heaps. Their commander remained completely calm and nodded to the brick, who in return whispered something into his sleeve. A second later every window on every floor erupted in a shower of breaking glass and then—

Clunk, clunk, clunk.

Smoking canisters were launched into the room, their great clouds of green gas instantly reducing those nearest to slumbering heaps. There were, however, some amongst the Darklings and Hidden who were immune to the effects, and for that lucky handful, the fox-haired man had soldiers. Heavily armoured men of a darker grey attire in riot gear and gas masks burst into the room. In place of sub-machine guns, they all carried long-poled electric batons and high-powered dart guns. This was nothing like the raid Ned had witnessed at the Circus of Marvels – the BBB worked the room with ease. With a jolt of their batons, a blast of their darts, one by one resistance was quashed. All, that was, except for Mavis, who launched blow after blow of her great arms at the mounting assault of grey.

One of the more heavily armoured intruders spotted Ned at the edge of the fighting and began to stride across the room towards him. Ned focused – focused with everything that he had – on the small band of ring at his finger. But just as before, the air shimmered in front of him as he tried to draw it together, then… nothing.

"Dad, over here!" he yelped.

Terry Armstrong, meanwhile, had no such problem when it came to his ring and was about to unleash a shower of hardened projectiles when one of the many Mavii reared up behind the man in grey and proceeded to break a teapot over his helmet. Reinforced alloys are lightweight and durable, the perfect material for special-forces armour. No match, however, for Mavis's best china, and the man hit the floor hard.

"You lot – with me, before this gas gets the better of us!" she ordered and quickly led Ned and his family back down the corridor. "The door knew who you were the minute you knocked, it always does – the Lady de Laqua indeed!"

"I thought Mavis's tea shop was neutral? Why are you helping us?" rasped an out-of-breath Ned.

"You have more friends than you know. From what I hear, what's coming doesn't care about neutral!"

"Thank you, Mavis – or what do I...?" started Terry.

"I'm Number Six, and you're welcome."

Heavy footsteps pounded after them and a quick glimpse over his shoulder had Ned witness the great ooze that was Gorrn surprise two of the dark-grey tanks by dropping on to them with a toothy and painful *flup*. The men screamed through their masks and the Armstrongs rounded the corner. Just as they did, they came face to face with Sur-jan, but not as they'd seen him before – reformed to his true flame-licked self. Sar-adin was the only Demon Ned had ever seen in his true Demonic form, but Sur-jan was quite different. His size and shape were similar, though his mouth was wider, and from it hung a snake-like tongue that forked at the end. A layer of fire crackled and spat over him like a sheet of armour and what little of the creature's skin Ned could see through the flames was red and brittle, as though made of rough glass. Only his eyes remained as they were, and they were all the more unsettling for it, as though somehow through all that power and magic a part of him had remained human.

Sur-jan nodded to Number Six, who nodded back, and on the Armstrongs hurtled, down another corridor that ran behind the main tea room, Whiskers scurrying ahead like a wind-up rocket.

There were more screams behind them as the Demon dealt with the few men who had managed to get past Gorrn.

Finally Number Six ushered them into the last room

in the corridor, inside which was a tall mirror framed by two high-backed chairs.

"Emergency exit. We've never had to use it before today – oh, the shame of it!"

She handed Terry a sliver of glass and the Armstrongs were just readying themselves to walk through when everything went a little bit wrong. From behind the wall they heard:

"YOU BRUTES! I'LL FEED YOU TO MY WYVERN FOR THIS!"

And in a last violent outburst, Mavis – the original and far larger Mavis – struck out at her assailants. Unfortunately for Ned and family, she struck out at the other side of the wall, on which hung the mirror, and instantly both wall and mirror were destroyed.

In a spray of plasterboard, splinters and mirrored glass, their emergency exit was turned to rubble. As the dust cleared, a dumbfounded Ned and family could only blink through the hole in the wall at the once again silent tea room.

Mavis lay sprawled over her counter. She'd been peppered with hundreds of darts and whatever liquid they'd carried to make her slumber had finally taken its hold. Every single one of her tea-drinking customers lay like Mavis, out cold on the floor, or sagging at their seats and tables.

Staring at Ned was the BBB's fox-haired leader, behind him at least thirty armoured men, each and every one with a dart gun pointed at the Armstrongs. Tears of frustration began to well in Ned's eyes even as he focused on his ring. Ned had no powers to call on, and his dad had no time as the grey-suits pulled their triggers.

Pfft, pfft, pfft.

A short blow of air, a sting at Ned's neck and everything turned to black.

CHAPTER 7

Old Faces

Ned was barely aware of the jolting motion of the transport, of the blindfold that had been placed over his eyes or of the muffled voices discussing "the boy" and his parents. *We're captives* was all his bleary mind could muster, and everything was lost.

After more than an hour of travelling, they were led from the vehicle and into a building, then finally into a room of some sort, though where in the world they were now was anyone's guess.

"Mr Fox will be with you shortly," announced the grey-haired wall of an agent they had seen at Mavis's as he took off the Armstrongs' blindfolds and left them in what turned out to be a windowless concrete room.

"Ned, Terry, are you OK?" asked his mum just as soon as the door was closed. Red-eyed from the dart's effects and clearly ruffled, Olivia Armstrong still managed to look beautiful as she ran round the room checking the walls for some hint of a weakness, some way in which they could escape.

"Fine, Mum," managed Ned. "Still a bit groggy, though."

His dad, on the other hand, looked beaten. For one thing, the clothes they'd had to buy him after their last run-in weren't quite big enough and his hair was now completely on end, but it was the look of utter dejection that finished off the picture.

"We were so close!" he howled. "Months, months of looking, of hunting and being hunted – for nothing! Do those fools have any idea what they've done?"

"Don't get worked up, Terry – you're no use to us when you're worked up, and I'm going to need your skills to break out of here."

But Ned's dad was "worked up" and in no hurry to un-work himself.

"That's the fifth time they've caught up with us now. How are they doing it?"

Ned had to admit, the BBB had been impressive. He thought back to the way they'd taken out the tea drinkers, how deftly they'd worked their batons and guns.

"I was there when they raided the circus," said Ned. "They were a hopeless bunch of jossers! But this time and the last few times they've caught up with us, they seemed to know exactly what they were doing. It's like someone's been teaching them."

Olivia was now wrestling with the door handle to their room and, as she did so often, switched off to her two men's ramblings.

"And anyway," agreed Ned's dad, "Mavis's is one of the most closely guarded secrets in the entire Hidden underworld. If the Hidden can barely find it, how does a squad of suited jossers even know it exists in the first place?"

And then the door opened.

"With help, of course."

Standing in the doorway was the grey-suited, fox-haired man Ned had seen at Mavis's – the same man he had seen some months previously during the BBB's raid on the circus. Just behind him was a gaunt, smallish agent who was again wearing a grey suit.

Ned's mum was glaring at them angrily, clearly annoyed that they'd removed the one obstacle between her family and the building's corridor with the simple turn of a handle.

"My name is Mr Fox. This is Mr Spider, my associate."

Mr Spider's eyes were wide and bulbous and he took in the Armstrongs carefully, eyeing each one with meticulous attention.

"I am very sorry about the darts but you have proved to be rather hard to talk to in the past."

It was only then that Ned realised his backpack was missing, and much more importantly – there was no sign of Whiskers! His heart started to beat violently. Whiskers, his dear old Whiskers, who had seen him through more scrapes than he could count – where was he?

"What have you done with my mouse?!"

And as the words burned on his lips, a shadow by Mr Fox's legs started to move. Mr Fox's eyes flitted to the floor.

"Please ask your creature to stand down, Ned. I really am trying to be nice. Your ticker has been taken to our R and D department to check that he's functioning properly."

Ned's dad formed a compact ball of ice by drawing in the air molecules around the room with an audible *fwup*. It was about the size of a walnut and Ned had seen the man blow holes through steel doors with far less. A second later and the ice had turned to hardened glass.

"Do you know, he said this might happen," said Mr Fox with an air of resigned certainty.

"Who said? Who's been helping you?" seethed Ned's dad, the newly formed glass ball now hovering between them both with clear intent. "Was it one of the Shar's men? Or Atticus and his tin-skins?"

"It was I," said a voice, as Mr Fox's informant appeared from behind him and walked slowly into the room.

There was a swagger to the way he walked, and a jolliness to the twitch of his moustache. He was wearing his signature striped trousers, a worn military jacket with broken braiding and tassels, and a severely beaten top hat. Aside from some deep shadows under his eyes, a clear sign that he'd had little sleep, he was the same wax-moustached Ringmaster as ever.

"Bene?" was all Ned could manage.

"Hello, pup," said Benissimo with a smile.

Which promptly fell away when he saw the look on the face of Olivia Armstrong, who then proceeded to pummel the man's arm. Ned and his father watched in awe, Terry's ball of glass having landed on the floor with a clunk as his wife administered Mr Fox's informant with swift and painful justice.

"*Months*, we looked, all of us!"

Whack!

"And all that time you were here with these men, these revolting men in grey?!"

Whack!

"Livvy, if you could just let me explain!" said Benissimo, who did little more than raise his arms in a useless and rather timid defence.

"Explain why you abandoned us?! Explain *this*!"

Whack!

"Madam, the man can heal, but he still feels pain – please refrain from hitting him," tried Mr Fox.

Olivia Armstrong, nun and agent, stopped. Her eyes turned to Mr Fox.

"How did you do it?" she shouted. "How did you turn the greatest leader of all time into an informant?"

What was quite clear was that Ned's mum had absolutely no interest in Mr Fox's answer, nor for that matter did Ned's dad, or the enlarging shadow that was Gorrn as he inflated to fill the rear of the room. The Armstrongs were about to blow when Benissimo decided to tell them what, exactly, was what.

"Livvy, you've got this all wrong. Mr Fox works for me."

CHAPTER 8

The Butcher and the Hammer

Barbarossa sat at his stone table, glaring out of the window. In front of him lay the great sweeping carpet that was the Siberian taiga. Down below in his fortress's iron belly the Darkening King stirred. The butcher could feel him, in the pores of his skin and the pit of his stomach. The Darkening King had a hunger that knew no bounds, a wish to devour, to rule, to reign. In that they were very much alike.

He looked down at the roasted pork that Sar-adin had so carefully prepared. It was, as always, just the way he liked it, its skin glazed to a perfect crackle, boiling fat oozing from its sides, and on a different day, in a different mood, he would have devoured it all till his chest was awash with grease and dripping. But Barbarossa had a different hunger and it would not be fed through his gut.

Atticus Fife sat beside him drinking from a goblet of fine red wine. For some strange reason the man did not show fear in his company – if anything, he seemed to consider himself an equal.

Barbarossa supposed he had been a little vague about the arrangements between them. Perhaps Atticus believed himself to be important to him? A partner, even? He had been the second-in-command to the great Madame Oublier after all – the Circus of Marvels' Prime, their one-time leader. Not that he'd done her any good. In fact, the tin-skin had betrayed her and the poison that had ended her life could not have done so without him. Well, Barba wouldn't let the same happen to him. The man clearly needed some chivvying up, which was just as well, as Barbarossa was in the mood for a little "chivvying".

"Walk with me, Atticus."

Barbarossa led him away from the great hall down a set of spiral steps. Behind them Sar-adin followed quietly. The Central Intelligence had done exactly as ordered. He had built them a fortress that could not be taken. But something still troubled the butcher, even now. Until the Darkening King returned to his full power, they could, conceivably, still be undone no matter how many tin soldiers he had, or fanged and wicked creatures fought for him. Barbarossa did not like "odds". So close to his prize, only certainties would do.

"The fair-folk will come, Atticus, and they will try to stop us."

"What remains of them, yes."

"And what does remain of them?"

"The pinstripes who still answer to me have heard word of a growing force in St Albertsburg."

Barbarossa grimaced but continued leading the way.

"A growing force… Do you know how a force grows, Atticus?"

"We have banned all flights between the Veil, Barba, and my men are—"

Barba raised a hand and the tin-skin quietened.

"A force grows when there is hope. It is your job to remove that hope, Atticus."

Barbarossa stopped by a heavy steel door and Sar-adin pulled out a set of keys.

"I am treading a fine line as it is, Barba. My men are beginning to suspect."

Sar-adin opened the door to reveal a dimly lit cell. There were no windows, only a withered figure chained to the wall.

"This, Atticus, is Sur-jan. Once he swore to fight for me, yet only this morning he met with the Armstrongs. You promised me that you would take away the fair-folk's hope and yet *it grows*."

Atticus's face dropped. The Demon looked to be in terrible pain. As cruel and as heartless as their kind was, he felt for it, knowing that whatever Barbarossa had done to the beast to reduce it so must have been unspeakable.

"Do you see hope in my captive's eyes, Atticus?"

"I-I…"

"You will feed them lies upon lies. You will confuse and befuddle them, till they cannot tell friend from foe, till they cower in their beds calling for their mothers. You will feed them and feed them, till all their hope, strength and vigour is swallowed whole."

"I will redouble my efforts."

"No, Atticus, you will push them till you have nothing left to push with."

And with that, Sar-adin shoved the tin-skin into the cell and locked the door.

"Barba?! Barbarossa, what is the meaning of this?"

"By the time they reach my forest, their spirits will already be broken. You will do the breaking, Atticus. You gave me your oath that you would. Your cellmate gave me such an oath once. A night with him should do plenty to remind you of what is at stake."

Barbarossa turned his back and retraced his steps, even as Atticus pounded on the door.

"Tell me, Sar-adin, how much longer?" growled Barbarossa.

"He grows stronger."

"But when will he rise, Sar-adin – *WHEN?*"

"Weeks."

"And the boy, his parents? I fear while they walk free that the fair-folk will continue to have hope."

"Sur-jan did not tell them about the stone."

"Then we are still safe. Find them, Sar-adin. Use the clowns and whatever else you deem necessary. The Armstrongs must not stand in our way again."

"Yes, master."

The butcher slowed.

"And, Sar-adin – when you end them, make them suffer."

CHAPTER 9

The Nest

Benissimo and Mr Fox led Ned and his family through the labyrinth that was the BBB's headquarters. Now somewhat over the initial shock of seeing their old comrade-in-arms, they followed with a keen eye on their surroundings, Gorrn clinging to Ned's shadow in silence.

"I still don't get it, Bene. How on earth have Mr Fox and the BBB wound up working for *you*?" asked Ned's dad.

"The BBB was set up decades ago. In many ways their purpose was not so different to the Twelve's or its circus. Our role was to protect the Hidden – theirs was to protect the jossers. The BBB knew about us fair-folk, though very little, and what you don't know is always frightening. They have been investigating us for years, trying to find out more. I simply set them straight – told them who the bad guys were and what sort of danger they posed to all living creatures, on both sides of the Veil."

"And then what?" asked Ned.

"Well, I think their brains rather melted – they went berserk. Had it not been for our red-headed friend here, they would have had me shot."

Mr Fox smiled.

"Not that shooting him would have worked. But you see, Mr Bear, my boss, well… he doesn't like surprises. I do think he mellowed after that first heart attack, though," Benissimo continued. "It turns out what you do know can be far more frightening than what you don't. But in any case, it's worked out rather well. Seeing as I became their topmost informant on all things to do with our kind, they have put me in charge."

Mr Fox promptly stopped smiling.

"A temporary measure, till we sort things out."

"But a measure nonetheless, Foxy."

An unmarked door slid open as they approached.

"Which, as you can see, has its benefits. This, my friends, is 'the Nest'."

Ned and family walked through the door and out on to a balcony, one of more than a dozen that circled several floors all looking down over a large indoor training ground. Far below, hundreds of grey-tracksuited men were being barked at by a severe-looking Frenchman and a rotund, slightly ageing Italian who had great curling horns protruding from his head.

"Special Forces, don't give me no-a rubbish. You couldn't climb your-a way out of a can!"

Several deflated-looking operatives were struggling their way up an admittedly treacherous wall that the ancient half-satyr was playfully skipping across. To one side the Frenchman was demonstrating the easiest way to neutralise a nightmonger. The terrifying creature was a blur of blade-like fingers, but was soon made quite harmless when the instructor launched two weighted nets from a gas-powered machine that looked very much as though it had been designed on this side of the Veil.

"Couteau and Grandpa Tortellini!" exclaimed Ned with the first truly genuine smile he'd given in months.

"The greys are coming along nicely under their tutelage and Tinks has been having a whale of a time mixing our tech with theirs — fascinating results."

"Tinks?!" grinned Ned. "Where is he?"

"Looking after your mouse, I should think. About half

of the old troupe has joined us. The rest are still MIA, I'm afraid."

"MIA?"

"Missing in action, Ned. You know as well as I do how bad things are out there."

A horrible thought struck Ned: *What about Lucy and George?* If they were here, Lucy would have sensed him by now and George would have been hot on her heels, knocking down any number of walls or grey-suits to see his old ward. He didn't need to ask – Benissimo spotted the look on his face immediately.

"George and Lucy are with the Viceroy. They've been delivering one of the old troupe, and I can't tell you more than that, I'm afraid. Don't worry – word's been sent and I should think they'll have threatened the nearest pilot by now and demanded passage back to the Nest."

"Delivering one of the troupe? Who?"

"All I can tell you is that he's a vital part of the plan – as are you, of course, Ned. And we have been trying to bring you in for a while now, as we have new intel that you need to hear. I needn't mince my words, especially not with you three. The Darkening King is growing stronger by the day. George, Lucy, all of us are scrambling to work with our allies, and telling friend from foe has never been harder. Come on, let's go to see the boffin – he'll explain our situation in more detail."

***

The boffin, known to Benissimo's old troupe as "Tinks", had been given a new laboratory to work in and it was to there that Benissimo and Mr Fox led the Armstrongs now. As Ned and his dad entered, they both went a little misty-eyed at what they saw. Ned and his father, both being Engineers – who had the power (when it was working, that is) to bend and manipulate atoms – had a different relationship with all things mechanical than most other people. Their powers hinged on understanding the structure of things, how they came together and worked, so that they could reimagine them into another form. And within these brightly lit walls were the most advanced examples of what modern-day science and technology had to offer, fused together with just a pinch or two of the Hidden's own magic.

The lab was big enough to house an entire circus troupe along with its cars and lorries. It was also teeming with smartly dressed scientists in matching grey lab coats. They were all building and testing equipment, and all of the equipment was designed, from the ground up, to fight Darklings.

Traps, snares, laser-guided harpoons, listening devices, scanning equipment… and data. Lots and lots of data, pouring out of printers, to be pointed at and argued over incessantly by teams of bespectacled analysts. They weren't all jossers, either. A good number of them were waist-height minutians, just like the Tinker, and no doubt, Ned guessed, refugees from the ill-fated city of Gearnish, now under the control of Barbarossa's ghastly machine-mind, the Central Intelligence.

Ned gawped in wonder at a man clicking a device on his belt that made him turn invisible and visible again, with varying results. At one point his head disappeared while the rest of him stayed visible; at another he appeared to be floating off the ground with no legs. His dad, meanwhile, was mesmerised by an aged minutian who was talking to a flea. He wore a large trumpet-ended device on his ear, while the flea responded by hopping up and down on a minuscule sensor at its feet.

Everything had the touch of the Tinker to it, but the Tinker himself was nowhere to be seen.

"Where is he?" asked Ned's mum, who, unlike her two "boys", found the gadgets on display extraordinarily dull.

A contained explosion in a room off to the far corner was to be her clue. The closer they got, the less josser and more "Tinker" their surroundings became – reams of paper and blueprints stuck to the walls, shelves weighed down to breaking point, and a trail of spinning, whirring and bubbling devices on every single surface. Through a door they came to a great sprawling mess and at its centre was the genius who had made it.

"Well, bless my toolbox, if it isn't the Armstrongs!"

CHAPTER 10

Tinks

He had the same unkempt whiskers, the same old lab coat heaving with screwdrivers, and he was the same old Tinker, though as far as Ned could tell he was in unusually high spirits, despite the burning something he was putting out on his desk.

"Hello, Tinks. Nice little set-up," started Ned's dad.

"Oh, indeed, Mr Armstrong, indeed. You never told me the jossers had such fantastic tech!"

"They're a clever bunch, once you get used to them," grinned Ned's dad.

A now teary-eyed Tinker proceeded to shake Ned's hand heartily and then gave his mum a rather elegant bow.

"The Armstrongs together – and here in our little home from home! You wait till the others hear about this. On second thoughts, I think I'll tell them."

Mr Fox patiently raised his eyes to the ceiling as the Tinker spoke into a watch on his wrist.

"Channel Alpha-niner, this is the big boff, over!" The little scientist was beaming now, though Ned sensed it had more to do with his watch than their arrival. "This thing is *brilliant* – so much quicker than a wind-modulator!"

"Big boff, over, this is the Beard. Can you please stop using this channel, Tinks. It's for mission-only comms and Scraggs is fed up with being asked to bring you biscuits – *OVER*."

Ned's ears pricked excitedly. "The Beard" had to be Abigail, surely – the wonderful bearded lady of the old Circus of Marvels troupe. And if she was there, then her lump of a troll husband, Rocky, couldn't be far away. How he'd missed them!

"This is a channel-wide announcement, over. That means you too, Tusky. The Arm—"

Before he could get to "strongs", Benissimo clamped a hand over his mouth and brought down the full weight of a moustachioed twitch.

"Later, Tinks! They need to be *brought up to speed*."

"Ah, right you are, boss." Undeterred, the little man broke into another enthusiastic grin. "We'll be wanting to fire up 'Big Brother' then."

"Yes, gnome. *Now get on with it.*"

"'Blinking Incredible Gateway', or 'BIG' brother (named it myself, as it happens), was devised to replace the Twelve's ticker network that Barba stole." Tinks was relishing the chance to show off to Ned and his dad, and pressed a button on his desk. A large monitor came down from the ceiling. "Live satellite feeds courtesy of Mr Fox here, and more than a hundred Farseers keep round-the-clock surveillance on just about everything. They're neurologically, metaphysically and outright magically connected, through a network that spans the globe. We use 'satter-light' and the 'interweb' – josser tech, you know – to send and receive the data. It really is clever stuff. In some ways it's an even better system, though I do miss the—"

"Hell's teeth, Tinks! Just show them Russia, would you?"

A second later and they were greeted by a satellite image of Siberia in Russia, which was when Mr Fox took over.

"Our eyes in the sky monitor everything, and had been doing so for a good while before the Tinker's 'Hidden' enhancements. We immediately noticed a sharp spike in activity around the same time your tickers went missing. Though of course back then we didn't know what it was. The truth is…" At this Mr Fox paused, clearly uncomfortable with what he was about to admit. "Well, the truth is, back then we didn't really know anything."

A few button presses later and they saw countless orange lines leading to Siberia with a web of dots at its centre that covered hundreds of miles.

"The Darklings – they're converging in the Siberian reserve," breathed Ned's mum.

"Indeed, ma'am. But why? You have other reserves – in the Americas, Asia and as far off as Australia – so why here? Why this one place?"

At the centre of the map, deep in the Siberian forest, was a large circular spot in black.

"This one area, large as it is, is also completely impenetrable to both our cameras and your Farseers. Apparently the tickers that Barbarossa has obtained not only keep a watchful eye but also scramble our signals. Benissimo and I – well, all of us – believe that that is where the creature is gathering himself. We have you and Ned to thank for that."

"Excuse me?" said Ned's dad defensively.

"You hurt the Darkening King, Terry, you and your

son – when you broke Barba's machine," rumbled Benissimo.

Ned had dared to believe, in all their months of searching, that the Darkening King *was* wounded, that in some way when they'd set it free they'd also managed to hurt it. If Benissimo and Mr Fox were right, maybe there *was* still a chance, still a way to undo what Ned and his dad had put into motion.

"If what we believe to be the case is true," continued Mr Fox, "Barbarossa won't need an army when the creature rises. And yet huge quantities of metal and machinery have been flooding into the area from Gearnish. A great part of those consignments has been the ticker soldiers we've heard reports of. Which means that we will be facing not one army but two."

Mr Fox paused for effect and the Tinker's face turned red. His people had unwittingly created a machine in the Central Intelligence that had not just strengthened Barbarossa and his Demons' forces but also doubled their ranks. Ned had only had to face one at the circus encampment and he shuddered at the memory of it.

"In any case, the Darklings that have managed to break free from their own reservations have for the first time let the world sleep soundly. Sticking to the shadows and dark places, they've quietly, slowly made their way to Siberia and the dark zone you see now."

"But why? Why any army at all? Surely Barba and that creature don't need them?" puzzled Ned.

Benissimo's face lit up.

"And that is exactly the point, pup! Why? Because they *do* need those armies, desperately – isn't it obvious? Until the Darkening King is fully restored there is still a weakness, a chink, a nook, a cranny that we can use to burrow through and defeat him!"

"Well then, what are you waiting for?!" said Ned's dad. "If he's weak and you know where he is, why wait? Why give him the chance?"

"Tinks, dig up the reports," ordered Benissimo.

The screen filled with a stream of photos – by the looks of it, of mostly military personnel.

"Andrei Galkin, thirty-two. Spetsnaz and best in class, only survivor of a mission into the Siberian taiga. Currently on leave due to emotional trauma," explained Mr Fox. "When we questioned him, all he could mutter was '*magic and monsters*'. The poor man was scared out of his wits. Not long after, we sent in a team of our greys. This time there were no survivors, though one of our operative's bodies was discovered some weeks later on the outskirts of the forest. This footage was retrieved from his headcam."

Ned and his family watched in ashen-faced silence. Even in low light, the video was shocking. At the centre of a clearing and towering over the forest's canopy was a fortress. At its foot and along its parapets and walkways were hundreds, if not thousands, of Darklings. As poor as the picture was, the multitude of creatures made the metal structure look as if it was alive, a living breathing "thing", and when its main gate opened, they saw them, bright and shimmering with reflections – an army of metallic tickers, man-sized and cold, pouring out and into the forest.

"I could go on, but I think the images are clear enough. Barbarossa has built his creature a castle and surrounded himself with an army to protect it while it grows strong. There is no clear way in, not without incurring extreme casualties."

"Bene, if there's a battle to be fought, surely we must fight it?" urged Ned's dad.

As horrific as the idea was, Ned couldn't help but agree. Surely any price was worth paying if it could stop the creature from rising.

"The battle will be fought, Terry, but we aren't ready,"

explained Benissimo. "At-lan was originally devised to rid us of the Darkening King and, as involved as you were in the latter part of its construction, Terry, we haven't the resources or time to rebuild it. Barba had been making its components in secret for months before he took you. We believe there are but weeks now till he rises."

"H-how do you know?!" stammered Ned.

"Sur-jan, the Demon you went to see – he's one of several. There are those amongst them that fear the creature's return as much as we do, maybe more. After all, they know what he's actually capable of."

And at this Ned's dad became visibly ruffled.

"Well, if your new pals here hadn't stormed in when they did, we'd know a lot more than we do now!"

"Calm yourself, Terry. Another Demon of his kind has made contact with us. About two months ago messages started to arrive, though the informant won't give us his name. We don't know who he is or where he's hiding, but he claims to be a Demon at any rate. If what he's told us is true, there is a way to destroy the Darkening King but it must be done at the precise moment he forms."

Mr Fox turned to the Armstrongs.

"The BBB represent just about every government body

there is, whether said body knows it or not. We are preparing to launch a full-scale attack, with Benissimo and his allies' help of course, but an outright assault is pointless unless we can actually destroy the creature once we get past its defences."

"And how *exactly*, Mr Fox, do we do that?" asked Olivia Armstrong.

Mr Fox looked to the Tinker and then to Benissimo. Benissimo nodded.

"We have no idea, though if this informant is to be trusted, there is someone who might."

CHAPTER 11

Who? What? Why?

"**W**ell?" urged Ned's mum.

"Yes, who? Who knows?" reiterated his dad.

Mr Fox looked rather awkward. It was clearly a state which he was not unaccustomed to being in.

"I'm afraid I can't tell you."

At this point both of Ned's parents, and in truth Ned himself, became more than a little irate.

"You don't trust us?!" said Olivia Armstrong in a dangerously quiet voice. "Well, of all the… First of all, you blow our mission moments before it comes good, then you kidnap us, then you lead us round your base and show us all this intel and now – *if I'm hearing you right* – you aren't going to actually tell us anything USEFUL!"

Olivia Armstrong was seething and Ned had no doubt that she was about to fly into another arm-bashing tirade.

"Madam, first of all I would like to remind you that, though Benissimo is indeed in charge of this operation, you are standing in the base that I built, and I am not one for emotional outbursts, unless coming directly from my superiors in the BBB, of which there are only two. More importantly, however, I am unable to tell you who holds the knowledge, because your unkillable friend here has not actually told me."

Ned's mum quietened. "Oh."

Benissimo signalled to Tinks and the network's screen turned black.

"It's not ideal, but the more people that are kept in the dark, the wider the chink in my brother's armour. Atticus is still trying to manipulate the Twelve and its pinstripes, though they're beginning to see through his lies, and the Hidden are more vulnerable than ever. We are on a knife edge – everything, and I do mean everything, depends on the secrecy of our operation. Barbarossa's arrogance is our best weapon, and the weaker he believes us to be, the better our chances. The Hidden have split into untrusting pockets, barely threaded together by their leaders. I've spent months reaching out to them in secret and few of them know what the plan of attack will be once they're called."

"Then who actually does know?" asked Ned.

"Me," said Benissimo.

At that Mr Fox looked slightly, if not openly, irritated.

Benissimo continued, "I leave tonight, and if this informant of ours is right, we will have ourselves a route to victory."

"And what are we supposed to do till you come back?" asked Ned's dad.

"Nothing, old friend, for now. When I return, *if* I return, I will – and not for the first time – be asking you all for everything."

CHAPTER 12

Little to Do about Nothing

As a young man Terrence Armstrong had dedicated his life to fighting evil, always by Benissimo's side and always in the thick of the fight. And though fatherhood changes a man and Terry's one true focus was now the safety of his family, the bond between him and the ancient Ringmaster was still as strong as it was deep. His wife had proved to be an equally capable fighter and the consummate spy. She had managed over the course of nearly all of Ned's life to remain completely hidden from the "Hidden" and to outwit both Barbarossa and every friendly operative working for the Twelve that had been tasked with finding her.

It was fitting then that Benissimo should need to talk to them. He did not, however, appear to want or need to talk to Ned, which as it turned out made Ned feel both furious and useless in equal measure.

He sat alone in a stark room; it had a bed and a sidelight, a sink at one end and no windows. It was far more like a cell than anything else. The Tinker had returned Whiskers to him, with a small but extremely useful upgrade. A tracking device had been welded into his casing. From now on, no matter where Ned was, as long as his trusty mouse was with him, the Tinker could use his network's "eyes in the sky" to locate him, which had the dual effect of making Ned feel both safe and irritated. What if he didn't want to be found?

Whiskers was staring up at him from the palm of his hand. Gorrn meanwhile was busying himself with Ned's sheets. Ned could only put his new-found helpfulness down to their change in surroundings; the odd creature was folding away his covers and stuffing them into a small drawer.

"Gorrn, they were fine where they were."

"Gru?"

"The sheets, Gorrn... Oh, never mind, I'll deal with them later. And, err, thank you."

"Arr."

Whiskers was still staring.

"Just like old times, eh? You, me and the shadow."

The Debussy Mark Twelve bobbed its head in a "yes".

Only it wasn't anything like old times, not really. He had his mum and dad, and nothing was more important than knowing they were safe. But for how much longer would any of them stay safe? They'd searched for answers for months, and now this informant had seemingly given Benissimo a route, however slim, of undoing Barbarossa's beast. Ned should have felt happy about it, but how did the Ringmaster even know the informant could be trusted? What if it was just a trick? A trap?

The Darkening King would be rising soon. George and Lucy were on some mission and Ned had been relegated to… well, *sitting*. And that was when he admitted what was really eating away at him. He placed Whiskers on the bare mattress and looked at his ring. No matter how many times he'd tried, it remained dormant, and for all Ned knew it would stay that way forever. Ned had gone back to being the boy he was before he'd found the Hidden.

Completely and utterly average.

If only he could talk to Lucy. She was bound to have some idea of what was ailing him. Maybe she was even suffering from the same problem? He sat with his two mute sidekicks, feeling in nearly every possible way both powerless and pointless.

But that was the thing about the Hidden, and most particularly about his friends at the Circus of Marvels: they didn't care what Ned could *do* – they just cared that he was there.

It came as a pounding of feet, a gabbling of whispers and excitable banter. By the time they'd reached Ned's door, they were in such a frenzy that Rocky, the Russian mountain troll, put his fist straight through it.

"NIED! Why for you hide in here?!"

They burst into his room in an avalanche of colour and noise.

"Ned, love, it's you! All this drab grey we've bin putting up with... Just this mornin' I was sayin' to Rocky how we needed a bit of colour, and here you are!" warbled Abi the Beard, and proceeded to hug him so hard he thought his eyes might burst.

With them were Grandpa Tortellini and a good half or so of his seven grandchildren, all whooping out a "Hey! How-a ya doin'?" and the occasional satyr-horned bleat. Scurrying along the ground were the three emperors, Julius, Nero and Caligula. The thieving pixies were far less jubilant when they realised there was nothing to steal, and decided instead to make up for it by harassing Gorrn, who hid in Ned's shadow with an "Unt". Monsieur

Couteau managed a less than sneery salute from the doorway before excusing himself, and was barged rather gruffly out of the way by Scraggs the cook, carrying a large tray of doughnuts that he'd baked especially.

"Extra jammy, Ned, just like you like 'em!" rumbled Scraggs, who, to Ned's wonder and despite their new pristine surroundings, had still not taken the time to wash his chef's apron.

Finally there was a welcome trumpeting and Ned's eyes lit up as Alice the elephant, who was too large to get into the room, popped at least part of her loving and leathery face through the doorway.

"Hello, girl!" he grinned and got up to pat her trunk.

"Arrooo!"

Breathlessly they launched a verbal assault of questions, to which Ned really had very few answers – mostly because of the speed at which they came.

"How are your ma and pa?"

"What's going on, on the outside?"

"You been eatin' properly, sonny?"

"Nedolino, and de-a training, tell us – how you-a doin'?"

"Once you rested, you come with Rocky, da? I show you base, very big, very interesting."

It was only when the fourth doughnut was shoved into his face that Ned realised why they were quite so happy to see him. His beloved old troupe, at least the ones that were here, had not been out of the confines of their Nest for months. Keeping the travelling kind cooped up for too long was like trying to bottle frogs and they were positively jumping out of their skins.

"You met the spider yet?" asked Abi.

"Mr Spider? Only briefly."

"Me no like 'googly' eyes. He always stick nose in business and always with de rules, Nied, *so many rules*."

"They're a serious ol' bunch these greys, Ned. Keen, mind you, keen to learn our ways – but ol' goggle-eyes is about as much fun as a wet rock."

Through all the banter and jam, the jeering and grins, Ned saw something else. The fate of the world was hanging in the balance, unimaginable evil poised to spring up from the ground and devour them all, but their eyes had never looked as clear or bright. Whatever the world was about to throw at them, the diminished Circus of Marvels would see it head-on and together.

Ned might well have lost his powers, but he had most certainly found his "point".

CHAPTER 13

Not Entirely Ideal

Ned wasn't quite sure what time it was when Benissimo woke him, or why the man was whispering. He was, however, quite certain that he was tired.

"Bene?"

"Yes, pup. Rise and shine — we've got a mission."

"What? I thought you said—"

"I have to say a lot of things when it comes to your parents, Ned. Most of all, I have to not tell them when I ask you to do something dangerous."

Ned rubbed at his eyes. "What kind of dangerous?"

"The informant's lead I told you about earlier — its location is not entirely ideal."

Something of an alarm bell sounded between Ned's still-waking ears. "And by 'not entirely' you mean…?"

"Russia, Siberia, Ned. It's in the reservation."

There was a low and rumbling "Unt" from beneath Ned's bed, followed closely by a "Scree" and some incredibly fast blinking from his mouse.

Ned, thankfully, was able to pick his words more eloquently. "Barking dogs, Bene! Have you lost your marbles?!"

"If we intend to beat this creature, it's the only way."

Ned would have gone in an instant but for one glaring factor that the Ringmaster had not taken into account. "Bene, it's not that I don't want to help you. The Darkening King is rising because of me and Dad. It's just that I don't know how much use I'll be."

"It's not because of you, Ned. And by the way, I know about your Engine – your parents told me everything, just before I drugged them."

Ned's ring finger buzzed and there was a slight shimmering in the air, before it fizzled away to nothing. Not even real anger could spark the thing, not any more.

"You did *what*?!"

"They'd never let you go, with or without them, and our best chance is to sneak in unseen. I can't say that your loss of power isn't an issue, Ned, but we really don't have any choice."

Another bell *ding*ed behind Ned's eyes. "And why is that?"

"The creature we are going to see will only help you, not me. Word has spread of your deeds, pup – it wants an audience with you *specifically*."

Ned wasn't entirely sure that he liked the sound of that, and he dreaded the answer before he'd even asked the question. "And this creature… is it a Demon?"

"Oh no, Ned. It's far, *far* worse than that."

"And I suppose you're not going to tell me what, because you aren't telling anyone *anything*?"

"That's the size of it, pup, but know this: if we do this right, if we get in and out of there without getting caught, and get the information we need, we will have ourselves the key to ending, once and for all, my brother and this monster he wants to unleash."

Ned sighed. "Not much choice then?"

"Is there ever?"

CHAPTER 14

Not Entirely Alone

Hurriedly and quietly, Benissimo led Ned along the base's labyrinth of corridors. Apart from the low hum of electric doors and devices, everything was silent.

"I don't know why I'm doing this. I'm not even sure I've forgiven you yet," started Ned.

Benissimo flinched, very slightly, before flitting back to his old bravado. "Oh, come on, pup, you think I'm brilliant."

"No, no, I don't."

Annoyingly Ned did think Benissimo was brilliant, completely and utterly, but he wasn't about to let him know.

"You'll see – you Armstrongs always come round in the end," grinned Benissimo, which was quite possibly the worst thing he could have said.

"Bene, Mum and Dad had every right to be furious. It's going to take a lot to gain their trust again and this isn't the best way to do it. You broke a lot of hearts when you disappeared, mine included."

"I regret that more than you know."

Ned stopped. "Then help me understand. This isn't your personal fight, Bene. You had no right abandoning us like that, not after everything Mum and Dad have had to go through."

"But it *is* personal, Ned – extremely. When there's time I'll explain, I promise."

It was then that Ned remembered what Barbarossa had told him on the *Daedalus*. According to the butcher, it was not just any Demon but the Darkening King himself that had cursed the two brothers and given them their immortality. What Ned still didn't understand was why. Was that what the Ringmaster meant? Either way, their mission came first. There would be time to talk when they returned. Ned had had the foresight not only to bring his trusty sidekicks but also the Tinker's perometer. From the look on the Ringmaster's face, there was little doubt that they would need it where they were going. Finally, at the end of one of the corridors, they came to a staging room lined with several mirrors. *Great,* thought Ned as Benissimo passed him his gear — a fur-lined coat, goggles and what looked like a small metal stick.

"One of the Tinker's modifications to BBB tech. It's a retractable Taser. It'll give whatever we run into enough of a shock for you to get away. Just twist the top to activate it. And make sure you button up the coat properly — it's still freezing where we're going this time of year."

"Dangerous *and* cold; Mum and Dad are going to kill me for this."

"I should think they'll try me first. If we're lucky, I'll get us home before they wake up."

"If we're lucky? Bene, are you sure this is a good idea?"

"Indeed, Mr B., are you sure?" said a voice from behind them.

They turned to see Mr Fox, dressed from head to toe in winter gear, sitting on a bench at the back of the room. Next to him was the bulbous-eyed Mr Spider, in his regular grey suit.

"Sneaking off in the dead of night without telling anyone? Well, it doesn't exactly glow with team spirit, does it?"

"Where did you come from?!" spat Benissimo.

"Actually, we were just behind the door when you walked in. I thought it might be a good idea if I tagged along."

"Mr Fox, you and I have done some great things in our short time together and I am very grateful to your organisation, but I think it might be better if you remained in the Nest."

The wording was polite enough, the coiled whip unfurling in Benissimo's hand far less so.

"Mr Spider, go and get some sleep," said Mr Fox.

"Sir?" said the thin-limbed agent. "I'm fine, thank you, sir."

Mr Fox's eyes rolled very slightly but he remained completely calm. "You are many things, Mr Spider, none of which is 'fine'."

Mr Spider grinned thinly, before excusing himself.

"Mr Spider has taken it upon himself to follow me of late and I'm not sure that I enjoy it very much. Now trust me when I say this, Mr B – I *really don't* want to come with you."

Ned watched Benissimo's whip closely. It was wavering to and fro and he was quite sure that it was almost ready to snap.

"You are a confoundingly difficult man to work with,"

Mr Fox went on. "Hot-headed, obtuse and with no regard for protocol. I hope you'll agree that I have tried to be accommodating. But here's the thing: for this partnership to work, for this entire operation to work, I need some 'certainties'. You can't, it seems, be killed, and for that I am – 'we' are – relieved. You can, however, be captured and being that you're the only one who knows 'the plan', well, if you're captured then we lose. I am not going to demand you tell me everything, but I'm afraid I must insist on making sure you return."

Mr Fox said all this with a calm, almost apologetic voice. He also seemed strangely certain that Benissimo would agree. The Ringmaster, however, got that stubborn look. His cheeks became flushed and his whip now rose threateningly between them.

"Mr Fox, I'm not sure that I like it when people 'insist'."

Mr Fox smiled, but remained seated and spoke into his wrist.

"Mr Badger, are you ready to wake Mum and Dad?"

"On your order, sir," crackled back his wrist.

"You wouldn't dare!" gasped Benissimo.

"Actually, it would be quite in character," smiled Mr Fox.

Ned flinched. If his parents found out before they left there would be trouble – bags of the stuff. "Err, Bene, maybe we should hear him out?"

"Nonsense, pup, I won't be blackmailed and I won't delay our mission."

"And besides –" Mr Fox pulled a sliver of mirrored glass from his sleeve – "you won't get very far without this."

It was a mirror key and no doubt the very one that they needed from the shelves to their left. Benissimo appeared to be in something of a checkmate, and all three of them knew it.

An angry twitch of a moustache later, and a powerless Ned made ready to step through the glass. He may well have lost his powers, but he had a mouse, a slovenly shadow, a Ringmaster and now a fox to help him on his way.

Ned pushed his face through the mirror and, a cool but clean tug later, found himself several thousand miles away, in a frozen and lightless wood.

CHAPTER 15

The Forest

The sun had yet to rise on a freezing Siberian morning. Benissimo got down on one knee and peered through the wood. Ned could feel the tiny hairs on his arms prickle and Mr Fox reached into his pocket.

"Soft mint, anyone?"

Despite where they were, the enigma that was Mr Fox seemed completely at ease.

"They're not standard issue, but I do allow myself small luxuries from time to time."

Benissimo's moustache twitched. "Mr Fox, considering our circumstances, I would appreciate you enjoying the 'small luxury' of keeping ruddy quiet."

Mr Fox stopped mid-chew. "I don't take orders from you, Mr B. I'd remember that if I were you."

"Actually, my unwelcome accomplice, right now I'm trying to forget you exist."

Mr Fox put away his mints and squared up to Benissimo. In his own clipped way he looked rather intimidating and was not about to give an inch to the Ringmaster.

"Well, like it or not, here I am."

"I think I've made it quite clear that I don't—"

Ned's eyes rolled. Clearly Benissimo and Mr Fox's alliance was being tested.

"Will you two belt up! I don't think any of us wants to be here, but being that we are and it's freezing, can we just get on with it?!"

Both men suddenly looked quite sheepish.

"Zeus's crown, you're right, Ned. I'm sorry and so is Mr Fox."

Mr Fox nodded reluctantly.

"Now, pup, would you be so kind as to summon your familiar?"

"Gorrn, sure, but what for?"

"Because between us and the folk I'm trying to get us to is the most dangerous stretch of forest anywhere on earth. Needless to say, I expect Gorrn will be about the only thing to keep us from being brutally savaged."

The worst part of Benissimo's explanation was that he wasn't smiling and Ned still didn't know what they were doing there.

"I'd feel a lot better about all this if I knew who we were trying to meet."

Benissimo frowned. "If we're separated and you or Mr Fox get caught, our contact must remain a secret no matter how long you're tortured for."

"Tortured? You didn't say anything about being tortured!" spat Ned.

Ned eyed the mirror nervously. Between the two men's face-off and the talk of torture, he was already regretting his decision to come.

"Keep your voice down! It won't come to that if you follow my lead. Now would you *please* get on with it."

Given their surroundings and the fact that he really had no choice, Ned did as he was told.

"Well, you heard him, Gorrn…"

Both of his sidekicks were uncommonly jittery at their surroundings and Gorrn at first pretended not to hear.

"Gorrn, you know I know you're there. I can see you oozing behind my leg." Which wasn't actually true.

Nothing.

"Please, Gorrn, oh great and dear protector, would

you kindly and in your own sweet time stop us from being *brutally savaged* or tortured, or even just a bit hurt?"

There was a tense moment when Ned thought Gorrn had actually fled, before he heard a low and unenthusiastic "Arr" from his foot. Inch by inch, the slovenly blob that was Gorrn began rising up from the cold forest floor, till their gloomy little spot became even gloomier.

"Thank you, Gorrn. Bene, Mr Fox, it works better if you're 'in' him."

Ned watched Mr Fox closely as he stepped into Gorrn's ooze.

"Well, this will be different," was all he said, though Ned noticed it was said with something of a tremor.

"We won't be invisible exactly, but Gorrn will make us blend in. We'll look more like a moving shadow than anything else."

Whiskers was unnaturally quiet even for a mouse, and Ned popped the little bundle of furred metal in by his neck. Even with just his faint *tick* rather than a real heartbeat, his mostly faithful companion was still a comfort.

The going was painfully slow. They had to make completely sure that no part of them was outside Gorrn's oozy embrace, which as well as making them look like a shadow, also made it harder to see. Benissimo led the strange group in total silence as Mr Fox covered their rear. The deeper into the forest they went, the more crooked and wild the trees grew. Their bark was as hard as stone and they rose up from the ground now, crowding and vast, like great armoured giants. Through the little light that made its way down here, Ned could see a wet blackness amongst the leaves and moss, as though some sickness was creeping into the forest or growing up from its roots. He had rarely visited a more foreboding place, made only worse because of its silence.

Slowly he began to notice, where long-dead trees had fallen and their bark had rotted, the telltale glint of slithering. Small creatures at first – worm, grub and beetle; then larger and more strange, black and scaly, or soft and with lidded eyes. He couldn't see them clearly enough to tell whether they were Darklings or not, and only prayed that they couldn't see him.

The ground began to slope downwards and Whiskers' fur stiffened at his neck. The little rodent was worried.

"You all right, boy?" Ned whispered.

Tick.

"Whiskers?"

Tick.

Ned didn't need to pull the perometer from his pocket. He could already feel its metal needle twitching.

Tick, tick, tick.

Finally he realised: the ticking did not just belong to his mouse.

CHAPTER 16

We Have Company

Benissimo slowed and pointed above their heads to the branches. Ned could quite clearly see all manner of winged birds. Pigeons, eagles, hawks and owls – and each and every one was scouring the forest with their beady ticker eyes.

Tick. Tick. Tick.

Tinks's Big Brother was right – the Twelve's eyes and ears had been plucked and now kept watch over Barbarossa's forest.

"Grr."

Ahead of them they heard several grunts and snarls, followed closely by a piercing howl. Gorrn's oozing form wobbled nervously and Mr Fox pulled the silenced pistol from his side as Benissimo edged forward.

The trees began to thin out and through the twilight

Ned could see that up ahead a small river crossed their path, and on its banks, a little upstream, sat a group of huddled, powerful creatures: four weirs, from the wolf-pack. Before the world had gone mad, their kind had been tasked with keeping the reserve's borders, but it was well known now that they had sided with Barbarossa and his cabal. Ned had been chased by a weir on Benissimo's flagship and had met others in St Albertsburg. They were gruff, violent creatures and their muscly torsos were covered in matted fur. Their combination of claws and fangs made them look terrifying, more so because their kind had quite forgotten what it was to be human. These were wolf-men and they lived for the hunt.

Benissimo put a finger to his lips and indicated in the opposite direction, downstream. Ned saw two more weirs coming to join the others. They were between both sets of creatures now and would be found before long unless they crossed the river. They had no choice. As quietly as they could, Ned and his party waded into the water.

Though the river wasn't wide, it was ice-cold, waist-deep, and its rocks underfoot were slimy and loose. As the water rose around him, Ned breathed in painfully. Step by tentative step they moved, Ned's heart and chest pounding, the river's cold current biting at his skin. There was now less than twenty feet between them and the second group of wolf-men. There was a flap of wings above them and a small kestrel swooped down low, first one then another. Was it one of Barba's tickers? Had they been spotted? One of the wolf-pack noticed, its keen ears pinned back and its slack jaw loose and wide as it sniffed at the air. The other three's fur bristled and they growled deep and low, scanning the riverbank for movement.

And that was when it happened.

Ned had noticed at various points in his life that when something truly awful took place, it appeared to do so almost in slow motion. As they approached the other side of the bank, he felt his foot give. It was slow and steady, but by the time he tried to counter the action, it slipped away from him entirely and Ned fell back into the freezing river with a loud splash. Gorrn's ooze muffled sound – but not, as it turned out, *all* sound. The weirs all stared as one, and as soon as they spotted the oozing shadow moving across the water, Gorrn began to shake.

A violent roar and all four weirs pounded through the river at a frightening pace, the other two closing from downstream. Benissimo and Mr Fox grabbed Ned by the shoulders and threw him on to the riverbank with a violent sweep of their arms.

"Odin's beard! RUN!" bellowed Benissimo.

Behind them the forest erupted and Ned, the Ringmaster and Mr Fox hurtled away as fast as their legs could carry them. Ned's clothes were sodden and his chest was pounding so hard he thought he might black out before the fang-toothed monsters caught up with them. Twice he stumbled and twice Mr Fox righted him. Branches broke underfoot and tore at Ned's cheeks as he charged forward, but it was no use – the pack's leader was gaining and fast, till Ned could almost feel his breath at his neck, his claws and teeth ready to gouge. Seeing the closing weir gain, Mr Fox turned deftly and unloaded his gun.

Pft, pft, pft.

Three successive shots and the weir howled, crashing to the ground in a jumble of angry limbs. The others stopped over him, enraged to see the life drain from one of their own.

"Silver bullets?" asked Ned as they surged on, and Mr Fox grunted a "yes".

"Arooo!" howled the other wolves, and the forest answered.

Ned couldn't see them, only hear the pounding of their feet as the ground shook. The taiga had come alive and it was speeding towards them. To their left and right branches snapped and trees shook, and from high up in the sky came the screeching of metal birds, flocking and preparing to dive.

"We can still make it. Just a few more feet – COME ON!" urged Benissimo.

And on they ran.

Ned couldn't or wouldn't look behind him but from the corner of his eyes he saw weirs gaining fast, not only wolf-men now, but the bear-clan, great hulking brutes of furred muscle barrelling towards them like trains – half man, half bear and all monstrous rage. Ned's limbs burned like fire. They couldn't hope to outrun them and there'd be no surviving if it came to blows – not without his ring!

"We're nearly there. *Move!*"

Ned looked ahead in horror. Benissimo must have gone mad. The sun's first rays were dawning and Ned could see that the forest had thinned to a clearing and beyond it a complete dead end – the foot of what seemed to be a steep cliff.

"Bene, what are you doing?! This is a dead end!" yelped Ned.

As the forest gave way to the clearing and daylight

spilled in from above, Ned could just make out a ledge in the rock face ahead; it must have been a good hundred feet above them. Just then two figures appeared at its edge and peered across the wood. The ground behind them thundered loudly as their enemies grew closer and Mr Fox turned and fell to one knee.

"Use your Taser, Ned – I'll down as many as I can. Bene, I trust you have a plan?" he shouted anxiously as he raised the gun's sights to his eye.

But Bene was just standing looking up at the ledge. A third figure had joined the other two on the ledge. He was far larger than the others, at least twelve feet in height, and Ned noticed that he and his two companions were wearing strange headdresses – until he realised that they weren't headdresses at all.

"Antlor and his herd, last of the great stags!" announced Benissimo triumphantly.

The mighty creature raised a horn to its lips and blew. *HUUUR!*

The forest behind them, every metal flapping wing and every snarling mouth, became quiet and still.

CHAPTER 17

Brother

The weir had run far and hard to reach the fortress. In the treaty his chief had made with Barbarossa, they had been promised freedom – a world without borders, a world where they answered only to themselves. Barbarossa, however, did not like bad news, and made ready to give him freedom of a different kind.

Breathless, the wolf-man had told him of two men and a boy in his forest – two men and a boy that had got away.

Breathless, Barbarossa had answered.

The familiars had poured from the butcher's arms like vengeful spirits, all gnashing and slithering, angry and wild. They were not like normal familiars. Barbarossa had changed them with some dark magic of his own making. Sar-adin, his Demon butler, watched without the slightest hint of compassion or remorse. In that both master and servant were the same.

"Are you sure that was wise, master? The weirs are our allies, are they not?"

"They think the taiga was theirs to give. They only made the taking easier. I will deal with the weirs; you will deal with my brother, the boy and the fool who joined them. They are not to leave the mountain."

"Capture or kill, master?"

"Bring my brother to me. Feed the boy and his accomplice to whoever wants them."

CHAPTER 18

The King in the Cave

King Antlor was nothing like the brutish creatures of the wolf-pack or bear-clan. Twenty feet tall and towering above everyone, he moved with poised majesty. Lit up by the flicker of torches, he seemed like a thing of dreams, a spirit of the forest come alive. He had two powerful legs in gold-brown fur, hoofed at the bottom, and above them a human torso, lithe but muscular, with strong arms and a pair of impossibly broad shoulders. His face though was every inch a stag, the fur like spun gold at his neck and forehead. Above his ears were not one but three full sets of perfect white antlers, at least eight feet across. Somehow the torchlight seemed to brighten and dull again with every breath of the creature's chest. Ned found him more terrifying than any of the Darklings he'd come across. They had been simmering rage, angry dogs of war, but the Stag King was a different kind of beast, alert animal intelligence, completely aware of everything around him and all the more frightening because of it.

As he led them to his throne, Benissimo turned to both Ned and Mr Fox. "King Antlor is a proud creature and noble, but do not forget his animal side. *No sudden movements.*"

"He's terrifying! I'm not surprised the weirs all ran!" whispered Ned.

"They weren't running from him."

"Then who?" asked Ned, confused.

Benissimo looked away, his moustache and goatee clearly twitching with nerves. "If I tell you, do you promise to remain calm?"

Something went off in Ned's head. It sounded like the *ding* of an alarm bell, only louder and broken.

"Bene, what have you done? What were they all so frightened of?"

But before Benissimo could answer, King Antlor spoke, the torches in the chamber flickering with his every word. "What lies beneath."

Ned looked up to see that the Stag King had taken his seat on a throne of woven branches, and was looking right at him.

"Please, come closer," King Antlor said, still looking at Ned.

As Ned and his small party approached the throne, more stag-men came out of the shadows till soon they were completely surrounded on every side.

Benissimo got down on one knee and bowed his head, and Mr Fox and Ned clumsily followed suit.

What exactly lay "beneath" and why had Ned been stupid enough to follow Benissimo without knowing more?

"We had almost given up on you," continued the Stag King, and even though he barely raised his voice, it carried across the entirety of his stone courtroom.

"The boy has been hard to find," answered the Ringmaster.

King Antlor breathed heavily through his nostrils, eyeing Ned intently. "Nothing good comes easily. Welcome, Engineer."

Ned could barely speak. It wasn't fear exactly – more like awe. As powerful and frightening as the Stag King and his herd were, he could almost smell the magic in their fur and he couldn't help but marvel at it.

"Thank you, your, erm, Your Highness."

Antlor nodded regally. "Word of your exploits has

found its way to my cave more than once. We are all grateful to you, son of Armstrong."

He then turned his attention to Mr Fox, his great dark eyes poring over him as though reading the page of a book. "You are human?"

"Mr Fox, of the BBB, Your Highness. And yes, I am a human."

Antlor sniffed at the air sharply. "You smell of… *nothing*, no past, no magic – how sad for you. I was human once; I do not recall liking it very much."

Before Mr Fox could work out how to respond, Benissimo addressed the courtroom solemnly. "I see it is true, Your Majesty – the forest is no longer your home."

There was braying and the scraping of hooves from the rest of the herd and their king looked positively pained.

"We fought them for months, Ringmaster, but the world has gone mad and the grass we once walked on grown sickly and black. Now only what lies beneath keeps the dark ones at bay."

Ned could feel his bones shake. What kind of creature was so bad, so positively frightening, that not even Demons and Darklings dare come near it?

"This is our sanctuary and our prison. The forest holds

more metal than bark or bone, and the bears and wolves – our one-time allies – now hound us at every turn."

"If my informant is right, Your Highness, the old one will have the answer to our woes."

The old one! thought Ned, remembering what the Demon at Mavis's had said. His skin prickled with something between excitement and fear.

"Pray your Demon speaks the truth! We will need more than arms and hooves to win this war."

King Antlor rose from his throne. Towering over them now, he took the horn he'd blown earlier from his waist, before stooping down and passing it to Mr Fox. "Use this when you need us, josser – we will hear it and we will come."

Ned wasn't sure why he'd singled out Mr Fox, but when he looked at the BBB's most prestigious operative he saw that the unflappable Mr Fox was in fact beginning to flap. The poor man's face had turned a very slight shade of green.

"Err, thank you. That is, erm, very kind."

The great stag sniffed at the air again and closed his eyes. "Fear not, human. Where the Ringmaster takes you now, fear will do you no good. If the old one wishes to end you, he need only breathe it and you will end."

CHAPTER 19

Older than Old

Benissimo and his party were led away from the courtroom down a meandering, torchlit passageway. The two muscled stag-men at their front and rear moved in complete silence and Ned decided to remain similarly quiet. Whatever he was about to yell at the Ringmaster could wait till they were alone. Gorrn slithered nervously in the shadows along the stone walls. Ned's mouse sat perched in terrified silence on his shoulder, peering out at the darkness without so much as a tick from his clockwork heart. The ground sloped downwards continuously and the further they walked, the warmer the air became, till the ground felt hot under their feet.

Almost half an hour had passed when they came to a thick stone barrier that blocked the way forward. The stag-men eyed each other nervously, then one of them fumbled a hand along the wall till it came upon a lever; a lever that had obviously not been used in some time. He pulled it and the metal groaned, finally shifting with a grinding of rock and metal. Gears turned, and a section of the wall gave way with a blast of stifling hot air. Ned covered his mouth and nose – it stank of sulphur and burning oil.

Their two guides handed Benissimo and Mr Fox their torches and motioned for them to go on. Clearly whatever Benissimo was searching for was not something that either of the two creatures was willing to meet. Even more troubling was the grinding of rock as the entrance was resealed behind them.

By the orange lick of firelight, Ned could see that they were in a large cavern; stalagmites and stalactites, jagged and sharp, were pointing up and down from the ground and ceiling, like hungering angry teeth. With every step down the hot stone ground, Ned seethed. He had no idea what they had come to see or why it was so dangerous, but if there was even the slimmest chance of not making it back to his parents, Ned wanted to know why.

"Right, goat-face, you had better start talking!"

Somewhere at his feet there was an irate "Arr" of

agreement from his familiar, and Whiskers backed Ned up with an irritable "Scree" followed by some lightning-fast eye blinks. The Morse code message in the robot's lit-up eyes was unintelligible because he was flashing them so quickly, but the sentiment was clear. Ned and his sidekicks were not happy.

"Now now, pup – you promised to remain calm."

"No, no, I didn't. You *asked* me to, but I never promised!"

"All the same, this isn't the time or place."

Ned was quite beyond caring about timing, or anything else for that matter.

"Time or place?! Benissimo, outside this stinking hot cave are the world's most terrifying creatures, like, *the* most dangerous things on earth, only they're all scared to death of what's down here. WHAT ARE WE ABOUT TO MEET and WHY DIDN'T YOU WARN ME?!"

"Well, you see, the security of the mission, and… you know, et cetera et cetera…"

"And *what*?"

"I didn't think you'd come if you knew."

At this point Ned could feel his peculiar rodent's fur bristle as Whiskers arched his back and then hissed – actually hissed, like an angry cat. The Debussy Mark

Twelve was going into attack mode, and behind them both, Gorrn had risen up over Ned as an angry block of be-toothed ooze.

When Mr Fox spoke, it was with his polite yet certain demeanour, though every so often there was a notable crack in his voice. "Ned, I think it might be prudent to calm down. I know you're angry, and I am too, though to be honest I'm a little more peeved with myself for insisting on joining you. The thing is, your friend George has been very helpful in getting me up to date with all things to do with the Hidden, and I've studied his collection of books extensively, so I like to think I know my 'creatures' at least in theory if not in practice. Have you noticed the air in here?"

"Err, yes, it's hot and it stinks."

"Yes, and it's getting hotter and, well, stinkier. From this fact I would deduce that old 'goat-face' here, as you call him, has brought us to see a dragon."

Dragons in any form were famously dangerous. That much Ned knew. They weren't, however, unbeatable, so that didn't explain the reaction of the Darklings outside.

Even under torchlight, Benissimo managed to look quite sheepish.

"Well?" asked Ned.

"Roo?" oozed Gorrn.

"Scree?" screed Whiskers.

"Our polite ally is correct," Benissimo admitted, "though Tiamat is not just any dragon. Tiamat is the father of *all* dragons."

Ned suddenly wished he hadn't asked. *"The father of all dragons?"*

"Look, we really don't have time to get into dragon genealogy, but to explain briefly, while most people can track their ancestors back a few generations, some even a few hundred years, dragons, and I do mean *all* dragons, can track their entire ancestry back to Tiamat. He is as old as this mountain and unimaginably powerful."

"And that stone barrier is to keep him out?"

"Actually, just his breath, pup. I doubt at his age whether he could squeeze a big toe through that opening."

Despite the heat, and the breathlessness in his chest, Ned felt a shiver of fear as cold as ice course up his back and neck. "So when the stag thing up there said, 'he need only breathe it and you will end'…?"

"He wasn't referring to the creature's voice. Dragons breathe fire, and this one breathes the most."

"If we get out of here, my mum and dad are going

to kill you, Benissimo, and if they can't figure out how, then I will."

"If you need any help at all, please consider me at your full disposal," said Mr Fox, who was thumbing the handle of his sidearm.

"Thank you, Mr Fox."

"Fox will do, and the pleasure really will be all mine."

There was an appreciative "Arr" from below and a bob of Whiskers' head.

Benissimo pursed his lips as though chewing on a rock. "When you two have quite finished becoming buddies, I suggest we crack on with our mission."

Step after step they went, the torchlight casting sinewy shadows in all directions. Ned had the horrible sensation of being watched. It was different from the forest. That place had been alive with eyes and ears, beaks, feathers and claws. As the sweat soaked his back and he pulled off his steaming winter coat, Ned was quite sure that only one set of eyes and ears was waiting. The big question was: waiting where?

They had come to the bottom of a steep incline when the rocks beneath them shifted. Their path was going gradually uphill now. Ned pulled the perometer from his pocket and checked the needle. It pointed forward. Nothing to fear yet then.

"So, Mr Fox," said Benissimo quietly, "glad you came?"

"I must admit the sensation of unrelenting fear and curiosity is a mixed bag, Mr B."

Benissimo chuckled. "They didn't train you for stag-men and dragons at your academy?"

"I wouldn't really know."

Benissimo turned to look at Mr Fox. "You don't know?"

"None of the BBB's operatives know anything – that is to say, anything about their past. I am something of a blank canvas. Which is why I can perform my job so well, without fear of distraction from anything or *anyone*."

Ned looked at Mr Fox too. He was every inch an operative, the consummate spy and soldier because, as Ned was just beginning to understand, he didn't know anything else.

"That... that must be awful?" stammered Ned.

"Protocol. The BBB is our entire life and I mean that literally. Friends and family are considered to be high risk, completely forbidden. We undergo years of extreme training, or brainwashing depending on your point of view. Our thumbprints are removed, our teeth replaced and finally, just to put the icing on the cake, we go through a twelve-month course of extreme hypnosis until we don't remember anything."

"But why?"

"I should think you'd know the answer to that, Ned? Didn't you have to do something similar to your friends?"

Mr Fox was right, and the memory of it hurt. Dear old Gummy and Arch back in safe cosy Grittlesby no longer remembered him. He had set the de-rememberer device to "ten" and any notion of Ned or their friendship had been permanently erased.

"To protect them *and* the mission. And you really don't remember anything at all?"

Mr Fox stopped walking. "I remember one thing, vividly, from before I became an operative." His expression suddenly grew dark. "And that's where I'd like to stop the conversation – thank you."

But before Ned and Benissimo were able to wonder why, from all around them, echoing back and forth along the cavern's walls, ceiling and ground, came a rumbling, deep and low.

"AND IT WAS JUST GETTING INTERESTING."

Benissimo's whip began to coil wildly and the ooze that was Gorrn sucked itself into Ned's shadow in a gurgling *shlup*. Whiskers made no sound at all, because the small rodent was simply too frightened to move. Ned checked the dial – its needle was spinning round and round! Either the thing had broken or the dragon was moving and fast.

"Tiamat?" started Benissimo.

"YES."

"Where exactly are you?"

"BENEATH YOU."

"Beneath us where?"

"YOU ARE STANDING ON MY NECK."

CHAPTER 20

The Stone Dragon

Benissimo had seen every wonder and horror that the Hidden had to offer, and of the latter he had fought most of them. Even so, as they climbed down past the dragon's ear and below its cheek, the Ringmaster was uncharacteristically quiet. Mr Fox was also mute, though in his case Ned got the sense that faced with such an unprecedented terror, he simply gave way to training and moved like a well-oiled machine, no foot or hand out of place, his mind remaining firmly on the mission.

Focus, thought Ned. *Stay calm*. But it did no good. As his trembling hands gripped on to the stone, he couldn't get away from the fact that the stone was in fact alive. So ancient was Tiamat that the dragon's scales and hide had fossilised to rock. Finally down on the ground, it was hard to see clearly which part of the rock before them was the dragon and which was the cavern in which he lay.

Then right in front of them a great vast eye blinked open, as high and wide as a house. Ned stopped breathing. The eye was green and blue, with a single black vertical slit down the middle that eyed them as though they were ants.

"LIGHT?" asked the dragon.

"Please," said the Ringmaster.

From far ahead of them, the dragon's nostrils blew and two perfectly aimed plumes of fire shot out. They landed at a far wall hundreds of feet away and some oily liquid there erupted with flames. All of a sudden the cavern filled with hot, orange-yellow light and the temperature in the already stifling air soared.

Ned squinted from the sudden brightness, his eyes adjusting slowly, and as they did so he could see that the stone that was Tiamat's skin was reflective, like polished black marble. It was like looking at the face of a shattered mirror, come alive with glistening reflections, and it was only when the dragon raised its head to look down on them properly that Ned could make out its shape and size. Tiamat was a great spiked behemoth with curving stalagmites rising from its head, neck and torso as tall as redwood trees and just as thick. Most of its body filled the cavern, though at the opening's highest point there was room for it to move its head and neck. The dragon's features were not so different to a dinosaur's, much like the pictures of T-rex that Ned had pored over as a child, though far larger. Every angle from which it studied them caused Ned unrelenting fear. The Stag King's words to Mr Fox rang out in Ned's head again.

"YOU ARE BRAVE TO COME HERE, RING-LING," boomed the dragon.

"Desperate times call for desperate deeds, old one," said Benissimo, who had regained his composure and removed his top hat as a show of respect.

"SO MY CHILDREN'S CHILDREN TELL ME IN THEIR SLEEP."

"Then you know of what goes on beyond your cave?"

"I DO NOT NEED THEIR SONGS TO TELL ME OF THE DARKENING KING. I FEEL HIM AS HE STIRS. IT IS THE ENGINEER THEY SING OF – IS THIS HE?"

"Yes, old one. I was told it was to him you wished to speak."

Tiamat lowered his head with a great rushing of wind so that he could eye Ned more closely. Hot air and burning sulphur filled Ned's nostrils and his cheeks reddened with heat. He'd been wrong to fear the Stag King, to be in awe of the creature. Tiamat was all-encompassing, his head large enough to blot out the cavern, his breath hot enough to peel away Ned's skin. It didn't matter that Ned had lost his power; nothing mattered in the face of Tiamat. In his gaze you were his to do with as he wanted.

"I am…" Ned mumbled.

"YOU ARE *SMALL*."

Ned winced. He was quite sure the creature had said it the way someone might say "snack". And, powers or not, he was truly small, truly insignificant under Tiamat's gaze.

"Yes, I-I suppose I am."

"THEN YOU MUST GROW STRONGER!" boomed the dragon. "OR YOU WILL FAIL."

As Ned looked into the creature's eyes, he sensed the cave and his companions slipping away from him as though he might be swallowed into the creature's mouth without it even moving.

"Fail *how*, Tiamat? What is it we must do?" asked Benissimo, and the dragon's gaze thankfully turned away from Ned and on to the Ringmaster.

"YOUR DEMON DID NOT TELL YOU?"

"Only that you knew of something, some ancient magic that we might use to fight the Darkening King."

Tiamat reared up angrily, pointing his great mouth to the top of the cavern, before blowing – and blowing hard. A huge pillar of molten, spittled fire poured out of him and into openings in the roof of the cavern. Far above them they heard the mountain tremor like a volcano as the dragon's fury was unleashed outside and into the cold Siberian air. Boulders began to tumble and break around them, till Ned thought the dragon might bring down the entire roof.

"TIAMAT WAS FIRST AND EVERYTHING BELONGED TO TIAMAT." Then his voice grew quiet and his great eyes closed. "*Until they tricked me.*"

"Who, old one? Who tricked you?" asked Benissimo.

"THE ONE YOU CALL THE DARKENING KING CAME *AFTER* ME! HE WAS NOT 'FIRST'. BEFORE BOOKS AND KINGS, BEFORE MAN-KIND, THE FEY WERE MY SERVANTS, TO DO MY BIDDING WHERE I WOULD NOT GO. BUT THE DARKENING KING WHISPERED TO THEM, TOLD THEM HOW THEY COULD GAIN THEIR FREEDOM AND IN DOING SO MAKE ME WEAK." His great eyes opened again and were full of rage. "THE

HEART STONE – *MY HEART* – THEY STOLE IT AS I SLEPT. IT IS THE SOURCE OF THEIR MAGIC AND IT IS *MINE*."

"You wanted to tell the boy this? How they wronged you?"

"YES AND NO. I WANT REVENGE FOR THE WRONG THAT WAS DONE TO ME. JUST AS HE WHISPERED TO THEM, I NOW WHISPER TO YOU: FIND THE HEART STONE. IT IS OF A PARTICULAR MAGIC, ONE THAT EVEN *HE* DOES NOT FULLY UNDERSTAND."

Tiamat swayed his great head left and right, like a snake being charmed.

"USE IT AT THE MOMENT THAT HE RISES AND YOU WILL DESTROY HIM."

"Will you help us?" asked Ned.

"DO NOT ASK ME – *ASK THE HEART STONE*. NOW LEAVE ME – I AM WEARY."

And the great dragon began to settle at the bottom of its cave, its head hitting the rocks with a thunderous crash. But there was one burning question that Ned needed to have answered.

"Before we go, could you please just tell me… why did you ask to see me?"

"MANY SONGS MY CHILDREN HAVE SUNG OF YOUR DEEDS. I WANTED TO SEE WHAT YOU ARE MADE OF."

"Why do you care?"

"BECAUSE IT IS YOU WHO MUST USE THE HEART STONE."

And with that, the great dragon closed both eyes completely and, with a signal from one of its mighty claws, indicated both that they should leave and where their exit lay.

Ned wanted to tell Tiamat that he was wrong, that the old Ned might have been the one to do it, but that *this* Ned had lost his powers. But he was far too frightened of the creature to disagree with him, or disappoint him, and besides, he could tell by the trembling snore that shook the cavern that the mighty and ancient Tiamat was now fast asleep.

CHAPTER 21

Trapped

Ned, Benissimo and Mr Fox emerged on the other side of the mountain at the top of a steep hill and away from the protective antlers of the herd. The sun had fully risen and as Ned laid Whiskers on the ground, his wind-up rodent let out a squeak.

"Oh, so you *do* have a tongue, do you?"

The Debussy Mark Twelve ignored Ned and peered down at the forest beneath them. Its little head bobbed one way and then the other. When he turned around, the rodent's eyes were blinking like furious bulbs and in frantic Morse code. Just as worrying were the telltale rumblings from the Tinker's perometer, and for maybe the first time Ned wondered if the little device did more harm than good.

"What is it, boy? What have you seen?"

Ned and Mr Fox deciphered the message together.

A long blink: "T". A dot, a dash and another dot: "R". By the time Whiskers had finished, "TROUBLE" had been clearly spelt, but not nearly as clearly as the sound of the ground trembling at the foot of their side of the mountain.

"Ground thumping and blinking mice, not an agreeable mix," said Benissimo. "Mr Fox, binoculars are standard issue with your lot, aren't they?"

Mr Fox already had them pressed up to his eyes.

"They're still in the forest's cover but I can make out Darklings, and what would appear to be… oh dear. I think they have the metal Guardians that Tinks told us about with them."

"Where?"

"Everywhere, Mr B."

"No obvious exit then?"

"No, nothing obvious," said Mr Fox.

Benissimo's whip unfurled itself and the Ringmaster's face hardened.

"Pup, I'm not sure that this will end well. Fox and I will carve you a way out of here. After that, head west and don't look back. May Odin protect you."

Ned gulped before cursing his ring. If only he could

still use it, harness its power somehow, he could help them at least.

Down below, the forest seemed to grow up the foot of the mountain, moving slowly at first, then faster and faster.

"Gorrn, I think I'm going to need you – rather urgently. Whiskers, old chum, stick with me, would you?"

Whiskers turned his head to one side. It was the turn of his little metal gears thinking. Finally he bobbed it in a "yes" and sidled up to Ned.

Down below the creeping shadow of forest became more detailed. It had arms and legs and teeth and claws. A row of yellow-eyed gor-balins walked slowly up the hill and at their front: a Demon. It was not disguised in human form like Sur-jan had been in Mavis's. It had deep-set eyes like firepits, a great set of horns as wide as its shoulders, and grey-black skin to match its grey-black teeth. Black armour covered its bulky muscles and it carried two curved scimitars, one in each hand. On its left and right were a pair of the Central Intelligence's Guardians. The Tinker's intel was right. The two machines marched in ordered silence, quite like the one that had almost flattened the troupe back at the Circus of Marvels all those months ago, though these ones were newer in design. Their frames were of burnished steel and chrome, more rounded than the angular scrapheap he'd fought before. It was like looking at an updated car design. These were faster, lighter and built for improved combat. They had no need of weapons – their arms were serrated and each of their metal hands ended with blade-like fingers worse than any claw Ned had seen. The one identical feature of the Guardians was their faces, moulded to look like protective angels, and all the more unsettling on their deadly frames.

Mr Fox put away his binoculars and started to grin.

"Why in Zeus's name are you smirking, Mr Fox?"

"Fox will do, Mr B."

In the air behind them there came the sound of distant thrumming.

"No first name, Fox?"

"Not that I know of, and I'm smirking because of Ned's mouse."

"Whiskers?! Hell's teeth, man, I really don't think now's the time to be marvelled by a wind-up pet!"

"Oh, I wouldn't know about that, Mr B. We jossers have our own magic though, and you might be interested to know that some of it was put into Whiskers by the Tinker before we left. Nanites, they're called, and they're more than enough for our friends in the sky to find us."

Above them, well over a dozen twin-bladed helicopters loomed out of the night, their powerful blades roaring.

Mr Fox looked up. "CH-47s – Chinooks, and I imagine with quite a useful payload."

Benissimo's moustache rippled as he broke into part of a grin. "Mr Fox, I have absolutely no doubt now that my brother will know of your involvement *and* that we are in alliance."

"Unavoidable, Mr B."

"Do you know, as much as it pains me to admit it, I'm rather glad you came along after all."

Seconds later, they were hammered by the beating wind of Mr Fox's cavalry, hanging over them in a controlled hover. When the first hatch was flung open, it was not a grey-suited operative of the BBB that Ned saw, but a focused wall of fur and muscle, and one that he dearly loved.

"George!" he yelped, and a second later, "Lucy!" as, next to the great ape, he spotted the golden hair of his friend and Medic.

From the sides of the swarming Chinooks came men, women and fair-folk, some suited in heavy grey armour, others with no need. Two trolls as large as granite rhinos pounded down the hill and hot on their heels came three dryads. As they ran, the ground at their feet erupted in green-vined chaos. Jossers and fair-folk ran together as one, and Mr Fox and Benissimo's strange alliance was about to be tested for the first time.

Two members of the cavalry held back: a bright-eyed Lucy and her hulking sidekick, George.

"Hello, old bean. Did you miss us?"

CHAPTER 22

Alliance

Gor-balins prefer better odds and their gaunt faces dropped as the grey-suits and fair-folk charged. Now emboldened, Benissimo and Mr Fox joined George and the three of them hurled themselves at the Demon, George knocking it to the ground with his shoulder as Benissimo's whip turned to flames and caught it about its neck. At its sides, grey-suits with their electrical batons were firing bolts of electricity at the Guardians in great arcs of blue light, and the creatures, though unable to feel pain, shuddered and stopped mid-strike.

Heart racing, Ned stole a moment by the Chinooks and their spinning blades with Lucy. Gorrn was undulating protectively in the shadows and Whiskers had already crawled up her leg and hopped into her readied arms.

"It's all right, Whiskers, everything's going to be fine," she hollered.

Ned watched her as she peered at the chaos. She looked different somehow – there was a sureness to her gaze that he hadn't seen before.

"Thanks for coming, Lucy. It's good to see you."

"You know, none of this would have been necessary if you'd just told us where you were. Now come on, quickly – let's give them a hand."

Ned's heart sank. Whatever trouble he'd been having with his Engine was clearly his alone. Lucy was already pacing down the hill and he hadn't the courage to tell her about his issue, or that he'd be useless in the fight.

"Ned?" said Lucy, turning back. "Don't just stand there – they need us!" But her face quickly paled at the sight of something behind him. "NED!"

He turned too late. A clenched fist came at him at a pace and struck him in the cheek. Dazed and confused, he fell to the floor, pain searing up the side of his face, and the world for a moment became black and blurred. Not all the gor-balins had cowered from the charge. In the clash that had followed, four of the creatures had used the chaos to circle round their flank and they now launched themselves at Ned and Lucy. Ned heard the squeak of his mouse as it leapt from Lucy's arms towards him, and saw Gorrn rise up, his vast mouth descending violently on one of the assassins.

"Grak!" he hollered, and the gor-balin was gone.

Lucy stood her ground, closing her eyes in deep thought, and another of the creatures howled. Ned could only guess at what she'd done inside its mind, but her powers proved more than enough to bring it to its knees.

The other two separated, one thrusting at Gorrn with its sword.

The other, to Ned's horror, pulled out its dagger and held it to Lucy's throat. It smiled. Even with its comrades fallen and the battle behind it all but lost, the gob's yellow eyes and sallow cheeks oozed with delight.

Lucy tried to pull away but the thin-limbed creature held strong, the claws from its hand digging at her arm.

"Ned?!" she cried.

His voice wouldn't carry over the din of the Chinook's blades or the raging battle, and even if it could, Benissimo and Fox would never reach them in time. Ned could only watch, just as he had outside Mavis's, just as he had a dozen times before.

"Lucy, I—"

"Squeak!"

Whiskers bit at the gor-balin's ankle and it howled before kicking the brave rodent away. Finally it laughed, eyes locked with Ned's as it drew the dagger so close to Lucy that her skin flared pink. He was going to cut her, to kill poor innocent Lucy right then and there, and there wasn't anything that Ned could do about it.

A fury fired inside him and he screamed, "STOP!"

And just as he did so, a pain shot up his arm, as bright and white as lightning. He could feel the atoms in the air with his mind, feel them fusing and growing in mass, hurtling at one another to be reshaped and *whoosh!* – his ring fired.

The gor-balin screamed and his scream was matched by another dozen down the hill. Ned refocused his eyes and saw that the ground by the Darkling's legs had erupted with great barbs of metal and ice. They'd shot up his body in an instant, forming a cocoon round it so complete, so complex and strong, that the air had been kicked from the creature's lungs, and the gor-balin stood helpless and frozen in place. Further down the hill, other gor-balins had met the same fate, encased where they stood and with no hope of escape. Knowing that the battle was lost, the Demon and its Guardians retreated from sight and back into the forest.

Giddy, ecstatic and very slightly delirious, Lucy fell on Ned and hugged him.

"Ned, that was amazing!"

Ned paused to catch his breath.

"I, erm, I'm not sure that I know how I did that," he finally managed.

"Told you we'd see them soon enough!" grinned Benissimo, as he came running back up the hill.

He inspected the cocoon-like prison that Ned had trapped the gor-balin assassin in with a whistle.

"Well, pup, whatever trouble you were having, it appears to have been fixed."

Ned looked at the Ringmaster. The man had led both him and Mr Fox into the worst imaginable danger and it was only because Ned's Amplification-Engine had for some unknown reason decided to work again that Lucy wasn't dead.

Ned flexed his hand slowly and tried his ring again, just a small test to see if it still worked. The air around his ring shimmered feebly, before sputtering away to nothing. The next time they came across the butcher's minions, both Engineer and Medic might not be so lucky.

"Benissimo, I think you and I need to talk."

CHAPTER 23

Brothers-in-arms

Benissimo was not a man that felt uncomfortable, not even when fighting Demons or meeting with kings. Yet, as the door to the twin-bladed helicopter closed and the Russian taiga fell away, he looked decidedly less like himself and more like a man about to face a firing squad.

That firing squad was Ned, and it was a one-man squad, Ned having asked the others to board one of the other transports and let him and the Ringmaster travel alone. George had looked utterly crestfallen, but Lucy gave Ned a knowing nod and boarded their Chinook in silence. Ned had gone so far as to ask his mouse to travel with Lucy, which the Debussy Mark Twelve was only too happy to do, having not seen her in months. Ned even ordered Gorrn to stay in his shadow and away from earshot.

"Bene, Lucy could have been killed!" Ned shouted.

Benissimo did not speak.

"We *all* could have been killed."

The Ringmaster pursed his lips very slightly and thumbed at his top hat.

"Do you ever think about anything except your mission? Anything except your holy crusade against your brother?"

Benissimo stopped thumbing his hat and his moustache visibly sagged. For a minute Ned thought he'd gone too far, when the Ringmaster finally answered. "No."

"I knew it. You don't care about—"

"APOLLO'S FLAMING CHARIOT, PUP, WILL YOU LET ME SPEAK?!"

Bene was on his feet, his whip lashing at the seat like an angry snake, and Ned thought he was about to hit him. The man looked heartbroken or crazed, or somewhere in between. His great chest heaved and he exhaled before taking his seat again.

"I don't care about anything else, Ned, because I do care about you, about Lucy, what's left of the troupe, about every living thing, man or beast that my brother has harmed or intends to harm. You are and have always been my responsibility. Now, I said I'd explain and I will, but what I am about to tell you remains between us, Ned.

Not even Kitty ever heard these words pass from my lips, though I think she had a sense of it."

Ned quietened down. He'd never heard Benissimo talk like this before. Every word looked pained, as though just forming the letters in his mouth was a torture he couldn't bear.

"To know why this is so personal, I need to tell you about my brother and I, how we came to be what we are."

"Bene, I know. I know it's the Darkening King that cursed you. Barba already told me."

The Ringmaster raised a hand and Ned stopped.

After a long pause, he finally spoke. "I have always known that the curse came from a Demon, but it wasn't until Jonny Magik told us about the Darkening King that I suspected. You see, my brother and I are old, Ned… very, *very* old."

Ned gulped. "How old?"

"I was born in Venice. The year was 1572."

"1572!"

Benissimo frowned. "Ned, this is hard enough. At that time the doge ruled the city, but behind him were its wealthy merchants. My father was one of them. The world was in his hands – he had a great estate, ships that sailed across the Mediterranean trade routes carrying silks and glass and coffers filled with gold. But it wasn't enough."

Benissimo rubbed at his scalp, as though trying to massage out the words.

"A strange thing happens when a man feels success – he wants to bask in its splendour, to revel in it. My father wanted to do so forever, to count his coins till the end of time. A woman came into his life who told him of a way he could. My father thought she was a wise gypsy. I knew even then she was a witch, and no Farseer like Kitty or Lucy but one embroiled in the dark arts. She told him that life eternal could be granted if he were to make a sacrifice, but only if it were great enough to break his heart."

"You?" gasped Ned.

"Please, pup! She told him that to live forever he would have to take the life of the thing he loved most… my mother."

Ned felt the bitter taste of horror in his mouth, but managed this time to hold his tongue.

"He spent weeks labouring over his decision, torn between love and his lust for power and immortality. I found out his intentions and was rushing to stop him, but my brother intervened and we fell to blows. I still carry the scar and he the wounded leg. Barba loved our mother, but like my father thought that power was more important; that, however dear, the price was worth paying. They could not have foreseen how wrong they were – when he took my mother's life the gift of immortality was granted, but not to my father. The witch had tricked him and the curse of eternal life fell to us instead."

Ned had never heard anything more ghastly in his life and if it had been any other man he would have reached across and hugged him.

"Bene, I'm so sorry."

"You still need to know why it's personal, pup. For a Demon to cross the Veil and walk on the other side takes an act of true wickedness, true evil. It took me time to see what Barba already knew. To make the Darkening King cross would take, and has taken, a dozen lifetimes. The Demon who told me about the Heart Stone told me many things, things that only their kind could possibly know. That witch didn't understand what she'd set in motion, but somehow the Darkening King had guided her hand and tongue from within its prison in the earth's core. Barba has walked the world spreading war and murder for hundreds of years – and for hundreds more,

I have fought him. Those battles, those lives lost, have fed the beast, enough to enable him to cross over when At-lan fired."

"Bene, are you saying it was all part of his plan?!"

"One of many, no doubt, but our lifeblood is his own. I know that now. After our battle in Annapurna, I thought my brother was dead, I thought the curse was lifted, but now I understand. It can never be lifted, and as long as we live, so will he."

Benissimo's moustache was trembling now and he looked to the floor.

"The Darkening King is my responsibility, just as my brother is. The three of us are linked, our lives and fates intertwined. So in answer to your question: yes, it's personal, and yes, it's all I care about – ending our cursed lives so that yours and the rest of the world's may go on."

CHAPTER 24

Headquarters

By the time Mr Fox's wing of Chinooks had returned to base, it was long after sunrise on the British coastline, near the cliffs of Dover. It was only when the helicopters touched down and their blades stopped that Ned understood where the BBB's base actually was. As he stepped on to the tarmac, he was met by Mr Fox, closely followed by Whiskers and Gorrn. Benissimo went over to debrief George and Lucy and what it was – *exactly* – that they should all be telling Terry and Olivia Armstrong.

Suddenly the whole compound, with its warehouses and lorries, started to tremble. Every inch of tarmac, every lamp post and every brick slowly and noisily lowered.

"What's going on?" breathed Ned.

Mr Fox looked worn out from the journey, but still managed to smile. "We may not have a Veil, Ned, but we do have a few surprises of our own. You are standing on the single largest 'lift' ever made."

Ned watched in wonder as the entire compound lowered into the earth, foot by foot, floor by floor, of the BBB's hidden base. Each concrete level was at least fifty yards high and housed different machines, from jump jets to tanks, jeeps and transports, and each and every floor cut deep under and into the British countryside.

"It's amazing, but don't people ask questions – you know, about the sinking?"

"We're in a military zone, Ned – regular people don't get to see it. Our 'lift' is for satellite surveillance. Seen from space it looks as though we haven't budged an inch."

"Clever."

"I'm glad you think so," said Mr Fox, who began to whistle as the giant lift sank further into the ground. It was a strange sort of a tune, not really a tune of any particular sort, but both soothing and jaunty nonetheless.

"Mr Fox?"

Mr Fox stopped.

"Why are you whistling?"

"Whistling calms my nerves."

The hairs on Ned's arm rose. "And why are you nervous, Mr Fox?"

"It's Fox, Ned, just Fox. And I'm nervous because I know what's going to be waiting for us on the other side of those doors."

Which was when their giant lift came to the thirteenth and last floor of the base, the one that housed the Hidden.

They were greeted by the sight of his mum shaking her head very slowly from side to side while sucking the air in through her teeth. Her arms were folded and her foot tapping on the ground. He'd only seen her take that pose once before and the ensuing outburst had been truly terrifying. Ned's dad, on the other hand, did not look like his dad at all. Terry Armstrong was a kind man, *too* kind even at times. But Ned had seen him flatten Barbarossa with a single blast from his ring and it had been in order to protect his son. His eyes were wild and his face red, and there was no doubt he was gearing up for some flattening.

The worst part, though, the part that made his predicament quite clear, was Lucy Beaumont. His friend had caught up with him and looked at Ned with such sincere sympathy that he felt that moment might very well be his last.

"Ned?" said Mr Fox.

"Yes, Fox?"

"You were very brave back there, in the forest – this shouldn't be too bad in comparison."

"Thanks. You were very brave too."

"Not sure I would have been at your age, Ned, not up against those… those *creatures*."

"Course you would."

"Well, I'll never know now, will I?"

As they waited for an onslaught of a different kind, Ned realised that the man was a true enigma, not only to Ned and Benissimo, but also to himself.

CHAPTER 25

Mr Bear

Mr Fox's room was completely bare. Operatives of the BBB had no knick-knacks or family photos with which to decorate their rooms. There was only the work. After a shower, Mr Fox had laid curled up in a ball for more than two hours. He had not slept. Of all the memories he had to have kept from "before", why this one? Why one that filled him with so much fear?

His laptop was dinging and had been for more than ten minutes. He sat up, shook his head and pressed the green button to "accept".

"Fox?!"

The man in the window of his screen was a ruddy-cheeked man, with a bulbous nose, huge greying eyebrows and hair that was as wild as it was thick. In the time that Mr Fox had known Mr Bear, he had never seen him in any state other than unrelenting anger. It was as if he was quite incapable of any other emotion.

"Bear, I'm sorry, I was in the shower. You've read my report?"

"Of course I've read your blasted report – that's why I want to talk to you! A dragon, for pity's sake?! And f-f—"

"Fairies, sir?"

"Yes, blasted fairies!"

"Well, it is a lead, sir. If Benissimo can get his hands on this stone, we may yet have a way of stopping this thing."

Mr Bear calmed. "You've done well, Fox. Keep at it and report everything you see. If you miss anything, Mr Spider will, I'm sure, fill in the gaps."

Mr Fox did not like being reminded of the ever-watchful Mr Spider, but he let it go. There were more important matters to discuss.

"Bear?"

"What?"

"This stone, sir… if it doesn't work?"

"Then we finish things the old-fashioned way."

Mr Fox said nothing.

"Do you have a problem, Fox?"

"No, sir. It's just… so extreme."

"There are always casualties, Fox, *always*."

Mr Fox looked away from the screen and began to hum, very softly.

***

Ned, Lucy and George sat in the corridor outside the briefing room on a grey plastic bench.

The corridor was like all the corridors in the BBB's base. Grey for the most part, immaculately clean to the point of being sterile and with the kind of peaceful lighting and orderly layout you might expect from a futuristic base hidden hundreds of feet underground. Doors here opened and closed with airtight silence, and the walls were thick and well insulated – but not, it seemed, quite thick enough to completely mask out sound. There was little in the world more formidable than an angered Armstrong parent, except perhaps for two. Olivia's furious outburst when they had discovered that Benissimo was working with the BBB now felt like a mere warm-up.

"*Oww!* That hurts! Terrence, can you please ask your wife to calm down?"

"Calm down?! I'll show you calm, *you snake!*" roared Ned's dad.

Crash!

Something on the other side of the wall broke.

"Do you think we should do something?" laughed Lucy.

"Honestly, dear girl, I should think if I go in there now it'll be like throwing petrol on a lit match," said George.

Crunch!

"That sounded like filing cabinets," grinned back Lucy.

Smash!

"Glass; that was definitely glass."

Ned felt dreadful. He was still reeling after what Benissimo had told him. The poor man quite literally carried the weight of the world on his shoulders. Lucy and George and the others knew of his curse, of course, but they had no idea of the extent of it; that it came from the Darkening King himself, the very creature they were all so desperate to defeat.

"Terry, we've been friends a long time… If you'd just let me explain!" pleaded Benissimo.

"Wow, he sounds genuinely frightened!" said the ape. "Benissimo, fearless leader of the Circus of Marvels, ageless, unkillable and—"

"Olivia Armstrong, I'd like to remind you that besides being a deft hand with a blade, you are also—"

"You kidnapped MY SON!"

"He came of his own accord!"

CRUNCH!

The briefing room went eerily quiet. Suddenly panicked that his parents might actually have gone too far, Ned stood up and went for the door handle.

"Don't worry – they're not actually going to kill him, Ned," said a smiling Lucy. "They know they can't anyway, and he's not really frightened. I think they're just going through the motions because they sort of should."

"Are you sure?" asked George, who was still loving every minute of it.

"I'm a Farseer, remember? If it was really going to end in tears, I'd know by now."

Ned sat back down again and looked at his friends. "It's good to see you both. It's been rough out there these past few months."

"I know, it's been rough on all of us. It's like the rules have changed and no one knows what the new rules are," said Lucy.

"I think, and not for the first time, that our illustrious leader is making them up as he goes."

"At least someone's trying, George," snapped Ned.

"I'm only teasing, old bean. I love Bene as much as any of us."

Lucy sighed, all the good humour gone from her voice for a moment. "I know he's doing his best, but he's so alone, in every possible way. He's lost Kitty, Madame Oublier and half the troupe – and he's too afraid of failing to let anyone else near."

If only they knew, thought Ned, and as much as he felt a true friend would tell them Benissimo's secret, he also knew that if he really cared for the man, he couldn't and wouldn't.

"At least he's got us," was all he managed.

"LIAR!" shouted Ned's dad through the wall.

"I think he's going to need a bit more than 'us'," smirked George. "Your dear old mum and dad are going to give him the walloping of a lifetime."

But Ned wasn't smiling. Aside from Benissimo and his parents, what was really troubling him was what the dragon had told him. Despite his fluke on the mountain, he had tried his ring continuously on their return journey and as before it had remained completely dormant. Ned simply wasn't the boy that Tiamat thought he was – not any more.

"Lucy, George, please keep it to yourselves but I'm—"

"Worried about your powers, about the ring," cut in Lucy.

"Yes! Ever since At-lan, since we sparked the weapon—"

"You haven't been able to use it, at least not until just now. It starts but drops the connection and you have no idea if or when it will work again."

Ned's eyes crossed. In the past Lucy had finished his sentences as though she was reading his mind. This was different: Lucy actually *was* reading his mind.

"Lucy, I—"

"I know, I know, we're friends and I shouldn't be using my gifts on you, Ned, but in a few seconds this wall is going to break and we really don't have a lot of time."

"What? Lucy, I—"

"I know, you're a bit annoyed with me right now, and you're right. I *can* help you, Ned, and no, I haven't heard the voice either."

Ned gave up talking and simply gawped like a startled goldfish.

"It's all right, Ned," said Lucy with a smile. "I've got you, and so has this big lump of fur." George grinned. "Oh, and by the way, DUCK!"

Lucy pulled Ned to the floor suddenly, when – *BOOM!* – the wall right by their bench broke apart before turning to shards of ruptured steelwork, its plastic and plasterboard vaporised to dust. Ned's dad had let his ring run wild.

The lighting in the now silent corridor flickered on and off erratically and there was a faint smell of burnt wiring coming from the newly made gash. Through the hole and its fizzing atoms, Ned heard his mum.

"Terrence, dear, I think we've made our point. Now, what's all this about a Heart Stone, you old goat?"

CHAPTER 26

A Brief Debrief

Ned sat between George and Lucy, across the table from his parents. They had made it quite clear that they wanted to have "words" with him, and Ned in kind had made it quite clear that he did not. Whatever they thought of his disappearing act would have to wait. It was time to move on to the subject of Tiamat's Heart Stone, and the small issue of how to get their hands on it.

A defiant-looking Benissimo sat by the Tinker and Mr Fox. He had survived the Armstrongs' assault with his usual bravado and looked at Ned as the room droned on with something approaching a grin, before giving him a wink. The unfortunate Ringmaster had already been wrongly accused of Madame Oublier's murder, forced to live in confined secrecy for months and, as Ned now understood, he also carried the full weight of the world on his shoulders. But Benissimo wasn't beaten, and Ned suspected that if the day ever came that he was, the Ringmaster would just wink at it and crack on regardless.

"How do you know the dragon can be trusted?" asked Ned's mum.

Benissimo paused. "We don't, but our informant was very clear in stating that Tiamat knew something that we could use against the Darkening King, which seems to tie in with the dragon's story."

"The informant who's a Demon and who *you have never met*."

Benissimo was doing his best to remain calm, though Ned sensed from the way his whip was currently curling on the table that it would not last.

"Yes, Livvy, *that* Demon."

"And it does also tie in with what the Demon in Mavis's tea room said, to find the 'old one'," said Ned, coming to Benissimo's aid.

"So if both dragon and Demons are telling the truth, and if we do manage to prise this thing away from the Fey, my son is supposed to use it *how* exactly?"

"I don't know," said Benissimo, who was now grinding his teeth so hard that Ned could hear them.

"And if we do figure out what he's supposed to do, how does Ned get near enough to actually do it? With his powers as they are, teleporting in there is absolutely out of the question."

Ned's eyes rolled. His current state really didn't need any more highlighting and it sounded like she was purposefully trying to shoot down Benissimo's plans before they'd even been made.

"We have a growing army in St Albertsburg led by the Viceroy, and those willing to fight alongside us are flocking there as we speak. The Viceroy's word still holds weight amongst fair-folk the world over and his fleet is being rebuilt in earnest. Besides the men Mr Fox here has promised us, there are pockets all over the Hidden that will answer our call."

"Ahem," started the Tinker quietly, "I have something that might help. It strikes me that one of our biggest hurdles is the swarm of ticker sentries now inhabiting the taiga, along with the army of Guardian-class machines Barbarossa has placed in the fortress."

"Not counting the vast gathering of Demons and Darklings that appears to be growing by the day," said Ned's dad.

"Yes, Terry, not counting them. I have a great-uncle,

ancient by anyone's standards, who I haven't seen in decades. We kept in touch loosely over the years, but when Barba stole the Twelve's tickers… well, he started to make contact more regularly."

Benissimo's shoulders finally dropped, if only a little, and he sat forward in his chair. "Go on, Tinks."

"He's been working on something, something of a breakthrough, and wants to meet."

"What kind of a breakthrough?"

"All I know is that it has something to do with Tickers – *all* Tickers."

Benissimo pushed his chair back. "Fox, we're going to need transport."

"I shall make arrangements. How many men do you need?"

"None."

"*None?*"

"If Barba didn't know about us working together, he certainly does now. The smaller we keep this, the better our chances of going in unseen. Olivia, Terry and I will pay a visit to the Fey. Ned will join George and Lucy as they chaperone the Tinker on his family reunion. By blood and thunder, we may well have a way out of this mess before the week is out!"

Benissimo's chest was now puffed up with swagger and his whip wriggled like an excited eel.

Ned's mum, however, was not satisfied. "Now you look here, Bene, I haven't agreed to any of—"

"Mum!"

Olivia Armstrong turned to Ned. "It's not up to Benissimo, *or* you. None of this is up to any of us."

"What are you talking about?"

"Yes, son, what are you saying?" added Ned's dad.

"We've spent months in hiding, like everyone else in this room, and for what? To find a way of undoing the Darkening King. Well, Bene's got one – better than anything *we* came up with – and if we don't all pull together then we may as well walk into the taiga and tell Barba he's won."

Ned's dad's eyes shimmered with what looked like a glint of pride, but Olivia Armstrong still needed convincing.

"Ned, you're just a boy and—"

"Mum, I'm going, and that's final."

George chuckled nervously and Mr Fox stared at his notebook and hummed. Things were about to go one way or the other.

"Ned, I…" began Olivia, but as she looked at the

faces round the table something shifted and she sighed. "Fine."

Lucy didn't say anything but put her hand on Ned's with a gentle squeeze that said: "well done".

CHAPTER 27

Father and Son

There was a time before the Hidden, before circuses, before Ned had found his mum, when his world had consisted of Terry Armstrong and a decidedly odd mouse.

Ned stood on the runway, with the very same mouse on his shoulder and a worried but loving father unable to let go. Everything had changed and yet so much was the same.

"I'll be all right, Dad."

"All right isn't the same as safe."

"None of us is going to be safe until this is over."

His dad peeled away, eyes misty but brimming with pride. "It takes a brave boy to do the right thing, even when he's scared."

"Takes a brave dad to let him."

His dad's stare flitted to Lucy and George, who were helping the Tinker board their Chinook.

"You really think Lucy can help you?"

Ned turned to look over his shoulder. "I don't know what I'm supposed to do with the stone, or even why it has to be me, Dad, but if it does, and if it's linked in any way to my ring, then yes, I'd say Lucy is the only person who can help me."

"Keep her close, son, her and the ape."

***

Elsewhere, in the Siberian taiga, three clowns made ready. Sar-adin eyed them disdainfully. Barbarossa had insisted he send them and it was only when his master explained why that the Demon understood. Eanie, Meanie and Mo were in turn cruel, stupid and grotesque, but together they had a strange way of getting things done.

"Find them, or the master will have you skinned."

"No skinny-do, Sar-adin. Mo findee boy, Mo good clowney," simpered the big one.

Barbarossa understood the importance of his underlings' weaknesses. Of all the traits that the three unwashed creatures had, cowardice was their most useful attribute. They would do absolutely anything to please Barbarossa and his Demon – they were simply too frightened of what would happen to them if they didn't.

CHAPTER 28

Clockwork Museum

As the van trundled through the streets of Amsterdam, Ned found himself missing the sway and tilt of an airship. There was something in the purr of their propellers and the yawn of their rigging that gave him a sense of calm. That said, George's snoring had much the same effect.

Holland is known for many things: the flatness of its land, its football and its tulips. The capital, Amsterdam, has a complex web of canals and an abundance of bicycles that weave and dodge through its cars and trams, but there is one thing it does beyond compare: museums.

Down a lesser-known street in one of its lesser-known suburbs is an almost completely unknown museum, mostly because nobody knows it's there. Mr Cogsworth's Mechanarium had sat in quiet obscurity for decades and when the Tinker parked down an alleyway to its side,

Ned could see why. The sun was setting and under its gentle orange glow it was almost impossible to see into the museum. The windows were black with years of grime, and what might have been a signpost was so riddled with cobwebs and dust that its brass lettering had turned to a greying blob of meaningless shapes.

"Come on," said Tinks. "He said to be here before closing and we've only a few minutes."

There was an apish rumble from within the van. George had woken up.

"I don't like it. Not one bit," he muffled.

Ned patted the van's rear doors affectionately. "It's all right, George. It's his great-uncle and we don't want to scare the locals now, do we?"

"I'm not scary; I'm perfectly polite."

"Don't worry, any trouble and we'll squeal," said Lucy, and she joined Ned and the Tinker as they made their way to the entrance.

"Dear old Faisal. We minutians have a longer lifespan than most, but it's a wonder he's still going. He was such a character in his day, always about to discover the next big thing," explained the Tinker, who was on this rare occasion excited to be in "the wild" and out of his usual lab coat.

As they opened the front door, they were met by a mass of miniature musical instruments, seemingly welded together into a single machine: a piano keyboard no larger than Ned's hand, cymbals the size of ears and tiny trumpets the length of fingers, amongst others. They were all arranged round an opening in the wall and doing their best to play a rendition of "Happy Birthday to You". Sadly the brass section blew out little more than dust and the piano was completely out of tune. Little bulbs lit up at the machine's centre round a doll-sized conductor. The doll turned on its heel and gave a metallic rasp.

"*One visitor, one coin,*" came the recording.

Then the doll held out its hand.

The Tinker grinned and produced three coins from his pocket.

"You know, before we made Tickers we used to make toys. Great-uncle Faisal's house was full of them."

He placed a coin on the conductor's hand and the mechanical wonder flung it over its shoulder, where it was caught by a flapping metal purse. Sadly, with the third and last coin, the little automaton's arm broke clear off and the metal disc spun to a standstill by its feet.

"I'm guessing he doesn't get a lot of visitors," smiled Lucy.

All the same, the turnstiles turned and beyond them the museum sprang to life. Countless light bulbs buzzed with light, spelling out the words MR COGSWORTH'S MECHANARIUM – WELCOME. The "W" of WELCOME promptly blew a fuse and there was a moment when they thought the whole room might go dark. A voice rang out through speakers in the ceiling with much the same metallic twang as the entrance's conductor, though it did seem a little more human somehow.

"Welcome, visitors! You are on a tour both historic and wondrous. The life and times of Faisal the Magnificent. Oh, and please do not touch the exhibits."

What came next really was wondrous, though Ned wasn't entirely sure it was historic. The walls, floors and ceilings came alive with tiny clockwork people, and only four of them malfunctioned before completely falling apart. They busied themselves with the moving of stages and props, some large, some less so, and all spinning in and out of view in a dizzying rotation of sound and moving metal. Ned's ring finger hummed ever so softly and his thoughts went to his dad. Terry Armstrong would have been in his element.

"1862 – Rocket-mail," announced the voice over the speakers.

And in front of them a small rocket on wires was dragged through the air, dropping tiny paper envelopes that the automatons caught with varying success.

"Oh, I remember my father telling me about that one!" grinned the Tinker excitedly.

"*1877 – the Underwater Bicycle.*"

Out of an opening in the wall came a half-sized bicycle ridden by an equally small pilot, who gasped for air as he rode along a metallic ocean floor.

"Possibly not his best," whispered Tinks, who Ned noticed was looking more and more misty-eyed by the second. The entire exhibition was devoted to the inventions of his great-uncle.

Everywhere they looked, exhibits went by, lit up by spotlights in the ceiling, and it took Ned a few moments to realise that they were standing on a conveyor belt. They passed by three more rooms with a never-ending display of contraptions.

The Auto-chewer was incredibly messy and spat out bits of half-munched biscuit all over the automaton it was supposed to be chewing for. Mr Moppit was an early Ticker design that had mops for arms and legs but made more mess with its "multi-hose" than it was able to clear up. As they approached the late 1800s, something changed. There were fewer exhibits to do with helping people get about or chew their food, and more and more exhibits to do with the advancement of Ticker design itself. When they passed the 1900s, everything suddenly stopped and the lights grew dim.

"Thank you for coming. Please make your way to the exit."

"Now what?" asked Lucy.

"I'm not sure, Miss Lucy. I suppose we wait."

The room was eerily quiet, its contraptions lifeless and still. Ned was just beginning to think that Tinks's great-uncle was no more than a footnote in a museum when a door opened at the far wall, and a brass Ticker stepped into the room.

The Ticker was about Tinks's height, with brass eyes, a wire-brush moustache and a round, barrel-shaped belly. Every step from the old machine caused a tiny puff of steam and one of its legs clearly needed oil, judging by all the noise its joints were making. No detail had been spared. It had a monocle lens at one eye, and a rather friendly multi-jointed face that seemed quite capable of turning a smile. And in fact, at the sight of Tinks, it did smile, and Tinks himself looked positively close to tears. Whiskers too, who had till then been sitting very quietly on Lucy's shoulder, hopped down to the ground and ran up to the old machine in a scurrying blur of rodent excitement.

"Mr Cogsworth!" exclaimed Tinks. "By the Great Gear, he actually finished you! I remember old Faisal building your parts. He said you'd change the world. Said you'd be a bigger deal than the Auto-chewer."

"Hello, Tinks. Let's hope he was right."

CHAPTER 29

Mr Cogsworth

Ned and his two companions found themselves sitting in Great-uncle Faisal's cosy living quarters. Family pictures covered the walls and a much younger Tinks was in several of them. A kettle boiled on a wood-burning stove that looked as if it hadn't been used in years, and the Ticker that was Mr Cogsworth rummaged away steamily in a cupboard for some teabags. As he did so, Whiskers continued scampering between his legs like an excited puppy.

"Do forgive me, it's been an age since I've had to brew tea," croaked the machine.

Aside from the comfy chairs and pictures, the rest of the room had been given over to become a workshop of sorts, with a similar appearance and organisation to the Tinker's.

"Home from home, eh, Tinks?" whispered Ned.

The Tinker smiled so wildly it looked as though he might hurt himself.

"Tell me, Mr Cogsworth, where *is* my great-uncle?"

"If you don't mind, sir, there are a few things I should discuss with you first. For one, the reason that he asked to see you."

Mr Cogsworth closed the cupboard and his shoulders sagged. "I'm so sorry, I'm afraid we don't seem to have any tea."

Ned had had Whiskers all his life, and he must have seen hundreds of Tickers since discovering the Hidden, but Faisal's invention really was quite unique. The only Ticker he had ever heard speak was the Central Intelligence and the thought of it doing so made him shudder. Mr Cogsworth, on the other hand, was rather polite and moved with a certain slowness that made him seem almost gentle.

"Can't Faisal tell me himself?"

"Of course, but before you see him, you really must hear what I have to say."

And at that, Mr Cogsworth moved rather stiffly to one of the armchairs before sitting down with a rusty groaning of his springs.

"Do you know why your great-uncle left Gearnish?"

"My father wouldn't speak about it, but I later found out that it was not under the best circumstances."

Mr Cogsworth's bulb-like eyes dimmed. "You're quite right. You see, Faisal was one of the very first to really push advances in Ticker design. He was way ahead of his time and within a few short years his creations were being produced all over the city. Great advances were made by your great-uncle and later by others. But his focus soon turned to the pursuit of AI – artificial intelligence. He wanted the machines to think for themselves. He envisaged a future where Tickers might replace farmers, doctors and factory workers; food and medical attention for *everyone*. The Central Intelligence was his very first experiment in that field."

The Tinker's face turned to ash. "Great-uncle Faisal? He-he developed the Central Intelligence?"

"Yes and no. When he published his findings, the ruling Gears who ran the city immediately went into production, despite his warnings that they weren't ready. Furious, he locked himself away to continue his studies till, more than a year later, he came upon something. He realised that AI, by its very definition, was dangerous in that a creature without a soul could not truly determine right from wrong. But it was too late, the Central Intelligence had already been built, and it quickly set about automating the city's factories – seemingly without any problems. Only your great-uncle foresaw what would happen."

"And then, Mr Cogsworth? What happened then?" demanded the Tinker.

"Your uncle expressed his concerns to anyone that would listen, but those in charge did everything in their power to ridicule him; to make sure that his findings were thrown out as nonsense by anyone he took them to. A broken and discredited man, nearly at the end of his days, he left Gearnish and came here."

The Tinker looked truly devastated. "Well, it's just awful – poor Great-uncle Faisal, all those years locked away in this museum, and for what?"

Mr Cogsworth's metal face rippled into a smile. "To crack the AI problem and learn how to undo the machine that his research had helped create."

The Tinker's little brow wrinkled. "And did he?"

"Oh yes, Tinks, he did. He knew that without a soul, an AI was just a set of numbers, a code. But your great-uncle is a very tenacious man. He discovered – with a little magical assistance – a way to duplicate the soul, to make a digital copy, so to speak, the first of which he put into a wind-up mouse."

At this Whiskers leapt on to the automaton's lap, his little head bobbing up and down happily. Ned's eyes grew wide – surely he wasn't talking about *his* mouse?

But before he got a chance to ask, Mr Cogsworth continued. "After many years, he went on to further his findings, in me. You were right, Tinks, I am indeed a bigger deal than the Auto-chewer."

"I'm sorry, Mr Cogsworth, I'm not sure I understand. And where *is* he? Why can't he explain all this himself?" demanded the Tinker.

"Oh, but he just did, Tinks. I am your great-uncle Faisal, and the one thing capable of bringing down the Central Intelligence."

CHAPTER 30

A Decent Pub in Dublin

Terry and Olivia Armstrong could not be a more formidable force, especially when combined with the enigma that was Benissimo. There was very little that Terrence, with the help of his ring, could not "amplify" into existence, and in turn, there was very little that his wife did not know about how to fight, what tools to use, what strategies to employ and with what mindset to do the fighting. Before Ned's birth, Terry and Olivia Armstrong had followed the Ringmaster into the fray countless times and the "old-goat", impervious to harm as he was, had never let them down.

Today, though, was not that kind of day.

"I thought you said the Seelie Court were friendly?!" roared a red-faced Terry Armstrong.

"King Oberon was – his son's another matter!" panted back Benissimo.

Their party of three had been running now for more than thirty minutes. The streets of Dublin had a turning, twisting way to them that seemed to go on endlessly and the screaming Fey behind them did not know the meaning of tiredness. An angry fairy could chase its target indefinitely. Sweat pouring, chests beating and tempers flaring, Benissimo and the two Armstrongs stopped to look back down the street at the approaching throng of crazed magic. It was three in the afternoon and the busy shoppers going about their business couldn't see through the Fey's glamours. Had they been able to, they would have screamed at the tree-men, twenty feet high, with jagged branchy spears; they might have marvelled at Oberon's Nightwatch, a magical battalion of inch-high knights riding on the back of hummingbirds; or perhaps been petrified by the sight of magic-wielding spell-casters with the body armour of insects, barrelling between the tree-men's legs in blurs of green, lilac and blue. Luckily for the innocent shoppers of Dublin, all they saw was an eccentric-looking man in a top hat and an out-of-shape Englishman with his increasingly hot-tempered wife tearing down the street.

Just a normal day then.

"We've got about thirty seconds before that mob catches up with us. Ideas?!" snarled Olivia.

Benissimo's eyes scoured the street ahead till they finally rested on the pub coming up on the right. It was old with something of a bell tower at its roof.

"I say we make a stand and pray that Mr Fox ignored my order to have no back-up at the ready!"

A second later, Benissimo kicked the door of Flannigan's Sports Bar and Brewery clear off its hinges. The barman was alone and eating a bacon sandwich, or at least would have been had his mouth not fallen open at the sight of the wild-eyed Ringmaster and a broken door lying limply on the floor.

"Excuse me, barkeeper, how exactly does one gain access to your roof?!"

A hummingbird came careering in from outside, and was promptly flattened by Olivia Armstrong and a well-aimed bar stool.

"Well done, Livvy," smiled Terry.

"You're welcome, darling."

The bartender, however, was far from impressed. "M-my door…"

As the buzz of thrumming wings grew louder,

Benissimo's whip tore across the bar area, vaporising the man's sandwich into a cloud of bready bacon.

"APOLLO'S FLAMING CHARIOT, MAN – THE ROOF?"

CHAPTER 31

Tick-tock, the Mouse and the Clock

Mr Cogsworth, or rather Great-uncle Faisal, explained in great detail how the switch had come about. His body was failing him and if he was to continue his research, there was to be no other way. Shortly before his real body had drawn its last breath, the scientist and marvel that was Faisal transferred his soul to the rusting construct before them.

Tinks was speechless. It wasn't sadness or joy, or even the shock of what had become of his old relative: it was pure scientific wonder. His great-uncle Faisal had crossed the line between man and machine and had become something of both. He was a complete anomaly, and even stranger in his uniqueness than the Central Intelligence, though thankfully for Ned and his friends a good deal nicer to talk to.

"And you've really found a way to bring down the machine?" managed Ned, who was in as much awe as Tinks but was at least still capable of talking.

Faisal's brush-like moustache smiled and his eyes glowed a little brighter. "Better than that, young man. I can bring down his entire network – every ticker from fly to hawk, every soldier-class Guardian, the whole blasted lot of them!"

Whiskers, who was still perched on Faisal's lap, gave out a loud "Scree".

"Not you, my little friend – you're *different*."

"How is Whiskers different?" asked Ned. "You two know each other, don't you?"

"Oh yes, I should say so! Your Whiskers here was the prototype for my Debussy Mark Twelve – my absolute finest creation. When I bought this museum, the owner was in a right old state. His faithful guard dog was terribly unwell and about to be put down. I took it upon myself to give its soul another home at the moment of its passing. So you see, it was Whiskers who paved the way for me to live on."

Lucy slapped her hand on Ned's shoulder and threw her head back with laughter. "Ned's mouse is a *dog*?" she said.

"A St Bernard – absolute whopper of a thing," laughed back Faisal.

"I *knew* he was special," said Tinks, "but a *dog*?"

"Whiskers?" murmured Ned. "Is it true?"

His wind-up companion bobbed its head up and down proudly and for the first time let its tiny tail wag.

"That is too weird," said Ned.

"I've seen weirder," grinned Tinks, who was now looking squarely into the bulb-like eyes of his great-uncle.

"Before you were born, Ned," Faisal went on, "the tales of your parents' exploits at the Circus of Marvels were a thing of legend amongst the Hidden. I sent Whiskers here as an anonymous gift to your dad in the hopes that he might be useful."

"He is," smiled Ned, "sometimes."

The monocle at Faisal's eye suddenly turned, focusing now on Ned's shoulder. Suddenly the old Ticker's arm flew out to where he'd been looking, its pincer-like fingers snapping angrily shut round something.

"But not useful enough, it seems!"

Very slowly Great-uncle Faisal opened up his palm to gasps as he revealed a twitching, broken ticker fly. "Where might this have come from, I wonder?"

Ned racked his brain – he'd only been at the BBB's Nest. Surely it couldn't have come from there?

"You realise this probably means you've been tracked here?" said Faisal.

"Master Armstrong, when you came back from your mission with Bene, you were scanned by the Nest's security detail, weren't you?" asked a suddenly alert Tinks.

"Scanned? Well, no… Mum and Dad were so angry I just waited outside for them to finish with Bene and—"

BEEEP. "INTRUDER ALERT."

The room turned red as emergency warning lights flashed in time with the recorded message.

BEEEP. "INTRUDER ALERT."

BEEEP. "INTRUDER ALERT."

BEEEP. "INTRUDER ALERT."

CHAPTER 32

Trouble and Strife

Great-uncle Faisal moved from his chair like a rocket. Hands whirring and eyes flashing, he took to the brass console on his workbench. Whiskers was perched on his shoulder with all the tail-wagging concentration of a robotic dog-mouse. Ned didn't need his perometer to know – danger had found them. The question was: how much and from where?

"Console – enact safety protocols," said Faisal.

"*SAFETY PROTOCOLS ENACTED.*"

And with that the lights stopped flashing red and the museum went eerily quiet.

"Hmm, sensors are picking up multiple signals. Don't worry, this little home from home of mine has a fairly robust set of tricks up its sleeves."

An old-fashioned curved telly by the console blinked

into life, the image on its black and white screen flitting from room to room. It stopped by Faisal's storage area, somewhere near the first exhibit.

"*Multiple life forms, section 1-A.*" This time Faisal's security announcement spoke in something of a whisper.

The picture was hard to make out, the only source of light being the sliver that was coming in from a newly forced window. Even so, the three silhouettes Ned saw there were unmistakable – a shrunken bowler hat, an oversized shoe. One tall, one small and one impossibly fat.

"Clowns!" spat Ned.

There were few sights Ned hated more than that of Barbarossa's hideous clowns, Eanie, Meanie and Mo. He could almost smell the reek of them coming through the monitor. Ned had had several run-ins with them before and knew well what they were capable of, how fast they could run and with what cruelty they worked their gifts.

"Faisal, your security 'tricks', how good are they exactly?" asked Lucy.

"Oh, quite capable of dealing with clowns, I assure you."

On cue, Ned watched as Faisal's clockwork exhibits showed themselves. From under chairs and tabletops, from shelves and storage boxes, his tiny wind-up men sprang to life, an army of angry dolls. And they were fast – but the clowns were faster. As the throng of little mercenaries closed in, Eanie nodded to Meanie and the tallest of the three opened a small box from his pocket. Ned could barely see them, but he could hear them through the speakers well enough.

Bzzzzz...

Ticker flies poured out of the box and on to Faisal's security detail. One by one the little creatures stopped in their tracks, before turning to the three intruders and standing to attention with a salute. A large plume of noisy, boiling steam erupted from the top of Faisal's head.

"If they can do that to my wee men, they can do that to the rest of my system!" said Faisal.

"T-that would seem to be the case," stammered the Tinker, who was watching the three clowns lead the throng of tickers through his great-uncle's museum towards his living quarters.

On the screen, Mo turned to the little wind-ups. "Quick flick, little soldies, open doorsy. Big bruvvers wants to say helloo."

They all watched in abject horror as Faisal's security

system turned on itself and opened the locking mechanism to Faisal's quarters.

A door swung open and through it stepped Eanie, Meanie and Mo, evil smiles on their painted faces.

But it was what stepped through after them that turned Ned's blood to ice. Great hulking slabs of polished and buffed iron marched through the door till the room was filled with the sound of the clattering, chattering and ticking of at least ten Guardian-class tickers. And unlike in the taiga, there was no fleet of Chinooks flying in to save the day, and there was absolutely nowhere to hide or run to.

Eanie turned away from his metal warriors, both large and small, and stared directly up at the security camera. Cracked make-up and low lighting did little to hide the clown's excitement as he smiled, displaying a row of stumped teeth.

"Jossy boy come vit cloons noo. Live or deady, it noo matter."

CHAPTER 33

Sharp Exit

"Revolting little thing, isn't he?" puffed Faisal. "I think we'll be wanting to use the exit strategy."

"I'd say that might be prudent, Great-uncle. And said exit would be…?"

"There, on the monitor – see the room the clowns have just walked into?"

Ned, Lucy and Tinks peered at the screen.

"There's an emergency exit behind the stage."

"Ah," said Ned. "Not much immediate use then."

"No," said Great-uncle Faisal, "perhaps not."

"Where exactly is that room?" asked Lucy nervously.

"Just the other side of this door."

Right then from under the doorway came the telltale sound of the padding of oversized shoes.

A spring audibly broke in the old machine's head.

Great-uncle Faisal picked up a large adjustable spanner from his workbench and handed it to Tinks.

"You need me to fix you?"

"No, Tinks, I need you to hit clowns with it," he said. He then took Whiskers from his shoulder and placed him on the floor. "Now, young scamp, before you were a mouse you were a dog, and this was once your home. We have intruders – I think you know what to do."

The Debussy Mark Twelve's fur bristled, its little clockwork gears beating with the brave soul of a mighty St Bernard, ready to protect its lair.

"Scree!"

"That's the spirit, ma boy!"

Ned grabbed a wrench from the table. He might not have had his powers any more, but he could still take a swing at Eanie and his cronies.

"Everyone, get either side of the door. I've got a plan," said Ned and promptly flicked the light switch to his side.

Great-uncle Faisal went to one side of the opening as quietly as his aged pistons would allow; Tinks and Lucy took the other side, while Ned held back in the shadows.

"Gorrn?" whispered Ned.

But the familiar was already ahead of him, oozing flat to the ground and stretching along the floor of the doorway. To anyone else, he would have looked like a shadow across the floor. Their trap was almost ready to spring. Finally Whiskers got himself into position, his tiny mouse bottom on the floor, his back upright and little chest heaving. For a moment Ned could almost see the St Bernard that he'd been, till the "Woof!" he'd no doubt wanted to bark came out as a minor "Scree!" instead.

Then the door swung open.

Eanie was the first to approach.

The passing of time had done little to dull the revulsion Ned felt for him. Even smaller than a minutian but with none of their kindness or cleverness, the clown's silhouette came across the doorway. He wore the same bowler hat and oversized shoes, had the same straggly orange hair. But it was the smell that made Ned want to wretch.

It was a smell like rotting fish and pickles, bin juice and malice; he would recognise it anywhere.

Eanie looked down and saw Whiskers, just as planned.

"Mousie, is it? I members you. You da boyz friendy."

Whiskers knew as well as Ned what the creature was capable of, but he didn't budge, not even an inch.

Eanie may well have been a coward, and dumb, but dumb cowards can make for cunning adversaries when it comes to the setting of traps. Eanie peered through the doorway carefully, eyes squinting at the dark.

"Jossy boy? I knows it's you – I sees your mousie. Come out and I makes it quick-r-snick, no needs for smashin' or bashin'."

Ned's muscles tensed and knotted. Every fibre of him wanted to lash out and attack, but things were different now. His powers had left him and they needed the advantage of surprise – of a trap.

And as the clown stepped through the doorway and bent down towards Ned's mouse, the trap was sprung.

Eanie's eyes crossed with pain as Gorrn rose up from the ground and all around him like a black tidal wave. A second later and his muffled scream was pulled into the darkness by Ned's familiar, before fading to a sickening silence. Whatever Gorrn might have done to him, Ned was glad of it and so were the others, Tinks, Faisal and Lucy all sighing with relief from the shadow of the doorway.

One down, two to go. But the others came fast and Gorrn, Ned guessed, was still digesting, or whatever it was a familiar did after swallowing a clown whole. Meanie found the lights and Mo barrelled into the room with an angry snarl, eyes wild and arm ready for punching.

"Wotcha dun wit' Eanie?!" he hollered. "Mo makes

sneaksie boy pay, Mo grind your bones ta bits 'n' bobs, and then he end da girlie!"

Ned looked at the creature in horror. Great loose lips stretched over a red and greedy mouth. Nothing the creature wore fitted him, because nothing could fit the unbreakable ball of blubber that was his belly. Every stitch and seam was frayed to bursting and his tiny bowler hat made his face look even larger and more eager to catch his prey.

Behind the creature, Meanie was struck from the side by Tinks's spanner. But the clown was built of stronger stuff and turned on the minutian violently. Two swings of his blackjack club and both Tinks and his great-uncle lay motionless on the floor.

Immediately, Ned struck out at Mo with his wrench but it just bounced off harmlessly.

"Silly jossy-boy. You can't hurts Mo – no one hurts da big one."

"Yeah, silly sneaksie jossy-boy," said Meanie, and where there had been one clown there now stood two.

"Lucy, get behind me," seethed Ned. The creature's belly might be impenetrable, but Ned was quite certain that the two clowns' knees would feel a wrench if it was swung hard enough.

Lucy brushed by Ned quietly and approached the clowns. Meanie grinned and Mo's tummy rumbled as if he'd just sat down to a Sunday roast.

"Gentlemen?"

"Girlie?" grinned Mo.

"You have frightened, bullied and shot people that I care about deeply," said Lucy.

"What's it to you, prissy whissy?!" barked Mo.

Lucy raised her hand and closed her eyes. "I would like you to STOP."

And that's exactly what they did. Both of the clowns froze in motion – mid-chew, mid-breath, mid-moody and menacing glare. It was as if time had stopped, but only for the clowns.

Ned couldn't believe what he was seeing. "Wha-what did you do?!"

"I've been practising. Their minds think they're asleep, so they've stopped moving. I can't fool them forever, though. Quickly, we need to get out of…"

But her words trailed away.

At the door was a horror in metal, pointed and sharp, with arms for pinching and cutting, and soulless eyes fixed wholly on Ned.

Tick, tick, tick.

CHAPTER 34

No Exit

"That's it," said Ned. "That's the only way out, Lucy. We're trapped."

And as he said it, both Mo and Meanie started to break from Lucy's hold. Whiskers was standing mournfully over a passed-out Great-uncle Faisal while Gorrn had slithered his way back to Ned, his great form bellowing and wobbling like a nervous jellyfish. Gorrn was frightened of few things, but metal did not feel teeth, at least not his teeth – that much the familiar knew.

"Dum-dum," came Mo's bass-bellied drawl. "We nots here for catchy, we's here for crush an' smush. No more jossy-boy, no more girlie-girl."

The eyes of the Guardians turned red and the automatons paced towards Ned, gears whirring and sharpened claws at the ready. Defenceless, he backed up against the wall behind him, now desperately trying to fire his ring. He thought of metal, of fire and stone – anything that he could use. The air spat and crackled in front of him… and then just as quickly fizzled to nothing.

The clowns pushed their way to the front.

"Smush an' crush, frik an' frak," grimaced Meanie, with Mo snarling beside him.

The clowns had just raised their clubs to strike when there was a rumbling from behind Ned, on the other side of the wall.

CRASH!

Something burst through the old brickwork like a furred bulldozer. Bricks were flung out in a violent spray to Ned's side, striking the clowns hard.

"George!" Ned and Lucy shouted in unison.

"ROARGHH!" George bellowed, leaping into the centre of the room.

As the brick dust settled, George took in the situation – the Tinker and his uncle on the floor, Lucy and Ned backed against the broken wall. His eyes met Ned's and for a moment they softened, before all semblance of Ned's kind friend vanished.

Their great ape protector beat at his chest wildly, his nostrils snorting with rage, biceps bulging and back arched. To anyone else, the sight of the enraged beast would have turned them as white as sheets. But the Guardians weren't anyone, and they had no skin to do the turning.

George was too angry to see how outnumbered he was, too lost in protective fury. As the Guardians moved closer, George pounced. In the scream of fist on metal, two of the Guardians were knocked sideways, only to regain their balance and strike back at the ape.

"GO, BOY! TAKE LUCY AND GET OUT OF HERE," roared George.

But Ned couldn't leave him. Two of the Guardians now held his great protector's arms, and a third struck at his chest. George kicked hard and the Guardian was knocked back, but only for a moment, then it was on him again. Red eyes blazing, its arm shot out and clutched George's throat violently. George kicked and roared as more of the metal monstrosities pinned down his arms and legs.

The clowns were regaining themselves too – bruised and battered as they were, their clubs were ready to swing.

"Ned!" gasped Lucy. "What do we do?"

Lucy's control over her gifts had clearly grown, but

against the Guardians and their metal minds she had no power.

And something in Ned's mind snapped, just as it had in the taiga. Something close to anger, but more focused and controlled. And at the same moment, his ring fired, without him trying to make it, almost as though it was acting on its own. A blur of physical pain shot from his ring up his arm, to his head and back down again.

The room filled with static as every hair on each of the bodies there stood on end. What came next was a blast of finely focused energy, an unravelling of sorts. In less time than it took to breathe a lungful of air, the Guardians, every last one of them, came apart. The welding of bolts were undone, screws unwound themselves, and piece by meticulous piece the Guardians stopped being machines or robots, and became a sum of disbanded, floating parts. Countless components hung in the air – the separate glass lenses of their eyes, the housing to their skulls, the ribs of their chests, the wiring, the cogs, the pistons and fuel chambers – then all clattered to the floor in heaps.

The clowns, like their butcher master, did not like the "odds", and were out through the hole that George had punched in the wall before Ned could refocus his eyes.

The first thing he saw when he did was that, to his relief, Whiskers had miraculously remained untouched by Ned's disassembly.

The second thing he saw was that Great-uncle Faisal had not.

CHAPTER 35

Dearly Departed

The whirring of twin-bladed helicopters in the skies above them came as a welcome surprise. It was a small wonder that the authorities of Amsterdam had let such intimidating machines hug the canopy of its rooftops and canals. It was raining hard now and through the downpour, Ned watched the Chinooks come in to land as he peered through the great hole in the wall made by George. Ned had visions of his parents stepping out on to the street, smiles in their eyes with tales of the Fey, Heart Stone in hand and ready to take their son home. Even if home for now meant a concrete bunker somewhere along the British coast.

While they waited for it to land, the Tinker carefully picked up his great-uncle's separate parts and placed them in a large plastic container.

"Tinks, I'm so sorry."

"It's all right, Master Ned," said the Tinker. "It wasn't your fault. If you hadn't done what you did… well, I'm quite sure it would have been the end of us – *all* of us, that is."

Despite his kind words, the heaviness of his brow told a very different story.

"If you wouldn't mind, Master Ned, do you think I might borrow Whiskers?"

Ned's dog-mouse, wonder that he was, was looking rather sad, head down on Lucy's shoulder.

"I guess so, Tinks, but what for?"

"Oh, just a hunch. You'll get him back soon enough."

As two Chinooks came in to land, it wasn't his parents that Ned saw but an ashen-faced Mr Fox. Into one of the choppers went Tinks and Whiskers, and the escorted remains of Great-uncle Faisal. Mr Fox ushered Ned, Lucy and George to the second.

To Ned's dismay, he noticed that Mr Fox was humming.

Ned didn't like it when Mr Fox hummed. The BBB's operative smiled at him, far too sweetly for Ned's liking. Something was very wrong.

"Mr Fox, what's going on?"

"Why don't we talk on the chopper, eh?"

CHAPTER 36

Best-made Plans

Barbarossa stared at the crystal in front of him. An invention of the Central Intelligence, it had a distinct advantage over air-modulators in being able not only to transfer messages but pictures as well. The jossers had many such things on their phones and gadgets, but phones and gadgets could be hacked – his crystal could not. The spidery torso of the Central Intelligence filled the frame and its soulless eyes loomed closer.

"Faisal – tsk-brrdzt – lives!" it howled.

"You never told me of this Faisal before."

"He should be long – brrt-ching – dead."

"My clowns assure me that he is quite dead now."

"He is not – crdtz – flesh, but ones and zeros."

"He is a pile of parts, nothing more."

The crystal seemed to shudder as the Central

Intelligence jerked its head left and right, spidery and crablike, with gushes of oil bubbling at its maw.

"Grddzt – ones and zeros DO NOT DIE!" raged the machine.

Even as they spoke, Barbarossa could feel the Darkening King beneath him. His words came more frequently now. And only the Darkening King's words mattered any more.

The butcher turned away from the crystal and looked through his window over the canopy of the taiga, down towards his fleet.

"Faisal, the Armstrongs and my brother – none of them matter. Not to you and I. You want a soul, do you not? And I the world. Stay the course and when the Darkness rises we shall both have what we want."

The image in the crystal quietened.

"Tsk – yes."

"My brother is raising an army. Do you know what a general is without soldiers, without pawns to send into battle?"

Hot steam blew from the Central Intelligence's head, its many-pistoned mind clattering for the answer.

Barbarossa turned and stared deep into the crystal.

"*Nothing*. Prepare your metal men and we will rout his army before they stand."

CHAPTER 37

The Fey

"Captured?!" seethed Ned over the din of the Chinook's blades.

"It would appear so," said Mr Fox apologetically.

Lucy squeezed Ned's hand. Opposite them a recovered George filled the entire width of their transport. Lost at sea yet again, without his parents, there could be no better anchor than George or Lucy. George would have reached out to pat him on the back but was currently gorging on bananas to settle his nerves.

"But why? I thought the Fey were neutral?"

"As did your parents, Ned."

"The Fey do what suits them, old bean," rumbled George, "with no rhyme or reason, at least none that I've ever fathomed, by book or face to face. The Heart Stone is no doubt more important to them than we understood."

"I'd say it's pretty important to all of us right now," said Lucy. "And Olivia and Terry – Benissimo too? – have they been harmed? Are they OK?"

"As you can imagine, they put up quite a fight. We were messaged some hours ago by a Lemnus Gemfeather. Lemnus claims that they are being well treated, though being held in the Seelie Court. He is also quite certain that the aim is not to harm them but to detain them."

George nearly choked on one of his bananas. "Lemnus?! I'd take anything that bounder has to say with a pinch or two of salt."

Ned's mind went back to a lifetime ago, to Switzerland, and a certain Fey named Theron Wormroot. The greedy creature had very nearly drugged Lucy and had intended to do the same to the entire troupe while they slept.

"I don't suppose he's any relation to Theron?"

"No relation and far better or worse than that bounder, depending on his mood. There was a time when 'the Twelve' were 'the Thirteen'. Long before even Madame Oublier's time, if my books read true. Lemnus led the Invisible Circus, as they called themselves, each and every one of them Fey by birth and powerful with it. Their role was to try and police the more magical realms of our Hidden. Well, their exploits are things of legend, both for the good and harm they wound up causing. After nearly six years of running riot, they were forcibly booted from the Thirteen and sent back to their own kind."

Mr Fox nodded and one of the agents at the front of the helicopter's interior produced a map.

"Thank you, Mr Gull, as you were. Dublin – home of the Seelie Court," said Mr Fox, holding the map out flat for the others to see, "the hub of the Fey and the seat of their rule. According to this Lemnus character, their realm is *under* the city. Here in the centre, not far from where Benissimo told me he was going, is where Lemnus proposes to meet us tomorrow morning."

Ned had only dealt with the Fey once, and once had been enough.

"In the morning? Wouldn't we be better off going in at night?"

"George?" said Mr Fox, and the ape cleared his throat.

"Not necessarily, old chum. You see, day and night, time itself, works differently in their realm. The greater question is whether Lemnus can be trusted. I should think Lucy will be better able to answer that when we get there."

"Oh yes, it'll only take a minute or so," said Lucy, "once I get a proper look at him."

She answered so confidently, so truly, that it threw Ned. He turned away to look out of the window to the sea below, dark and brooding by night as it was, and it suddenly dawned on him: in the time they'd had apart, Lucy had grown stronger, more in control of her powers than ever, and him? Well, Ned was unable to control his at all. It wasn't jealousy exactly that he felt – more that the balance had shifted, and especially now Ned longed to be who he was back then, to be as useful as he once was.

"You all right, Ned?" asked Lucy, as always a step ahead of him and where his head was going.

He smiled and it was a smile that said, "not even a bit", which he knew only Lucy would pick up on. He needed to talk to his friend and desperately.

"In any case," continued Mr Fox, "once inside, we'll have a guide to take us to the Heart Stone and then on to your parents and Benissimo."

There was something about the way that Mr Fox said it that annoyed Ned. For one thing, the order was wrong – his parents and the Ringmaster needed freeing first – and for another, he sounded so matter-of-fact, so sure that Ned would agree.

"You know, people always tell me what I can and can't do," said Ned. "Who I should help and why. But they never ask me – they never actually ask me what I want. And what I want is to get the old goat and my mum and dad out of there. *Then* we can talk about the Hear—"

"Ned, this is an infiltration mission. Our chances of obtaining the Heart Stone will be far higher with fewer numbers."

This time Ned's temper boiled over. "You're as bad as Bene! The mission always comes first, doesn't it? You don't care about Mum and Dad, about *people* – you just want your stone, don't you?!"

Lucy stared open-mouthed. Even George, who was never at a loss for words, said nothing, and Ned and his two anchors waited to see what the fox-haired josser would say.

Mr Fox didn't say a word, not at first. All that training, all that control started to visibly drain, till his whole face began to twitch.

"Mr Gull?"

"Sir?"

"Join Mr Hawk and Mr Sparrow in the cockpit, would you?"

"Yes, sir."

The map in Mr Fox's hand trembled and as soon as the agent left them, he threw it to the floor.

"You don't know anything about me!" he shouted.

To Ned's amazement, the cool-headed operative's voice was shaking.

"Well, according to you, you don't know anything about you either!" spat Ned.

Mr Fox sat back and composed himself as much as he could.

"You're wrong about me, Ned. Being an operative, being an agent, none of us has memories – that's to say, almost none of us. Before this madness, I had a life and there was someone in it. I don't know her name, only that we were together and then we weren't. She was taken from me. I will never forget her face for as long as I live, or the face of the creature that took her – *a Darkling*."

The words poured from his lips like poison and the agent rolled up his sleeve to reveal a livid red scar, long and wide, that ran all the way up his forearm. It had clearly been made by tooth or claw.

"I didn't know what it was, not then. But now I do. I joined the BBB for two reasons, Ned. Firstly, to stop that happening to anyone else – *anyone*. And secondly, because they told me that I'd forget her, forget the pain. I didn't and I can't, but I will never stop fighting the Darkness – fighting to save others the pain of losing someone they love."

Ned could see from the tear in Lucy's eye that Mr Fox must be telling the truth.

"I will do everything I can to save your mum and dad, Ned – to save Benissimo. I'll do everything I can to save all of us."

CHAPTER 38

The Liffey

The River Liffey flowed right through the centre of Dublin. Red-brick and brightly painted buildings lined its edges, and so did the undercover operatives placed there by Mr Fox. Beyond the river was a city teeming with busy Dubliners marching to work. Ned might have enjoyed taking it in – the cobblestones, the old parts, the new – but today, like every day stretching back for months, he was a ghost of sorts. Buildings, places of interest, whole cities had lost their meaning in the wake of the Darkening King. They were now just facades hiding older truths – tinpot men with living souls, or here and now, somewhere beneath their feet, a Seelie Court that held both Benissimo and his parents.

To an untrained eye, it might have been hard to spot, but Ned could see plain-clothed BBB operatives everywhere. In the coffee shops, begging on the streets, reading papers, or simply ambling down the road by the Liffey, Mr Fox's agents watched and waited. Not long ago they had been looking for Ned. Now they were trying to help him, or at least keep him safe enough for long enough to carry out his mission.

George had bellowed at having to go on to the Nest and neither Ned nor Lucy relished the idea of their mission without him. But Mr Fox's contact had been clear: he would only see the Engineer and the Medic.

"While you're in there, keep your wits about you, old bean, and if you can't keep yours – *hang on to Lucy's.*"

Lucy had had to prise the gorilla's fingers from Ned's back and they were quite sure that they heard a stifled sob as the Chinook's blades spun for the next leg of its flight. Mr Fox led the way while his seemingly mute number two, Mr Badger, covered their rear. Ned made sure he was a good distance away from either of them so that he could talk to Lucy in private.

"Do you think George is all right, Lucy?"

"I don't think anyone's all right, Ned. You've been gone a long time and I know it's been bad for you, but George and I – we've seen the other side. The Hidden are divided and terrified and no one knows who to trust or what they should do. We all know what's coming and I think protecting us, in George's own sweet way, is the best thing he can think of to make sense of it all. We're his family, Ned – you, me and the troupe."

"Dear old George."

"Don't worry, he's as strong as he is soft," said Lucy. "It's you I'm worried about."

Ned sighed. "It was close back there, like, *really* close. I tried to fire it and—"

"And it fizzled. Till you saw the Guardian grab George's throat."

"Lucy?"

"Yes?"

"Stop doing that."

"Stop doing what?"

"Stop reading my mind and finishing my sentences. It's really annoying."

"Sorry."

Lucy blushed very slightly, though there was a mischievous sparkle in her eye that suggested she only "might" stop.

"We could have all been killed. What if the Fey put up a fight? How am I supposed to help get us all out of there if my ring won't even listen to me?"

"You've got me and Mr Fox too, remember. He might be just a josser, but he's good at what he does and I trust him. If this Lemnus character is true to his word, we'll get your parents and Benissimo *and* the Heart Stone out before anyone notices."

Ned's heart sank even further. "And what if we are successful… If I can't rely on my powers then how am I supposed to even use this Heart Stone when we get it?"

Lucy's face soured. Ned hated it when it did that, because even though he wasn't a mind reader, he knew enough to know that it usually meant an outburst was coming. Lucy bit her lip and checked that Mr Fox wasn't listening.

"You really are the most self-centred boy I have ever met."

"What are you talking about?"

"Oh, Ned!" And at this point, her proud, pretty blue eyes seemed to blaze. "You don't get it, do you?"

"Get what?"

"*You're* not supposed to do anything – *we are.*"

"But Tiamat…"

Lucy was in no mood for "buts".

"You met an old dragon, a really *really* powerful old

dragon, but that doesn't mean he knows everything, does it? Sure, he knows about the Heart Stone – it was his, after all. But he didn't know you were having trouble, did he?"

"No," said Ned a little sheepishly.

"Well, I did, before I even saw you, Ned. We're linked and that link can't be broken. You and I are in this together because of our gifts, because of our rings, and our rings will end this together. Just as soon as you work out how to use yours again."

And at last, Lucy smiled.

"Well, whatever I have to work out, it needs to happen quickly. I can't wait for everyone to nearly die every time I need to use it!"

"I should hope not! Something's holding you back, Ned. *We* just need to figure out what it is."

"What about his voice, Lucy – why haven't we heard it?"

Lucy stopped walking.

"The Darkening King is rebuilding his strength, that's all. Trust me, when we get close, *if* we ever get close, we'll do more than hear him."

Up ahead Mr Fox stopped and signalled for Mr Badger to wait. Mr Badger nodded and then placed himself by a shop window, blending in, Ned thought, with as much subtlety as a pillar in a pond.

Mr Fox led them on, down a narrow alley where a fairy was waiting for them. The strange creature bowed and as his lips parted, Ned could have sworn he heard distant bells as old as churches along with the smell of blackberries and sage.

"Lemnus Gemfeather, at your service."

CHAPTER 39

Lemnus Gemfeather

He had great plumes of wild red hair shimmering with what looked like spun gold, and eyes of brightest green and blue, with flecks of burning violet right at their centres. He was a strange mix, with a kind fatherly look about him and thick untameable eyebrows that gave him an almost severe expression, all framed round a long hooked nose. His clothes were all in red and from another era entirely, though completely untouched by age. He looked like a rich courtier in braiding and sequins, luscious silks and scarves. But beneath it all was mischief, as clear and as bright as day. He bowed dramatically again, waving a small lace handkerchief as he did so, and eyed Mr Fox's party of three carefully.

"An honour, sirs and lady."

Ned watched as the odd creature sniffed at the air

inquisitively and his eyes narrowed to the ground by Ned's feet.

"A familiar? Welcome, little cousin."

There was an oozing and apprehensive "Arr", as Gorrn shrank further into Ned's shadow till there was very little of him left at all.

Behind Lemnus's smile and theatrical gesturing, Ned sensed a power that frightened him. A bolt of lightning was only a thing of wonder so long as it didn't strike you.

"Mr Gemfeather, I am Mr Fox. My associates here are—"

"Call me Lemnus, please," cut in the fairy. "I like your name, I do, I like it very much. Fox in name and nature indeed. Quite so, quite so, though of course your usefulness remains to be seen."

From the twitch of Mr Fox's eye, Ned guessed he didn't know what to make of the man, but decades of training took over and he simply smiled politely.

Lemnus turned to Ned next and stared into his eyes till he was close enough to touch. His expression changed for a moment, all the pomp and show quite drained out of him.

"The Engineer. It's true then: quite ordinary to look at, yet extraordinary to behold."

Ned wasn't sure whether the creature was being kind or rude, but either way, far more pressing matters were on his mind.

"Lemnus, my parents and Benissimo – are they safe?"

"Undeniably, dear child, sleeping like babes in a wood."

"Why? Why were they taken prisoner? They only came to ask for help."

Lemnus's features grew dark and he spoke in hushed tones. "To even know of the Heart Stone's existence and not to be one of the Fey is a heinous crime in our realm. The greatest of crimes… But to ask to *have* it? For use in battle?! Only a fool or madman would request such a thing! Prince Aurelin did *not* take kindly to it."

Ned suddenly found himself stricken with worry. Were his parents really safe? He'd met Prince Aurelin and as far as Ned could tell, the creature was devoid of any compassion, at least for those who weren't from his realm.

The fairy's eyes warmed and his face softened to a grandfatherly glow.

"Fear not, boy. I have seen them and they are well."

Ned could feel his entire body physically unwind, and with that Lemnus turned his attentions to Lucy, who gave him a piercing look. The fairy stiffened, before his face broke into an uncontainable smile.

"Pretty and true," he mumbled. "A firecracker, a spark of a thing you are, *you are*! A spark of a thing you are!"

Despite being relieved that his parents were safe, Ned couldn't help wishing that the creature had seen some kind of spark in him. Was he disappointed in Ned? Had he picked up on the truth that the dragon had missed?

"Come along, my brave knights, let us enter the fray!" said Lemnus excitedly before turning away from them all and approaching a door at the end of the alley. Ned could have sworn it wasn't there a moment ago.

"Ahem, Mr Gemfeather—" began Mr Fox.

"*Lemnus*, please," said the red-haired fairy, looking back.

"Mr Gemfeather will do for now," replied Mr Fox, and he reached to his side and placed his hand on a carefully concealed pistol. "These children are under my protection. I have somewhere in the region of three hundred operatives patrolling the street beyond this alley. Live satellite uplinks, radio and, well, a lot of eyes with which to watch – we're not going anywhere unless Lucy tells me that she likes you."

Lemnus turned to Lucy, raised both eyebrows and waited for her verdict.

Lucy's mind was already somewhere else and, for an

unbearable minute, no one said anything. Finally, she came out of her trance and smiled.

"Well, Lucy?" asked Mr Fox, eyeing the fairy threateningly, hand firm on his pistol. And not for the first time, Ned saw that the man's words held true: he would do anything to keep them safe.

"Well, I've never 'seen' anything like it. But then I've never tried reading the Fey. His brain's like a box full of frogs. It's noisy, jumpy, and it feels like it could tear open at any minute. But..."

Ned held his breath.

"Deep down inside, at his core, he's kind of... *funny*."

Mr Fox pursed his lips and frowned. He looked to Lucy, then to Ned, and finally back to Lemnus.

"*Funny?*"

"Funny peculiar, and just plain old fun, I think – at least he seems to be," said Lucy rather brightly. "And bad people, *truly* bad people, are rarely any fun."

Mr Fox chuckled – actually chuckled – before whistling softly, in less of a tune and more of a "think".

"Ned, Lucy, we appear to be at a crossroads," he said. "Your parents are prisoners, Ned, and Benissimo, the only man who knows who all our allies are, or how to contact them, is with them. As if that weren't enough, the one weapon we hope will be capable of bringing down the Darkening King is also with them. If Mr Gemfeather can be trusted, we have a chance, albeit a statistically minute one, of walking away from this alive with what we want. If we don't, the entire planet will perish. Do we follow on the basis that this man is 'fun' or don't we?"

Ned didn't need to be asked. Lucy was all right with him and Lemnus knew where his parents were being held. Nothing else mattered.

He and his friend spoke as one. "We do."

Mr Fox nodded. "Right then, Mr Gemfeather. Please lead the way, but do so knowing that if you try anything, anything at all, there is a giant ape not far from here that will make finding you and causing you pain his life's work."

"Quite so," smiled Lemnus and waved a hand.

The door in front of him opened.

The party of three could not have been less prepared. They looked through its arch and one by one their mouths fell open.

CHAPTER 40

The Glade Awakens

As Ned crossed the doorway, Dublin – at least the Dublin that the rest of the world knew – stopped existing. In its place was a wide glade of pure unbridled magic. Ned had crossed the Veil countless times and could never quite get used to it. Colours, sounds, even time were altered by the meeting of magic and non-magic in ways that never made sense and always filled him with awe.

Entering the heart and home of the Fey was another proposition entirely. For one thing, their realm did not need the Veil to stay hidden. The Fey had their own magic, a magic that was older and wilder, more untameable and strange. Silently Ned, Lucy and Mr Fox followed their guide into the glade, a glade that burst with colour and magic. Ned marvelled at buttercups the size of buckets; trees of turquoise, gold, ruby-red and lavender.

As they waded through waist-high grass, the smell of roses was mixed with honey then moss, peaches, magnolia and thyme. If smells could deafen! The constant change of scents, like notes of music, was intoxicating. And there was sound too, or at least what Ned thought was sound. Not quite music, but some wordless song, and one that he'd heard somewhere before. It was as though the glade – every part of it, from the plants to the air, even its light – was speaking to him, calling with words that made his heart fill with memories as old as time yet they were not his own.

It took a while to notice but Lemnus had stopped walking because, as it turned out, there simply wasn't any need. The glade, its trees and flowers, were moving closer and at an alarming speed. From every side great arms of twisting, knotting greenery grew up around them. Branches reached across the sky, and every flower, from foxglove to dandelion, grew and grew till their small party gazed up like ants in a living forest, so different from the taiga yet wilder and more strange. The ground at their feet began to soften, like moss-filled quicksand, and Ned felt himself lowering into it. His mind raced to a half-remembered biology lesson he'd had at school. He'd learnt in detail how the carnivorous Venus flytrap would welcome in a fly with its sticky sap and then violently snap shut round it.

"Lucy, why is the garden getting bigger?"

As the vines shot towards them, Lucy's hand gripped his own.

"Stay close," she whispered.

"Unt!" came Gorrn's muffled groan.

And just as he groaned it, Lemnus turned on them, his face quite changed and as serious as stone. Reaching into his dress coat and pulling out a small silk pouch, he poured a yellow powder into his palm and blew. A great cloud of pollen flew up into the air and smothered them.

And with that, Ned and his allies were swallowed up whole.

CHAPTER 41

St Albertsburg

Elsewhere, away from fairies and frozen forests, a great and desperate gathering was under way. Steel mills were rebuilding a fleet, with thicker hulls and more powerful engines. Troops were being trained, supplies stockpiled and all the many races and species of man, woman and beast were putting aside their differences for a single common purpose.

These gathered fair-folk no longer trusted what was left of the Twelve, no longer trusted Atticus Fife. On Barbarossa's orders, Madame Oublier's former second-in-command, now their new leader, had forced those remaining under his control to act in a way that was nothing short of cruel. At a time when they needed it most, communication of any kind amongst the many factions of the Hidden had been banned unless sanctioned by the Twelve, and travel had been outlawed completely. As a result, entire cities, towns and villages found themselves completely isolated, and any information they were party to heavily monitored and doctored by Fife and his men. It didn't matter that the Twelve no longer had the ear of its people. Fife was on a different mission: a mission to keep them separated. The more apart and leaderless they remained, the less likely they were to unite.

But that was the thing about the Hidden and its many factions – they needed each other both in peace and war, and the Governor-General of St Albertsburg, its Protector and Viceroy, was doing what he could to spearhead an alliance. They were now preparing to fight for their very existence. His beloved city literally groaned with the weight of new bodies walking its streets. St Albertsburg and its twelve isles had become a beacon of hope in a world where light had been all but extinguished.

With Benissimo's help and advice, the Viceroy had offered up St Albertsburg as a place to prepare for the coming battle, and those brave enough to make a stand had come in their thousands, in their tens of thousands, with many more ready to heed the call to arms when the time came. Every square inch of the isle's open spaces was now full to bursting with airships, supplies and tents – the greatest military gathering of the Hidden in living memory. Deep in the guts of the coal-heavy isle, furnaces burned by day and by night. But not for the making of arms – St Albertsburg had stockpiles of weapons that could arm any force of man or beast. They burned for glass – for the making of mirrors.

Carrion Slight and his network of mirrors had given them the notion. The plan was as follows: on Benissimo's command, the Viceroy's owls and any airship deemed battle-ready would go by air, as expected, to fight the Darkening King. Their ground troops, however, would arrive at the taiga by mirror. No amount of winged or legged ticker could warn Barbarossa in time, not if they arrived at once. Overseeing the operation from the painstaking creation of the mirrors, to their packing and transport to Siberian Russia, was Ignatius P. Littleton the Third, otherwise known as the Glimmerman.

The Viceroy's mind was ablaze as he made his way to the hangar. In every crevice, nook and cranny that he walked past he saw the same thing: hope, a desperate hope that their tireless efforts would be enough to win the day and that their faith in him would be answered with victory. The Viceroy also hoped – hoped that they were right, even though his heart told him it was madness. Everything now rested on the gambit of surprise – almost everything. Benissimo had assured him before travelling to Ireland that everything was in hand, though he still hadn't divulged what it was he was hoping to find at the Seelie Court. Whatever it was, the Viceroy knew that no amount of hope or courage would win the day without it.

The loading bay was frantic with last-minute preparation. They had built a special transport for the journey and several of his own carriers would travel in convoy to offer protection. Once the initial load of mirrors had safely made it to Siberia, the rest would go via the mirror-verse itself.

The Glimmerman was less rotund than when he'd arrived and the Viceroy had been informed that the man no longer slept. Gone was his cheerful jacket of tiny mirrors; in its place a white shirt long stained with soot and sweat.

"Well, Ignatius, how goes the glass?"

Despite the heat and exhaustion, the arrival of the Viceroy in the loading bay straightened up Ignatius and his group of master glassmen immediately. They were in one of the many loading bays that cut into the isle's side and all about them military personnel heaved at the vast mirrors as they loaded them on to the transport.

"A-another hour or so, my lord," said Ignatius, then, spotting something from the corner of his eye, his face turned bright red as he shouted, "Will you be careful with that? You have no idea what it took to make!"

The little man's nerves were clearly shot to pieces. Any movement of glass was a tense affair and Ignatius had never been tasked with creating so much and certainly not in such a short space of time.

"Ignatius, you've done admirably. Why don't you give yourself some time off? There are plenty of glassmen who can hold the fort for one night."

"T-time off, sir?" he answered as though the words were completely alien. "Time... *off*?" he mouthed again.

And that was when they heard it, muffled as it was, high above the city and its streets – a scream, and then another, till there was a long, drawn-out wail of hundreds and thousands. The rock above their heads shook and the air filled with sirens and the screeching of the Viceroy's giant owls. It was only when the first bomb dropped that His Grace, the Viceroy and Governor-General of St Albertsburg, the 37th Duke of de Fresnes, understood.

BOOM!

And one bomb became many. High above them the

crystal city shattered under hellfire, and beside them two vast planes of mirrored glass cracked from the ensuing tremors.

"My glass!" stammered the Glimmerman.

"My city!" roared the Viceroy.

To their left, the loading bay's open doors offered a clear view to the sky – a sky now peppered with the black silhouettes of Barbarossa's fleet. Each and every one of its *Daedali* loaded with the Central Intelligence's metal men and a hoard of Demons to guide them.

CHAPTER 42

A Ball of Vines

Ned found himself in a dimly lit tunnel, bordered at every side with knotted roots from the glade above.

Mr Fox was the first to speak and did so while raising his pistol.

"What did you do to us?! Lemnus, if this was all some elaborate trap—"

His gun was pointing squarely at the fairy's head and any sense of humour he'd had before stepping into the glade utterly evaporated.

"Trap? Oh no, sir, no trap to be sure. The pollen I blew was to protect you from the glade. You see, it likes new visitors and rarely lets them leave."

"Are you telling me that it can think?"

"Oh, quite so, though what it thinks we never know!"

"Then the Seelie Court must know we're here? You

promised me when you made contact that you could get us to the boy's parents undetected."

Mr Fox's face became entirely military. Gone were his polite mannerisms and in their place, focused, pin-sharp eyes locked on Lemnus, trying to read his every word.

"Our magic does not work that way. It is not ours to control but a living thing of its own. We merely understand how to talk to it, and even then only in ways that it allows. If I had not used the pollen, our glade would have fallen in love with you just as surely as you with it, and you would have lived out the rest of your days in its leafy embrace. The glade works to its own rhythm and yes, it knows you are here, but the court do not and will not, if you follow my lead."

Mr Fox eyed the tunnel mistrustfully, his keen senses picking out every detail till he concentrated on the only details that mattered: they were alone, no guards had come running, no weapons had been drawn.

Lucy's eyes were shut tight, though Ned could see from her lined brow that she was deep in thought; a single bead of sweat was trickling down the side of her face.

"Lucy? Lucy, are you OK?"

She opened her eyes wide, with a look of utter confusion. "He's telling the truth. It's hard to explain —

the Fey's minds are so… *noisy*. But all that noise, well, it's not directed at us, not at all. Something seems to have them in a tight hold; whatever it is, I can't read it."

On the ground Gorrn billowed nervously, half in retreat and half drawn to the walls and vines around them. Meanwhile Mr Fox's finger was still poised over the trigger of his gun.

"By noise you mean what they're thinking about?" he asked.

"Yes, and it's not us."

Ned watched as the agent relaxed his hold on his gun and then holstered it. However new Mr Fox was to the workings of the Hidden, one thing was sure: he trusted Lucy and her gifts implicitly.

"Lead on, Lemnus."

They moved through the network of root-encased tunnels, quietly and carefully. Their guide could not have seemed more relaxed, no doubt because he called this place home. As their path widened and lowered, Ned realised that everything here, from the walls to its doors and what he'd thought were carvings, was in fact not made by the Fey at all but formed by the roots of the glade itself. They passed by great halls, squares and balconies of vine and bark. It reminded him of their journey into Annapurna, how plants and stone had seemed to mingle. The Seelie Court, at least the warren that housed it, was alive and, Ned sensed, quite able to think. What came as much more of a mystery was that it was also, to his eyes, abandoned.

"Lemnus, where is everybody? Where are the Fey?"

"Far too busy to notice us, Engineer. They are at the ball."

And the fairy's face did two things – at first he smiled, lost in a long-loved memory, then he scowled at the thought of it.

"They're at a ball? Is that some kind of dance? How can all of them be there?"

"You'll understand when you see it."

"But we're not going to see it, right? We're going to avoid the ball and the fairies in it, aren't we?"

Lemnus stopped and pointed towards a series of windows.

"The Seelie Court works in reverse. These tunnels are what you might call a basement. The court itself is below us and the bedchambers of the courtiers lower down again. That throne room is where they are lost in the dance. The chamber that holds both your parents and the Heart Stone is in the adjoining room."

Ned, Lucy and Mr Fox crouched down low and peeked over the edge of the windows. Below them was the most extraordinary sight, even by the Hidden's standards. Hundreds upon hundreds of fairies were amassed in a single throne room. Along its edges were huge oak banqueting tables where fairies sat, row after row, feasting on great mountains of food. At its centre they danced, pirouetting endlessly to some silent music that neither Ned nor his companions could hear. Peering closer, he saw that once again nothing was made by hand. Even the vast chandeliers that hung over them all were leafy, and the lights at their tips were glow-worms instead of flames. Ned had expected the fairies amassed here to be different, but his limited knowledge of their kind couldn't have prepared him. Some were no larger than thumbs and ran across the tables; others were ten feet tall with limbs as thick as his wrists. Some had feathers for hair, others the wings of beetles or birds; and no two sets of eyes or skin colours were completely alike. They shimmered and shone, a few of them changing hue in the same way as familiars, and others yet seemed more animal than anything, with beaks and the ears of foxes, or hooves for hands.

Two things bound them together. Like Lemnus, they

all wore dated courtiers' clothes from another era, but unlike Lemnus, they were all lost in a trance. They laughed and ate and drank, but it was as though they were acting, or playing a part that never changed – or couldn't change, even if they'd wanted it to.

"What's the matter with them?" breathed Mr Fox, his training again fully stretched by what the Hidden offered.

"The magic in these walls has a power to it. It is nature unbound, as pure as a newborn spring, as deadly as a dying winter. They are listening to its song. It feeds them with power till they become giddy and unable to free themselves."

"No wonder there was so much noise," said Lucy. "But that's awful! How can they be set free?"

Lemnus seemed to sadden and anger at the same time. "They don't want to be free. The music feeds them and so they come – it is the source of their magic. Were it not for my bag of pollen, I'd be down there with them now."

As he spoke, Ned could see how much the creature meant it. His lips were trembling and his hands fidgeting wildly. For a moment, Ned saw Lemnus and his people in a different light. As powerful and wild as they were, they were also prisoners of a sort, drawn to the strange ritual like moths to a flame.

"How long does it last?"

"Time has little meaning to us. Sometimes a night, or days, sometimes a month, or a string of years. Wherever we are, there is always the music. It has made us cruel and selfish, because we care for nothing else."

Ned thought back to his meeting at St Albertsburg and how little Prince Aurelin had seemed to care for the Hidden's plight. Rather than make him angry, he'd felt sorry for them, all of them. Gorging on the glade's magic had ruined them – every one, except perhaps for Lemnus.

"You want it stopped, don't you?"

Lemnus's face sagged, his great red eyebrows crumpling round his eyes. "More than anything."

"When this is over, when we defeat Barbarossa and his Demon, we could come back here and help you somehow."

"Yes, Lemnus, there must be a way," said Lucy, who looked as close to tears as the fairy in front of them. "I'll talk to the other Farseers – they must know of something we can do."

"No need, little firecracker. And thank you, mind-maker. The tales I have heard of you are as true as your hearts, but I already know what must be done, and done it will be, here and now. In taking the Heart Stone you will break the curse. It is my job of jobs to keep it safe. But I'm simply going to give it to you."

Lemnus pointed to a stairwell and gave them a broad smile.

"Follow me, Fox, boy and girl. Whatever you do, eat nothing, drink nothing – or here you will remain till the song is sung."

CHAPTER 43

Breaking and Entering

Lemnus led them down a spiral staircase and into the Fey's courtroom. Ned's heart was pounding so hard he thought it might actually burst. They walked now as thieves, carefully dodging and ducking, as the spectacle continued around them. The fairies in the court were in a trance, but Lemnus made it clear that bumping into them or treading on their toes would rouse them just as surely as it would a dreamer from any dream.

"Gorrn?" whispered Ned.

"Arr?"

"Do not leave my side."

There was little chance – Ned's familiar clung so close to his shadow that he was almost completely invisible. As they walked, Ned looked at the food and drink on the tables. He'd never seen anything more appetising or so perfectly cooked. The apples looked juicier and the grapes brighter; goblets of drink seemed to call out to him till his throat ran dry with thirst. A cat-eared fairy walked by with a tray of drinks and before he knew what he was doing, his hand reached out to take one, or at least it would have done if his occasionally useful familiar hadn't bitten his calf.

"Unt!" he warned quietly.

"Oww! Err, thank you," mouthed Ned.

Gorrn went back to shivering in his shadow and Mr Fox was so overcome by his surroundings that he had gone completely silent. It was like being in a music video or a film without any sound, only there *was* sound – the fairies laughed and their feet shuffled, but all to music that Ned couldn't hear. Finally they passed by an empty throne and into the adjoining room. Wherever King Oberon was, he was not at the ball.

They found themselves standing in the hollow of a giant oak tree. Light spilling down from hundreds of feet above them shed a greenish glow over everything. And there, sitting on three chairs made of vines, were Ned's parents and Benissimo, eyes open but apparently asleep. The fairy had been true to his word – they were, at least to Ned's eyes, completely unharmed.

Ned ran up to wake them when Lemnus grabbed his shoulder.

"Steady, child – slow and steady, if you will. To wake them suddenly is to hurt them."

"Then how?"

"Take the stone and they will wake slowly, peacefully."

In the centre of the room was a small wooden plinth, and at its top sat a black stone just larger than a man's hand. It was perfectly smooth and shone gently with a light of its own. At the plinth's foot was a more worrying sight, though it was, like Ned's parents and the Ringmaster, sound asleep. It had deep red fur with bright turquoise stripes and looked to be some mix of both tiger and lion. Mr Fox's hand hovered over his gun.

"Lemnus, what exactly is that?"

"That, sir, is a ligron. Part tiger, part lion, but mostly magic. The only one in existence and utterly fearless. It is also mine."

"Handy," said Mr Fox and left his gun in its holster. "Well, Ned, I'd rather like to get out of here, wouldn't you?"

Ned approached the Heart Stone. The more he looked at it, the more it seemed to shine.

"When you take the stone, your parents and the

Ringmaster will wake from their slumber. Slowly at first, Mr Fox. I would suggest that you help urge them from their seats, then move at a pace. The court will also wake, you see, and you will have little time to escape."

"What?!" Ned's eyes bulged out of his head. "Lemnus, how are we supposed to get them through that blinking room if every fairy in Dublin wakes to find us running off with their magic pebble?"

"On the back of my ligron."

Ned stared at the creature. Even asleep it oozed power, but it was still no larger than a normal tiger or lion.

"No offence – I mean, he's a wonderful creature and everything – but we can't *all* get on him."

"He grows."

"*Very* handy," said Mr Fox.

Lemnus pulled a handkerchief from his pocket and passed it to Ned.

"Elven silk. It will protect you from the Heart Stone's power until you are ready to use it."

Ned took the handkerchief and wrapped it round the stone.

"Mr Fox, Lucy, get ready to help them," Lemnus said, indicating towards the three sleepers.

Ned approached the stone and slowly put his hand to

it. It was warm to the touch but otherwise surprisingly "stony". It was far heavier than it looked, but he was able to lift it from the plinth with little effort.

"Try not to drop it," grinned Lemnus.

There was a stirring from the foot of the plinth and in the chairs to their side. Ned's mum and dad, Benissimo and the ligron opened their eyes slowly.

At the sight of her son, Olivia Armstrong smiled giddily before getting up and falling flat on her face.

"Jeffrey?" she winced. "My darling boy, is that you?"

"Ned, Mum. It's *Ned*."

"Course it is, Cuthbert, I'd know your face anywhere. Peter, look, darling – it's our *darling*."

Ned's dad blinked over and over till he finally settled to take Ned and his companions in.

"Oh, yes, Daphne, you're right! How ever did he wind up here? Jack, my boy, we have so missed you."

Ned shot a look to Lucy and Mr Fox, before turning on Lemnus. "What has happened to them?!"

"Don't worry, child. I think you have an expression, no? 'Away with the fairies.' I'm afraid they're still a bit 'away', but fear not, they'll be back to their old selves in a moment or two."

Lucy was trying to help Olivia off the ground and Mr

Fox was doing his best to rouse Benissimo, who was still drifting in and out of sleep.

Suddenly the room began to rumble and the ligron rose.

"Hello, old friend," said Lemnus. "I have a job for you. You're going to carry my friends on your back and get them to safety. Can you manage that?"

The ligron bowed its head solemnly and stared at Ned and his party. His eyes weren't the usual orange-yellow of a big cat, but the same bright turquoise as his striped fur. He was beautiful, almost regal in the way he held himself, and utterly terrifying. Gorrn gave a low "Unt" to his gaze and promptly slid into the shadow of Ned's pocket, where he would no doubt stay.

"Coward," whispered Ned.

"Quickly now, I hear them stirring next door."

Ned and the others manhandled the sleepers on to the back of the ligron; as they did so, it started to grow, inch by stripy inch, till it was the height of a large stallion and the width of two bulls. Within moments a staggered Ned found himself looking down from its mane and only Lemnus remained on the ground. The fairy clearly had no intention of going with them.

"But, Lemnus, when they find out what you've done you'll be—"

"Dealing with a small rebellion, and not my first, young lady! Oberon, our king, has seen many such troubles, though this I'm sure will be the worst."

"Come with us!" urged Ned. "Oberon is going to kill you for this, Lemnus."

"Unlikely – it's on his orders that I have helped you. It is time to save our people. Though they won't thank us for it, and they will try to kill you to get the stone back until we can calm them down – *if* we can calm them down. Quickly now, back through the courtroom – my ligron will take you to the surface."

The extraordinary creature that was Lemnus Gemfeather put his hand up to the ligron's mane and led them towards the courtroom.

"Lemnus," asked Ned, turning back one last time, "the Heart Stone – how am I supposed to use it?"

"With courage and conviction, dear boy, and with the help of your friend!" He then turned to Mr Fox all mischief removed. "And, Mr Fox?"

"Yes, Mr Gemfeather?"

"Listen to yourself – your role is more important than you know."

Ned had no idea what the fairy had meant, and at first glance it seemed like Mr Fox hadn't either. As they entered the throne room, something in front of them stirred. The fairy put his cheek to the ligron's fur.

"Move swiftly, my pet, or your charges will be torn to shreds."

The first of the court to break from their curse was a thumb-sized hummingbird. It was thrumming its way towards them, a gentle flurry of green and yellow. Its minuscule rider looked to Lemnus and bowed with a smile. Then it took in the ligron's passengers. As its eyes honed in on Ned and the silken bundle on his lap, its tiny face turned to confusion then outright rage and the hummingbird's rider screamed. It was a piercing scream, a loud and desperate scream, and it was heard in every corner of the fairy king's realm.

CHAPTER 44

Magic Wakes

A horrified Ned could only watch as the vast throne room woke from its trance. Beneath him the ligron growled, its claws digging into the ground for purchase. Lemnus's pet was preparing to charge. In its way: every noble and knight of the Seelie Court. Plates of food were dropped and pirouettes abandoned in stumbled falls as the room followed the scream to its source.

"Fox, get them to hold on!"

"Easier said than done!" shouted back Mr Fox, who was doing everything to rouse the Armstrongs and Benissimo short of slapping their faces, until he finally did just that.

"Odin's beard, man, what are you doing?" spat Benissimo. Then his eyes focused on the room. "Oh…"

ROAR!

With a great lurch the ligron charged, smashing through an oak table and its gathered Fey like a bowling ball through a set of pins. The fairies there screamed and scattered, and the ligron continued its assault. Ned clung on to its fur with every ounce of his strength.

"Barking dogs, Lucy! Hold on!"

"WHAT DO YOU THINK I'M DOING?!"

Faster and faster the beast ran, piling through rows of panicked and angry Fey. Tables, chairs, dishes and jugs were cracked and smashed to pieces till one scream became a hundred and the room turned. At the far end, where the Fey had had more time to wake from their slumber, weapons were drawn and a hastily made barrier of tables raised. The ligron roared again, charging like a furred bull at the throng of waiting fairies. Ned ducked as a flurry of needle-thin arrows launched from the backs of hummingbirds narrowly missed him. Above them, the taller fairies threw spears of thorn-tipped vine.

"Argh!" yelped Lucy, as something tore into her, her arm now bleeding badly.

"BRACE!" screamed Ned.

CRASH.

The ligron lunged at the barrier of tables before them, nearly knocking Ned's dazed dad from its back. Mr Fox's arm shot out and pulled him upright again with a mighty heave. The ligron at last managed to claw its way up and over the barrier, Ned's heart leaping into his mouth as a dozen blades screamed by their legs and feet. They landed on the other side, crushing three larger fairies with a painful crack, and the beast sped on.

Up the spiral staircase and through the Fey's courtyards and squares it ran, behind them a tidal wave of winged and angry assailants.

"Ooh, so pretty," sang Ned's mum as another spear flew by their heads.

"Mum, wake up!" shouted Ned, face now turned to their pursuers.

Closing the gap was a buzzing, chattering throng of armed fairies. Some flew, some galloped, others sped along the walls and ceilings like angered ants protecting their nest. For a moment, Ned felt sorry for them. Their prized possession and the source of their magic had been stolen just as they had stolen it from Tiamat. Etched on each and every face was a hatred he'd rarely seen and never by so many aimed at so few.

A hummingbird dived from above, planting its razor-sharp beak in his cheek.

"Argh!"

His sorrow promptly left him in a spray of blood as he swatted at the bird and its rider.

"Ned! Watch out!" yelled Lucy.

Ned turned just in time to see a wall of vines thickening in front of them.

"STOP!" he yelled, pulling at the ligron's mane in a violent attempt to avoid their collision, but the ligron leapt forward, howling as the closing greenery stabbed at its sides. There was a burst of light and their mount stumbled, its paw tangled in some knotted snare, and they were all thrown violently over its head, landing in a painful heap at the centre of the glade.

Finally Ned's parents had been knocked back to their senses, as had Benissimo.

"Mr Fox, what are Ned and Lucy doing here?" said his mum as she pulled herself off the ground.

"I should think that's obvious, madam."

"Don't you madam me, young man!"

But the Ringmaster, as always, had other things on his mind. "The stone, man – do you have the stone?"

Mr Fox did not answer, as his eyes were fully focused on the gap beyond both Benissimo and Olivia Armstrong. Ned and his allies had kicked a hornets' nest. To one side of them was a growing throng of bloodthirsty fairies; to the other a mass of now thorny glade, rising and closing by the second.

The wounded ligron turned its massive bulk and limped in front of them.

"Lucy, Ned, I thought Lemnus said that the glade wasn't under the Fey's control?"

"Lemnus Gemfeather?!" stammered Benissimo. "He's been helping you?"

"Apparently by order of his king," replied Mr Fox, drawing his gun.

"Lucy, Ned, get behind us," ordered Ned's dad.

A suddenly alert Terry Armstrong blinked and a throng of stone projectiles hung in the air in front of him.

Benissimo unfurled his whip and Olivia had picked up a thick branch from the ground that she was stripping for use as a club. The ligron stooped its head low – wounded or not, it had at least one last charge to give them.

"Mum, Dad, don't hurt them! None of this is their fault. They just want their stone back."

"Yes, dear, and I am quite certain they will tear us limb from limb to get it."

Lucy stood by Ned and raised a hand to his cheek, and in a burning second the gash the hummingbird had made left him.

"Thanks. You may have to do quite a bit of that in a minute."

Almost on cue, Ned's familiar slipped out of his pocket and slithered to the ground. Gorrn was clearly terrified but would not let his master face the Fey or glade without at least a little fighting and biting of his own.

Lucy smiled at the creature then her eyes locked to Ned's, clear and bright.

"Now would be a good time to fire up your ring."

"Right," said Ned.

"Right," repeated Lucy and her face hardened.

Ned Armstrong, last in a long line of Engineers, stood by his friend and Medic, and turned to face the Fey. He could hear the yawn of the glade's stretching thorns behind them, and in front of them was a now slowing army of vengeful fairies, glowing with magic and menace as they prepared to charge. There would be no running.

Ned shut his eyes. He dug deeper than he'd ever had to. He thought of his parents, of Lucy, of everyone he'd ever loved or cared about, and deep in his chest something stirred. Defiance, bravery or sheer unbridled love — it moved in him like a tidal wave, and his ring finger burned... then suddenly fizzled to nothing.

The Fey charged and the ground shook. Ned looked

to Lucy in staggered disbelief, then to his dear mum and dad, his friend the Ringmaster. He could do nothing to save them, nothing but stand there and watch.

Closer and closer they came. Ned's parents looked back to their son. It was a look only a parent can make, a look that says, "Be brave – we have you," knowing full well that they would be the first to fall.

At the final moment, when the reds, greens and violets of the fairies' eyes were on them, Lemnus Gemfeather, protector and betrayer of the Heart Stone, pulled himself out of the ground and placed himself between them all.

As he did so, a great voice boomed through the air speaking in words that neither Ned nor his companions understood. Outraged and utterly perplexed, the fairies lowered their weapons in silent fury. Behind Ned, the glade withdrew till the door they had first walked through revealed itself once more.

Lemnus calmly walked up to Ned and his party, and bowed. "Go on – now, quickly. Through the door."

"Gemfeather," said Benissimo, giving Lemnus a reverent bow, "what in Zeus's name was that voice?"

"Zeus? No, no, Your Ringship – it was Oberon. In our realm a fairy king's bargain, no matter its edge, cannot be refused."

"What did he offer in return?"

"His life," said Lemnus sadly. "Do not waste it, Benissimo – defeat the Demon, and destroy the stone."

***

Perched on a windowsill above a dark alley sat a grey and white pigeon. It did not coo, nor did it fawn with any other of its kind, because under its feathers and beak beat a clockwork heart made up entirely of brass. The Turing Mark Three had sat on the exact same spot for more than two days. Occasionally its ticker mind would remember to do something "pigeony" and it would coo, or ruffle its wings, but its gaze had not left the Fey's secret doorway in the alley for even a second.

Its lenses clicked in quick succession as the door opened and four adults with two children walked through it, then refocused and clicked again at the silk-wrapped object in the boy's hand.

A ruffle of feathers later and the Turing Mark Three took to the sky. It would be a long flight back to the taiga and Barbarossa was waiting.

CHAPTER 45

The Fallen

Ned had his parents and the Heart Stone, but there would be no cheering, no hugging or joy. As Mr Badger started to speak, Lucy's eyes were already filling with tears, such was the power of her gift. The news could not have been more grave – St Albertsburg had fallen.

Back at the Nest it became clear that the BBB's secret base was no longer a secret, at least not to the Hidden. As they came in to land they passed over countless supply lorries and the skies across the cliffs of Dover were thick with unmarked grey helicopters, like a swarm of bees protecting their nest.

Ned and his family alighted from their transport in staggered silence as Lucy rushed ahead to help care for the wounded. If ever her powers were needed as a Medic, it was now. Everywhere they looked they saw haggard faces and hollow eyes that had seen too much. Barbarossa had done more than send a message – he had crushed their forces before the battle had even begun and its effect could not have been more plainly written than on the Viceroy's face. He had a thick bandage over his head, a swollen bruise on one eye and his nose was bleeding and cut.

"We weren't ready for them, Bene."

The Ringmaster looked aghast at what remained of his allies. "Odin's beard, Tom. What of the city?"

"Bloodstained rubble and shattered glass. The bombs came first and then the Demons with their metal men. I've never seen such violence, such unrelenting cruelty…" His voice trailed off. "My city, Bene, the city I swore to protect – it's gone."

All around them were the same ghostly expressions of shock and defeat. Men, women and children from all over the Hidden's domain had gathered at St Albertsburg because they believed in the Viceroy and because despite everything, they had hope. Those lucky enough to escape with their lives had had all the hope kicked out of them. Listless and broken, they were tended to by the BBB's grey-suited agents.

As the great lift descended, Ned could see that each and every floor had been turned into makeshift hospital wards. Abigail and her husband Rocky carried the wounded, two at a time under their great arms. Scraggs the cook and his army of kitchen gnomes brought soothing broths and bread and even the three emperors, Nero, Caligula and Julius, were for once not causing mischief but delivering bandages and medicine to those most in need.

Ned had never seen anything like it and neither had his parents. The three of them stood and stared, just as wide-eyed and horrified as the victims. But like Benissimo, the Viceroy and Mr Fox, their role in all this was different. They had to dig deep, to lead, to find a way through, no matter what.

"It's started, son," said Terry.

"Looks more like an end to me, Dad."

"Only the end is the end, and we've a few more forks in the road till we get there."

"But St Albertsburg, our allies… how can we still win?"

Ned's dad took his hand in his own and stooped down so that their eyes were level.

"Are you the same boy that only yesterday told us we had no choice? The same boy who has twice brought down the Darkness with little more than a ring and a chest full of hope?"

Ned looked away. "I don't feel like him any more."

"It's not about how you feel, Ned. It's about who you are – who we all are – and, like it or not, we have to fight for what we believe in, all of us, to the last man, or woman – *or boy*."

Ned's dad took his mum's hand in his other, and gave it a squeeze as she wiped the tears from her face.

Ned looked up at his parents, then beyond them to the mass of wounded and worn. Darklings were terrifying and Demons the stuff of nightmares made real, but the rest of the Hidden, as frightening and changeable as they could be, were also beautiful. Aside from the citizens and soldiers of St Albertsburg, gathered in the Nest were a myriad of the Hidden's folk, some new to Ned, some familiar. The Circus of Marvels when he'd first found it had taken his breath away, its satyr-horned acrobats and face-slapping Farseers. He'd learnt to love a giant ape that had made him faint with terror and had his heart broken by a man who could turn himself to mist. In front of him now were dryads and dwarves, witches and elves, creatures furred or feathered, on legs or hooves or borne aloft on glorious wings that stretched from their backs. As strange as they were, he loved them all for everything they stood for.

But what he saw right now was a defeated mess.

In that moment something happened in Ned's head. It was a nudging, nagging feeling and it felt a little like bravery, except that Ned was utterly terrified. What if he couldn't do it – what if he couldn't save any of them?

He picked up the case that Mr Badger had used to seal the Heart Stone and marched over to Benissimo, who was still deep in conversation with the Viceroy.

The Viceroy smiled at Ned as he approached and a little of the man Ned knew returned.

"Ned Armstrong? By Albert, you're a sight for sore eyes."

Ned bowed his head politely, then turned to the Ringmaster. "Bene?"

"Not now, pup," said Benissimo, looking slightly cross at the interruption.

"Bene, I need to talk to you."

He scowled. "Can't it wait?"

"I'm sorry, Bene, but it can't. Look around you – we're out of time! I have the Heart Stone and I know what everyone needs me to do, but I can't do it unless I know what this *thing* actually does and how I'm supposed to use it."

He shoved the case into Benissimo's arms.

"So shall we get to work?"

CHAPTER 46

Boffins

They had stood waiting outside the Tinker's lab for more than ten minutes. Benissimo had banged on the door hard, and Ned had shouted and shouted, but there had been no answer from the diminutive scientist.

Benissimo reached into his pocket and pulled out a rune.

"What's that for?"

"This one packs quite the punch. I'm going to blow his ruddy door off."

Ned had seen Benissimo use runes before. They were in essence like magical hand grenades and not to be used lightly.

"Are you sure that's a good idea?" asked Ned doubtfully.

Thankfully they were saved by a young lab technician carrying a styrofoam cup.

"Mr B, sir. Might I suggest this?"

Benissimo's eyes narrowed at the cup in her hands.

"He hasn't slept, or eaten. The only time he comes out is for coffee. Just tell him you have some."

And with that she passed them the cup and left them to it.

"Tinks, I know you're in there," shouted the Ringmaster, "and I know you know that I know you're in there, but what you *don't* know is that I have a cup of fresh coffee in my hands." He pretended to smell its aroma. "Nicaraguan blend, if I'm not mistaken."

There was a loud crash and a muffled yelp from the other side of the door, followed by the sound of tiny footsteps.

"Bene?"

"Tinks?"

"I take it *you* know how many explosives I usually have to hand?"

"Yes, Tinks, it's well documented."

"And the number of experimental weapons I've been working on?"

"Oh yes, and we all thank you for it, Tinks."

"You had better not be lying."

The door slid open with a pneumatic hiss and a barely recognisable Tinker grabbed at the coffee in Benissimo's hands.

"Neptune's trident, man, what on earth have you been doing down here?"

"Working?" offered Tinks.

To say that the Tinker's lab was in a state of chaos would be like calling water wet. Where his worktops began and his tools ended was anyone's guess. Reams of schematics covered the floor in ever thickening layers, and all of the mess – the bolts, the screwdrivers and screws, the ratchets, spanners and cutting tools – led to his central worktop, where what was left of his great-uncle Faisal's head had been disassembled into parts. These, unlike the rest of the lab, had been carefully and precisely laid out. Littered over everything were piles and piles of empty styrofoam cups.

The Tinker was now muttering into his new cup, unshaven, bog-eyed and clearly quite unhinged.

"Tinks, how much coffee have you drunk exactly?"

"Ha-he! Not enough, *never* enough." And as he said it, his eyes grew wild.

Amongst the carefully laid out machine parts, Ned spotted Whiskers. The Debussy Mark Twelve – part ticker and, as Ned had come to discover, part dog – was staring at a print on the table.

"Whiskers?! Hello, boy. How are you?"

Ned's beloved dog-mouse did not look up. At Ned's feet there was an almost imperceptible "Unt". It was the first sound Ned's familiar had uttered since leaving the Fey's realm.

Gorrn was rippling very quietly on the floor and something was definitely wrong. Ned turned to the Tinker, who was looking shiftier than ever.

"Tinks, what's going on?"

"I've been working on something. The code Faisal told us about – I'm close, really close."

Benissimo had yet to be fully debriefed on their mission to Amsterdam. All he knew was that Tinks's extraordinary great-uncle had told them of a code that could stop the Central Intelligence, shortly before Ned had turned him into a pile of disconnected parts.

"Gnome, sit down and speak clearly. I am in no mood for dithering."

The Tinker did as he was told, his face calming just enough to get the words out.

"The tickers that laid waste to St Albertsburg –" and for a moment Tinks's face turned to utter shame – "the tickers that were built in my fair city… there's a way to stop them, maybe even turn them, the same way the Twelve's eyes and ears were turned to work for your brother."

Benissimo's eyes narrowed and he leant in closer. "Go on."

"Code. Ones and zeros. That's what they listen to, besides their own programming. Ned will know from his time with the jossers that computers can be hacked. If we can hack the Central Intelligence, then we can control the orders that it gives."

Benissimo was a man of swords and muskets, not lines of data.

"And this 'hacking' – can you do it?"

"I don't know. There isn't a lot of Central Intelligence lying about to try it on. In principle yes, but it… he… isn't a normal computer. He thinks for himself, and essentially rewrites his code at will. Creating the right code, a code that can adapt to his mind as it changes, well… that's what all the coffee is for."

"Well, keep at it," said the Ringmaster, then he took Ned's case and handed it to the Tinker. "Tinks, this is the Heart Stone – get it under your lenses, would you."

The minutian did as he was told, taking the Heart Stone out carefully and placing it under a set of microscopes.

As the Tinker inspected the stone, Benissimo began to pace the room. It was slow and brooding to start with, but grew faster and faster. He circled both the Tinker and

Ned, till his feet were wading through paper like a truck through snow. If Ned hadn't seen him like this a dozen times before, he'd have thought he was beginning to crack.

"Bene? You OK?"

The Ringmaster stopped dead in his tracks and grabbed Ned by the arms.

"My dear boy, our allies are broken in spirit and bone, and until you rudely interrupted me upstairs I thought that all was lost. But your spirit has given me hope, not for the first time, Ned Armstrong, and I've no doubt not for the last either."

"Fascinating, utterly fascinating," muttered the Tinker, then looked up and blinked at Ned and Benissimo.

"What is it, Tinks? What does it do?" urged Ned.

The Tinker paused, looked back to the Heart Stone, then to Benissimo and Ned. "I haven't a clue."

At which point Whiskers turned to them all, his tiny eyes blinking brightly, and said, "If I were you, I would worry less about the stone and more about getting your powers back."

Ned's mouth opened and closed like a goldfish.

On the floor Gorrn billowed wildly.

"Tinks," said Ned finally, "WHAT HAVE YOU DONE TO MY MOUSE?!"

CHAPTER 47

Whiskers?

"**Y**ou put your great-uncle Faisal in my mouse?!" seethed Ned.

The Tinker had explained in detail how what was left of his great-uncle was failing; how the only way to keep him alive was to transfer the code of his "soul" into another ticker, and that the perfect conduit was Whiskers, given that he had successfully undergone the procedure before.

"You knew, didn't you? In Amsterdam, when you asked to take Whiskers with you?"

Poor Tinks looked very close to tears. "Well, I mean, you see… yes."

"Gorrn?"

His familiar did not need to be asked. The truth was that he had become rather fond of Whiskers. As Ned's sidekicks and companions, they had a certain bond. And now Whiskers was not only a robotic ticker in mouse form, *and* a dog, but also a geriatric minutian scientist, and the latter transformation had not taken place with anyone's permission.

Gorrn rose up as a mountain of undulating menace and grabbed at the Tinker's wrists.

"Unhand me, you gelatinous blob!"

"Pup, there's no need for that!" protested Benissimo, till Ned quietened Gorrn with a raised hand.

"How dare you treat my grand-nephew like that!" said Great-uncle Faisal.

Ned leant in very close, till his nose was almost touching the mouse.

"If I were you, Faisal, I'd button it. Whiskers, are you still in there?"

The little mouse's eyes blinked and his demeanour changed back to that of a tail-wagging dog-mouse. He nodded to Ned, then sat on his haunches.

"Are you all right, boy?"

The dog-mouse that Ned loved and knew shrugged.

"We'll get him out of there, Whiskers, when this is all over, I promise."

Whiskers wagged his tail contentedly and Ned turned on the Tinker.

"Tinks, how long till you and Faisal crack the code?"

"I don't know. Could take weeks, maybe months."

The walls of his lab seemed to close in around them as Benissimo roared back.

"We don't have months! Tinks, get your staff, and get all of them on this. I want that code cracking, and I want to know what that stone is and how it works." He marched to the door, his moustache in full twitch, adding as a final thought, "I would suggest installing a coffee machine before you start – no one in your team sleeps till I see some results."

Outside, the larger laboratory was empty, though no doubt it would soon be full. Every available hand in the facility was working round the clock to help house and tend to the Viceroy and his evacuees.

The Tinker had not had the answers he'd hoped for and Ned had never felt darker in his life.

"Well, that didn't go as I'd hoped," he sighed.

"He's right though, pup," said Benissimo.

"How can you say that?" replied Ned angrily. "I love that little ball of bolts. I mean, I'm not really sure I know what he is any more, but he's mine, and—"

"No, no, not about Whiskers," said the Ringmaster. "Faisal – what he said about your powers."

Ned sighed again. "In Dublin, when the Fey charged, I tried my Engine and it just *fizzled*. Nearly everyone I care about was on the brink of being torn to shreds and all I could do was just stand there and watch! Even if we do figure out what I'm supposed to do with the stone… what if I can't actually do it?"

Benissimo put a firm hand on Ned's shoulder and leant in towards him.

"Well, I would have thought that was obvious. Everyone who stands beside you, and everyone that stands behind them, dies."

"I think, Bene, that it might be time for some training."

CHAPTER 48

Mr Bear's Insurance

Mr Fox had been dreading the video call since their return from Dublin. The role of the BBB was quite simple really. Their job was to protect the human race at all costs. That's why, despite himself and the man's annoying habit of flying by the seat of his pants, Mr Fox liked Benissimo. He didn't like to admit it, and certainly not to the Ringmaster, but they were very much alike. Benissimo wanted to save the Hidden and Mr Fox wanted to save everyone else.

Mr Bear's face appeared on the screen, filling it in its entirety.

"Mr Fox."

"Mr Bear."

"Spider's reports do not bode well. Owl and I are anxious."

It was Mr Spider's job to report on Mr Fox's work with the Hidden, and to give up-to-date information on their mission. Since the Viceroy's arrival, his reports had been incessant.

Mr Bear spooned a great handful of peanuts into his mouth.

"Your ally, this Viceroy with his owls, has been defeated."

"Partly, yes, sir. But we are doing everything we can to repair what's left of their fleet."

"He was to be the hammer, and the ground forces the anvil. If this leader of theirs is so weakened by one attack, what hope does the mission really have?"

"To be fair, sir, it was a surprise attack."

Mr Bear glowered, and poured another handful of nuts into his mouth. "Fair?! Is war fair?"

Mr Fox knew where the conversation was going and tried his best to suppress a hum. There was no use feeling bad, he supposed. He *was* still an agent of the BBB, no matter how much he'd warmed to the Hidden.

"No, sir, it is not."

"And the boy – what about the boy?"

"He's a brave lad, sir. He's started training and his father insists that all is in hand."

"I don't have time for training, Fox – I need results. And as for this Tinker – apparently the man has lost his mind, inhabiting a small wind-up mouse with the spirit of his great-uncle in the hope he can crack a code for him? And *no one* knows how this fairy-rock works, is that right?"

"That's right, sir."

Mr Bear leant away and spoke to someone off-screen.

"A large number of Chinooks will be on hand throughout the battle. If the boy cannot do what we need him to do, you will leave the blast area with as many agents as you can. I will use the launch codes on your word, or on Mr Spider's should you fall."

A cold feeling crept across Mr Fox's skin. If Benissimo's plan failed, Mr Bear was going to drop a nuclear warhead on to the Siberian taiga. The man didn't care how many of the Hidden were killed, no matter how hard they fought or on what side.

"Sir, I…"

But the picture on his screen had already turned black.

CHAPTER 49

Dad

"Calm down, Ned!"

"Calm down? How can I calm down?!" yelled Ned.

Just a couple of feet away, a nightmonger stood completely frozen in a block of hastily made ice. The ice had been made by Armstrong Senior. The junior of the two had, and not for the first time, come unstuck at the last minute while trying to use his Engine. The nightmonger's claws had unfortunately found Terry Armstrong's arm before he was able to entrap the Darkling in ice, but luckily it was only a small wound and he was bleeding only very slightly on to his shirt.

Ned and his dad were standing in an empty hangar that would normally house a pair of Chinook helicopters. For the last twelve hours, it had only housed the

Armstrongs and whatever beast his dad could come up with to test his son's skills.

Ned looked at the encased nightmonger. The Darkling's eyes were turning this way and that, its face a picture of surprise and menace. It was almost amusing, the way his bitter bloodshot eyes darted back and forth. But only almost.

"It's looking at us again, Dad. You sure the ice will hold?"

Ned could only watch enviously while his dad blinked, then raised his hand to let the Engine at his finger fire. Around the ice block the air shimmered and turned till a newly formed layer of frost almost doubled its thickness.

"That'll keep him till George arrives with our lunch."

Terry Armstrong was many things to many people. On the josser side of the Veil he was a kind, unassuming salesman with a soft spot for charity shop jumpers. Behind the Veil, his actions as a young Engineer had been a thing of legend. To Ned, he was all of those things but first and foremost he was his dad. The scissor-like claw of a nightmonger was famously sharp and irritating to the skin, but you'd never know it from the patient expression on his father's face.

"Are you OK, Dad?"

"Never better."

"Liar."

His dad's face creased into a smile. It was the same smile he had given him when Ned set the toaster on fire aged seven. The same smile he'd given him every time he'd opened a school report and his grades were a never-ending C. It was the same smile Ned knew he'd get for the rest of his days, if there were to be any, so long as Ned managed to regain his powers.

"How do you always do that?"

"Do what?"

"Make me feel better."

"It's kind of my job. I won't lie, yesterday's band of gor-balins gave me a bit of a beating. But your ring almost fired then – it's only a matter of time now."

Ned remembered the hopeless puddle he'd made on the floor.

"I'm not going to beat the Darkening King with puddles."

"No, you're not, but it's a start. That wyvern had you going, and I'm sure your wall would have stopped him if—"

"If it had been more than three inches high?"

At the thought of it, Ned began rocking back and forth on his aluminium stool, his eyes two sinkholes of tiredness and worry.

"Son, I know you think the world of her, we all do, but do you still think Lucy's right?"

Lucy was sure that Ned's powers would return if people he cared about were in danger. After all, his ring had sparked to save Lucy in the taiga, and again to save George in Amsterdam. Yet here and now, to save his dad – who he loved as much as anyone or anything in the world – nothing seemed to be working.

"I wish I knew, Dad. It worked to save Lucy and George, but I don't understand why it's not working now. I teleported into a giant blooming weapon of mass destruction just to get you and Mum out – well, to stop Barbarossa too, but mostly to save you and Mum. But every time you unleash a Darkling and it tries to rip your head off, my Engine just fizzles. Dad, we can't win a war with fizzling, or puddles, or three-inch walls, and I can't work the Heart Stone if I can't use my powers!"

Terry Armstrong gave him that smile again, and again it melted Ned's heart. "Then we'd better get cracking. Perhaps we need to up the ante a bit..."

He motioned to a bunch of grey-suits at the edge of

the hangar. These men had been carefully selected amongst the BBB for their size. They wore specially altered riot gear, thick protective armour, reinforced helmets and each carried long, high-powered Tasers. It was said that their weapons could stop a charging bull elephant. Just as well then, because Terry Armstrong was about to make things noticeably more dangerous.

"Open up the big one."

One of the agents scratched his helmet and looked to the others.

"*The big one?* You sure, sir?"

Ned's dad looked to his son, then back to the agent.

"Not really," he said, "but after you've opened it, I suggest you find yourselves somewhere safe to hide and stay there."

A bead of sweat was beginning to form on his father's temple.

"Dad, what's the big one?"

"Benissimo wouldn't tell me," said his dad, "but I do know it's big."

"DAD?!"

Terry Armstrong smiled at his son and helped him off his chair.

"Let's hope Lucy's right, eh?"

CHAPTER 50

Dinner for Two

As it turned out, Benissimo's mystery cage housed a twelve-foot fire-breathing cyclops from somewhere in southern Greece. Despite only having one eye, the creature had honed in on Ned and his dad immediately, charging at them with a furious roar, and had nearly incinerated the pair of them. His dad, as ever, had borne the worst of it, succeeding at the very last minute in holding its charge.

Needless to say, Ned's Amplification-Engine had not fired.

A deflated Ned now sat in his room with Lucy. Scraggs was working round the clock to feed the Viceroy's wounded and everyone else had to make do with the BBB's standard-issue dinners. Ned stared at the carrots and peas in front of him. They'd had the life microwaved out of them and he had no idea what kind of meat the lump next to them was, or even if it was meat. Thanks to the Tinker, his mouse and sidekick now lived in the lab, but at least he still had Gorrn. Good old dependable Gorrn, the shadow in Ned's shadow, always there no matter what.

"You all right, Gorrn?"

A greying ooze rose up to the side of his table, till the two glowing slits for eyes blinked up at him like stars.

"Unt," said Gorrn and his head shook like a bowl of reluctant jelly.

"He's been like that all afternoon."

Lucy smiled. "Oh, Ned, he's just a bit tense. We all are."

"*He's* tense?"

Gorrn oozed back to a puddle on the floor.

"Dad nearly died, Lucy. We both did. Maybe that's what we deserve for letting the Darkening King rise in the first place. None of us would be in this mess if it weren't for our rings."

"Ned, don't be ridiculous. You were tricked, and anyway, I helped you get there, remember? No one knew what Barbarossa was planning, not even me, and I'm a Farseer as well as a Medic."

"It doesn't matter – I still provided the spark that freed him."

"Yes, you did, and then you and your dad hurt the beast. No one else could have done that, not me, or Kitty before me, not even the great Benissimo."

Ned brightened, if only a little.

"Your powers can cause harm, Ned. So can mine," continued Lucy. "But the Engine was passed down to you to *help* people, to save innocent…"

Her voice trailed off mid-sentence, and a light sparked in her eyes.

"Lucy, what is it?"

"You've got a big heart, Ned Armstrong," she said, getting up suddenly. "And sometimes big hearts have a way of hanging on to stuff that they shouldn't, but I'm going to find a way to fix you – just you wait and see."

And with that, Lucy walked at a pace for the door to his room.

"Hang on a minute, where are you going?"

"I'm searching."

"For what?"

"For a way!"

A confused Ned looked back down to his plate of

microwaved something, then to the floor and the shadowy puddle that was Gorrn.

"I'm not sure I always understand that girl. Oh well, it's just you and me then, eh, Gorrn."

"Arr."

***

Several miles away, and under the cover of a pitch-black night, a Demon and three clowns scaled the cliffs of Dover. Beneath them the chalk-white rock was peppered with sinewy black arms and legs. Gor-balins when climbing in great numbers look very much like an army of ants. The handful of Barbarossa's ticker flies that had made it into the BBB's base had discovered a single but brilliant flaw in its defence system. There was little point in using a hammer to break down a door, especially when one had found a key.

Sar-adin looked to the clowns as they made it to the edge of the cliff. Their mission had been made very clear – Barbarossa would not let them fail again, and had sent his finest to ensure their success. The Demon despised nearly everything about them, but for one simple thing: they would do absolutely anything he told them to.

"Mo?"

The largest of the two remaining monstrosities simpered towards him. Dressed all in black for their mission, he looked even more ridiculous than usual.

"Sar-ee-dins? Mo is ears for you, he is."

"Once we gain access to the compound you are not to leave my side. It must be done in front of me. Fail and you will…"

The clown's face shuddered. "No speaksie of toasty cloons, no needs to get hot and fiery. We's good cloons this time, Sar-ee-dins. You'll sees it all, all the smushin' and crushin' of da jossy-boy und his girl."

CHAPTER 51

Things That Go "Bump" in the Night

When Ned woke up, it was to his door being almost ripped from the wall in a tear of metal and fibreglass by a furred hulk of terrifying strength, eyes focused and nostrils flared for the doing of harm.

"George?"

"Quickly, old bean, they're everywhere."

A second later and Ned was hurtling down the corridor in a T-shirt and pants, his ferocious protector leading the way like a crazed bulldozer, Gorrn hugging the ceiling behind them. All around Ned could hear more shouting and guns being fired and as they passed by yet another corridor, Ned could see that it was filling with smoke.

"What's going on, George?!" spat Ned through gasps of air.

"Assassins, hundreds of them. They gained access through an old mineshaft and they're attacking anything with a pulse fitting your or Lucy's description."

As they turned a corner, a gor-balin came tearing towards them, a curved blade in its hands and a face brimming with malice. The creature's yellow eyes widened at the sight of George, but it continued its charge nonetheless, flecks of spit at its mouth, and muscles bunched for stabbing. George grabbed its arm with a painful *snap* before throwing it to the wall. There was a loud *crunch* and the gor-balin lay motionless where it fell.

"Come on, old bean, we've minutes before lockdown. After that every corridor will be closed."

But Ned was still staring at the gor-balin. This was St Albertsburg all over again – nowhere was safe from Barbarossa, not even the Nest! He meant to finish them all before the real battle had even begun, and if George was right, Ned and Lucy were his next target.

George grabbed a dumbstruck Ned by the waist and carried him at a gallop.

"Where are you taking me?!"

"To Lucy and Mr Fox. There's a safe room just a bit further on – I'll come for you when the fighting's done."

"What about Mum and Dad – where are they?!"

"In the thick of it, with Benissimo."

"But we have to get them, George!"

"I'll head straight to them once I know you're safe."

Ned's head filled with images of his mum and dad, surrounded by gor-balin assassins on every side.

"What about the lockdown?! Gorrn, go to them – *hurry!*"

"Unt!" grunted his familiar from above.

"PLEASE, GORRN!"

There was a reluctant "Arr", and Gorrn turned the other way, towards the battle. He might not have been the most conversational of familiars, but when it came to fighting and biting there was no one better suited to the task, and Ned prayed that he would reach his parents in time.

Ned turned to look ahead and as he did so, George suddenly slowed. Ahead of them a pair of gor-balins had just dispatched one of the BBB's guards, and now turned to face Ned and George.

"Hold on!" said George, who was about to leap at them, his legs flexed in readiness, when Mr Fox stepped out from a doorway. His face was red, angry beyond words, and he lashed out at the gor-balins violently.

"This is my –" the heavy Taser found one of the

creature's necks and it shook in a painful spasm — "COMPOUND!"

Ned had rarely seen anything like it. He was as fast as Monsieur Couteau, with his mum's flair and training, but the singular purpose with which he used his baton took Ned's breath away. Every strike was both clinical and violent, and as the gobs fell to a heap, he almost felt sorry for them. A staggered Ned could only wonder at the man as Mr Fox looked away to regain his composure.

"I'm sorry you had to see that, gentlemen. Inside, if you will," urged Mr Fox.

The BBB's foremost agent began talking into his earpiece, flicking from one comms channel to the next as his men provided a stream of garbled intel. His expression had completely changed now, the anger all gone. It was replaced by a face carved from marble — expressionless, alert and completely focused on the task in hand. He'd seen that look before and it had been worn by Benissimo. Both men would ride whatever storm to protect their own.

When Ned entered the safe room, he saw his friend and Medic waiting for him.

"Lucy! Have you seen Mum and Dad?"

"No, Ned, but I can 'feel' them – they're alive, I'm sure of it."

Ned let himself relax, if only slightly.

"She's right," said Mr Fox. "The heart of the fighting has been in the top floors and from what I'm being told, your parents and Benissimo have led a victorious counter-attack through the middle. It seems that Barba has, at least this time, underestimated the forces he needed for a proper assault... George, we'd best head up and help the others. I have the codes to get us through once the corridors are shuttered. There's a party forming to mop up what's left of the gobs. Ned, Lucy, this room is made of reinforced concrete and stainless steel. Nothing is getting in or out till I lift the lockdown, which will start as soon as these doors close again behind us. Don't worry, I should think you'll be out of here within the hour."

George and Mr Fox then exited the room in a hurry, the automatic door's pneumatic sliding mechanism opening for them on their way through. As it started to close again, there were two loud crunches from the corridor outside, followed by the unmistakable sound of falling bodies on concrete.

"What was that?" asked a terrified Ned.

He had just seen what Mr Fox was capable of, and he

knew that taking George out was an almost impossible feat. The hairs on his neck and arms began to prickle.

"I don't know."

Lucy moved quickly, drawing out a dagger that Monsieur Couteau had given her and turned to face the door. Very slowly, the door's heavy steel mechanism that had been closing started to work backwards.

"Stay behind me, Ned."

"Shouldn't you be behind me?"

"Do you have a weapon?"

"Fair point."

The door slid open and Ned's nose was hit with a vile and familiar smell. There on the other side was the unsightly bulk of Mo, club in hand and fresh from use, followed immediately by a grinning Meanie.

Instinctively, Ned raised his ring, but even as he did so his face fell. He thought of daggers, of ice and fire, of anything, and the more he tried, the more it fizzled to nothing.

"Gotchi-gotchi, jossy-boy," boomed Mo.

And he had. Ned wanted to scream – the two clowns were like something from a horror film, all in black but with their same brightly coloured hair and cracked make-up. Their new clothes did little to mask the stench in the windowless room, but it was their smiles that turned his stomach.

"You shouldn't have come here," Lucy warned and closed her eyes, readying herself to use her powers when Meanie raised his musket.

"No blinky-tink, twitchy-witch, or I's shootin' you deadsie."

There was literally no escape – not this time. Not even George could burst into the room, because his great protector was unconscious on the floor outside. It was then that another figure walked through the door and sealed their fate.

Sar-adin's eyes were glowing a fiery red. He was still in his human form, but there was no mistaking the power that rippled across his skin. There were few things Ned hated more than clowns, but one of them was standing in the room right beside them. This was the Demon who had destroyed Kitty in a final furious outburst. Back then, Ned and the old Farseer had defeated Sar-adin in battle. But that was a different time, and a very different Ned.

"Murderer!" he seethed.

"Jossy-boy's pet blob do murder! Blob kill weenie-Eanie. Only two cloons noo, two ANGRY cloons."

"Silence!" said Sar-adin, raising his hands. His eyes

glowed more brightly and his fingers began to smoke with the smell of burning sulphur.

"You failed! Your gobs are losing and you won't get away, not this time," said Lucy, hand gripped firmly on the handle of her blade.

Meanie, the tallest of the clowns, laughed. It was high-pitched and cruel, and Mo smiled greedily beside him.

"We not coomes for de odders. We only coomes for yous two."

Mo and Meanie closed the gap between them till Ned's eyes watered from their stench. Ned stepped closer to Lucy and took her hand as they shared a terrified look.

"Now, Sar-ee-dins, crushin' and smushin'?" begged Mo.

"Yes, now," said Sar-adin, and his hands erupted in a flash of blinding fire.

For a moment the room turned hot and white, and when Ned refocused his eyes he saw two small piles of burnt soot, smoking on the floor. Ned and Lucy stood speechless. The Demon had turned the clowns to blackened powder before their eyes.

Slowly, the fire playing across Sar-adin's skin died out and he lowered his arms.

"Repulsive creatures, were they not? Now, I wish to speak with you. Both of you."

CHAPTER 52

The Enemy of My Enemy is My Friend

The next morning the BBB was alive with the news – Barbarossa's Demon had risked life and limb to pass the Engineer and the Medic a message: the Darkening King would soon rise. Wounded or not, the Hidden were preparing for battle.

It turned out that Benissimo's Demon informant and Sar-adin were one and the same and they had let the creature escape so that Barbarossa still believed him to be loyal to his cause. Mr Fox had called an emergency meeting of the Nest's key decision makers. They all sat at the table and quietly listened to the two friends' story.

It was the first time Ned had seen Mr Fox since the attack. The young agent had till now been locked in his room and, according to Abi, he'd been heard arguing with Mr Spider on numerous occasions. In front of him were his laptop, a ream of notes in a binder and carefully laid out pens with especially sharpened pencils. He was an entirely different man from the raging machine Ned had witnessed the night before. Behind him was Mr Badger, who stood observing silently with his usual brick-like demeanour.

The rest of the room was barely listening. The Viceroy had not recovered from the attack. The poor man hadn't just lost men, and his fleet – he'd lost his heart in the crumbling debris that had become of his city.

"What do we have to fight them with? You've seen what's left of my men and our allies," he said.

"Barba clearly knows where we are and who we've sided with," said Benissimo. "There's no need to hide our plans any more. I say we put out a call to everyone this time. Every free and able man or woman of the Hidden. They'll come, Tom – they'll heed our call."

For a second the Viceroy quietened, mulling over Benissimo's words, but what he'd seen at the hands of Demons and their tinpot men would not let him free of its hold.

"You weren't there. You didn't see the Demons or their machines – you've no idea what they're capable of. The

Hidden will be too frightened to come, and with good reason. This Sar-adin and his visit changes nothing."

"It does if he can lead us to the beast."

"But a Demon, for pity's sake!" cried the Viceroy.

"The same Demon who told us about the Heart Stone in the first place," roared back Benissimo. "He had every chance to kill the boy, but he took the clowns instead."

"A ruse to gain their trust, nothing more. Clearly the object houses immense power. What if your brother wants the stone for himself? This could all be part of some elaborate trap. For all we know, Tiamat is in cahoots with Barbarossa, or even the Darkening King himself… By Albert, man, *think*."

From the other side of the table, there was a quiet *snap* from one of Mr Fox's pencils. Mr Fox did not look up, but his face was turning to a shade of red and he began to hum.

"Humph, hum – hurr." As he went on, the humming turned into a kind of huffing. "Hruff, rum, rar."

"Fox?" said the Ringmaster. "By the gods, man, what's got into you?!"

"Hrumph, frumph, frhur."

His face became a searing purple and then Mr Fox exploded. He threw his laptop across the room violently, and it shattered where it hit the wall. He grabbed at his remaining pencils and broke them all at once, then threw the contents of his binder into the air. As the sheets of printouts floated to the table, he finally spoke.

"You're all going to die!" he said. Then his face dropped. "We're all going to blasted well die, all of us, unless we take action *together*."

For maybe the second time since Ned had known him, Benissimo was at a momentary loss for words. He blinked, ruffled his moustache and leant back in his chair. He then cocked his head to one side, taking in the normally controlled agent, and smiled.

"Zeus's crown, I didn't know you had it in you, Mr Fox."

Mr Fox sat back in his chair again and cleared his throat. "My training does not allow for outbursts, but Darklings have attacked my base and *I do not like Darklings*."

Which, as far as Ned could see, was abundantly obvious.

"They have killed my men and women, the bravest and truest men and women in the world. I swore an oath not to let that happen and yet it has. We weren't the only ones attacked last night. There have been outbreaks of violence in every Hidden outpost across the globe. Don't you see? Your brother has sent us all a very clear message.

He intended to strike fear into all our hearts, to break us before the battle even started, and if the clowns had killed the children last night… well, he would have succeeded. Sar-adin stopped that from happening. This is *not* over. Not yet."

Olivia Armstrong put a warm hand on Lucy's shoulder, and addressed them all. "Seeing that he only spoke to Ned and Lucy, shouldn't they be the ones to decide whether he can be trusted?"

Lucy was the first to speak. "There's no doubt that Sar-adin is evil. I've never sensed anything like it before, not even in Carrion or the Central Intelligence. But as evil as he is, he's also frightened, and from what I know Demons can't feel fear. As he tells it, the Darkening King and Barbarossa have made a pact."

Ned looked to Benissimo and remembered what he'd told him about his brother and their curse.

"Your brother thinks that the Veil will be torn down and that he'll get to rule over the world in exchange for bringing him back, but he's wrong and he can't see it. Sar-adin can. The Darkening King feeds on suffering. If he comes back, he'll make everyone pay – humans, the Hidden, Darklings and Demons, *we'll all be slaves*." She paused, overcome for a moment.

Ned noticed, and took over. "Sar-adin says he can get us into the fortress – he'll get a message to us when the time comes. According to him, we have to strike the beast at the precise moment that it forms. Too early, and there will be nothing to kill; too late, and he'll be too strong."

"And how long do we have?"

"He rises in three days." And even as he said it, Ned's stomach turned.

Benissimo nodded and turned his attentions to the Tinker. "And is what the Demon told them true? Are both Medic and Engineer needed to draw from the Heart Stone's power?"

The Tinker's eyes were so bloodshot from tiredness that they'd turned almost entirely red. "Well, boss, it is an object of extraordinary power, there's no doubting it. I think Sar-adin is quite correct and I have a theory. The Heart Stone has very similar properties to the Source. It focuses magic, that is, it draws it from the earth itself, like a magnet. The Fey have been using it for generations to give them their powers, in the same way that the Veil draws its power from the Source in Annapurna. But they are different."

"Go on."

"I believe the First Ones – the ones who built the

Source, as well as Lucy and Ned's rings – based their technology on the stone and the way it works. The lines between science and magic blur often, but we mustn't forget that the Heart Stone is pure, primal magic, the likes of which we'll never fully comprehend. Ned and Lucy could in theory connect to the Heart Stone the same way they connected to the Source, but I have no idea what it will do to them if they do, especially if they're not, um, fully in charge of their powers."

Ned saw Lucy, his parents and Benissimo exchange a look.

"Well, let's not worry about that for now," said the Ringmaster hastily. "Thank you, everyone. Time is indeed our enemy and I suggest we all do what we can to prepare."

CHAPTER 53

Bananas

"George, this really is kind, but I'm not hungry."

Ned was in his room again, hiding away from training and the desperate looks of an entire military base, all praying that he would succeed. Seeing that he needed cheering up, George had made him an assortment of his favourite treats. Sliced and diced banana, banana fried and grilled, honeyed, sugared, caramelised and even George's old favourite – banana sushi. The great ape piled up so many dishes that they almost filled Ned's entire table and he had done so with the last of his private stock of "yellow gems".

"Not even a bite?"

"Sorry, George."

He nodded politely, though Ned could tell that the ape was disappointed. The oversized gorilla looked at the table and licked his lips nervously.

"What about Gorrn? Would he like some? We can't just let it go to waste."

There was a low "Unt" from the floor.

"He doesn't eat, George, at least not food."

"Right," said the ape, all the while his eyes remained glued to the table.

Ned smiled. "Oh, go on then."

George didn't need to be asked twice and almost jumped on the plates of food. He gnawed, chewed and devoured in a flurry of furry greed till halfway through he let out an enormous belch.

"Better?"

"Sorry, old bean, nerves make me a bit peckish."

"A bit!" smiled Ned.

More than half the table had already been devoured in less than a minute.

"I am *very* nervous."

"*You're* nervous? I can barely muster a puddle and the entire planet's depending on me!"

"I know, dear boy. It's you I'm nervous about."

George's wrinkled face sagged, despite the recent infusion of bananas. There was no one better than George at cheering Ned up, no one in the world, but even the great ape seemed to have run out of "cheer".

"George? I thought you came here to… what was it? 'Lift my spirits.' You can't just gorge on—"

But Ned didn't get round to finishing as just then Olivia Armstrong burst into the room, her eyes as wide as saucers.

"Ned, we have an emergency – come with me quickly."

George got up to follow but Ned's mum barred the door.

"Not you, monkey."

Olivia Armstrong was not a woman to be meddled with, and certainly not when it came to her son. But if anyone was up to the job, it was George.

"Madam, step aside."

"I'll do no such thing," said Olivia, eyes piercing like daggers.

George's chest puffed up and the fur on his back bristled. "If it's all the same to you, I would rather come, Olivia."

"He's my son and I'll decide what's best for him!"

George's eyes changed. Ned had seen that look before and what came after was never pleasant. When the ape spoke next, it was in a measured and slow rumble.

"Olivia, I know you are accustomed to being listened to and we have never had cross words before, but I would like to remind you that I love your boy and am sworn to protect him, and if you try and stop me, do so knowing that I weigh several tonnes and become violent when protecting my own, even when they're someone else's."

Olivia Armstrong looked as though she had just been slapped clear across the face. The gentle giant that was George had threatened her. She was about to launch into one of her tirades when Ned took her arm.

"Mum?"

"Yes, dear?"

"He's coming."

"But—"

"*He's coming.*"

A minute later, they were rushing through the BBB's corridors till they arrived at the mirror room.

"Mirrors *again*, Mum?! What's happened?"

"There's no time to explain… We've had a tip-off and we need to get there quickly."

Breathlessly they walked into the room that had led Ned to the taiga. This was to be a different mission altogether.

"Madam, where are we going?" asked George.

Ned's mum took a mirror-key from the wall and looked to her son. It was an almost apologetic look that made his stomach turn.

"Mum, what is it? Where are we going?"

"Grittlesby."

CHAPTER 54

Past and Present

Ned hadn't known what to expect when he'd stepped through the mirror, but he definitely wasn't expecting to find himself in his old bedroom at Number 222 Oak Tree Lane. When he'd left this life behind, he'd had to leave most of his junk here too. Strangely it was all still right where he left it – the abandoned projects he'd built with his dad, the scale model of the solar system, even his stripy old pillowcase and covers. For a minute he thought that he was still the same boy, the same boy who'd never heard of the Hidden or been fused to a ring that now barely worked. But back then he had no mother and had yet to meet a talking ape.

"Err, Mum, have we stepped through time or something?"

"Don't be ridiculous. The pinstripes use this place to keep an eye on your previous life, to make sure the Hidden stay hidden and there's no unusual activity. We've had a tip-off that something's out there and it's heading for your old friends. He failed to get to you with his clowns and we think Barba might want to use Gummy and Archie as leverage against you."

Ned was devastated. The last time he had seen his friends, he'd used a de-rememberer on them. The device had completely wiped any notion of who he was from either of his old friends' memories.

"But they don't even know who I am?!"

"No, darling, they don't – but you remember *them*."

His mum led Ned to his dad's old bedroom. Like Ned's room, it was almost completely unchanged, except for the mounting piles of surveillance equipment by the window. There was a telescope pointing through the curtains, and his mum immediately went to it.

"Where are the pinstripes?" asked Ned, his heart now racing.

"They went to investigate. We haven't heard a word since." She peered through the telescope carefully. "There, across the street – look."

Ned looked through the eyepiece. It was firmly focused

on a sitting-room window on the other side of Oak Tree Lane. In the room sitting on a sofa were Gummy and Arch, a soft flickering of light playing on their faces, between them a large tub of freshly made popcorn. Mrs Johnston was always good at feeding up her boy, though you'd never know it by looking at him. They were laughing, no doubt at some terrible film. Gummy loved action flicks; the cheesier the better.

"Movie night," he mouthed and nearly every part of him wished again that he could be the younger Ned, the one that had lived in this house, had normal friends, eaten popcorn and watched movies. Except that then he wouldn't have had the two parts of his life now standing beside him.

"George, open the curtains. They won't see us in this light," said Ned's mum.

Movie night was always on a Friday and the rest of Oak Tree Lane was completely quiet. Happy families were in their sitting rooms talking, playing or just contentedly watching their favourite shows.

That was, until they heard the first claw scraping along the lane's tarmac outside.

Scrrrr.

Ned's skin crawled. "What is that?"

George peered through the telescope, his enormous eye against its lens.

Scrrrrr.

"Nightmongers," whispered the ape.

Scrrrrrrrr.

"How many?" seethed his mum.

"Hard to tell in this light. Ten or more, I'd say."

"TEN OR—" yelped Ned.

"Shh! Keep your voice down, darling. I should have waited for Bene and your dad! We'll never be able to take them alone – oh, good God!"

"What is it, Mum?! What have you seen?"

Ned's mum looked frantically about the room, opening closet doors and searching under the bed.

"I forgot to bring any blasted weapons – tell me your dad kept a stash in here, somewhere, *anywhere*!"

"I don't know!" said Ned. "I had no idea we even needed them back then."

He looked through the telescope and his blood froze. Walking very slowly down the centre of the road and all along the kerb were more nightmongers than he'd ever seen. And he could make out others perched in the branches of the trees, each and every one with claws made for slicing. There weren't ten or more, but at least thirty!

"There's nothing here. Oh, where is your father?"

"Why would he have had weapons here?" said Ned, thinking it through. "He's an Engineer, right? I mean, he could amplify anything he needed."

"Oh, Ned! So could you…?" Her voice trailed off.

George began breathing heavily, nostrils flared, his face pressed to the glass.

"Ned, old chum. Those boys, their mother… you care for them deeply, don't you?"

"Very much."

"They're family to you, aren't they? Like the circus, like—"

"Like you, yes, George."

"Then they're family to me. I'll try and break through, at least warn them. Livvy, take Ned back to the Nest and get some help as quick as you can."

"George, stop!" tried Olivia.

But Ned hardly heard either of their words, even as the ape's fur ruffled and George prepared to charge downstairs and on to the street.

"There isn't time," mumbled Ned.

The road was filling and quickly. Ned stared at his two friends, and his throat dried. Mrs Johnston had just walked into the sitting room with another tray loaded with snacks. She'd never let the nightmongers touch either of the boys and they'd kill her for even trying to stop them. Dear Mrs Johnston, she was one of the kindest ladies he knew.

"It's not right, it's not fair…" he said, his voice shaking. "They've never done anything to anyone!"

He couldn't just stand there. He threw open the window and one of the panes of glass shattered noisily.

"Ned, what are you doing?" pleaded George, but Ned didn't hear him.

"STOP IT! THEY'RE INNOCENT!" he yelled into the night, and as he did so, something in the pit of his stomach began to smoulder, slowly at first, then as fast as lightning, it shot up from his belly and into his chest and arms, till it found its way to the ring at Ned's finger.

Ned held his hand up and his Amplification-Engine hummed. Second by second, it grew in force till his whole hand and then body trembled. The air around him whistled and blew and the road outside the house began to shake and then melt. This wasn't like Amsterdam, or the taiga or even St Clotilde's. There was a rage in him now so fine and focused that it coursed through him like a vengeful flame. He wouldn't and couldn't take any more.

"STOP!"

A surge of air poured out from around him, smashing through the glass of the window and down to the street below, where it knocked a path right through the nightmongers. With a flick of his wrist, another five were flung upwards violently, their twisted moans soaring into the air.

The remaining Darklings turned as one to look at Ned, then fled as fast as they could, hoping to escape before Ned fired his ring again. Their hopes were not granted. The tarmac from one end of the street to the next erupted, splintering to metal and ice in a violent, crashing wave. The nightmongers were crushed and frozen where they ran.

Next Ned turned his attention to the Johnstons' home. He blinked and a hundred corkscrewing blades were formed on the road outside, hovering and waiting to fly; he nodded and they were hurled at the creatures on the roof and in the treetops. Six more stood frozen in terror by the front door and living-room French windows, their faces pictures of stretched and leathery fear. They bolted, Ned letting them run for a moment, clambering over their fallen comrades.

"Stop," he whispered, then parted his arms and brought

them together again in front of him. As he did so, parked cars on either side of the fleeing nightmongers flew towards each other like magnets, violently crushing the remaining creatures between them. Ned had never known such control, such complete and focused power. He raised his arm again.

"Stop!" But this time the voice was not his own.

Standing next to him was Lucy Beaumont. Behind her were Benissimo, Ned's dad and Mr Fox. They were all smiling.

"I would say that puts you squarely back in the game, son!" grinned his dad, before flicking on the light switch.

"Well done, darling. I'm so sorry we had to put you through that."

"What's going on?" said Ned, looking at them.

He glanced back to the world outside the window and, as he did so, Lucy closed her eyes, just for a second, and all the fallen nightmongers shimmered and were gone.

"You tricked me!" Ned stood there in furious disbelief.

Lucy had used her powers as a Farseer to make him believe his friends were under attack. But the whole thing had been in his mind, except of course for what he'd done to the street. The road was still ruined, cars broken, their alarms mewling weakly, and from the water gushing up at the far end of the road Ned was fairly certain that he'd burst a major water pipe.

"What…?"

Lucy looked at him apologetically. "It was my idea, Ned."

"But why?"

"It was what you said the other night in your room… about how maybe you and your dad deserved to die in training for bringing back the Darkening King. That's when I finally understood why your powers only worked sometimes – why it worked to save me and George, but not yourself or your father. Because they only work to save innocents, and part of you thinks you and your father – the powers you share – are responsible for bringing back the Darkening King in the first place."

"Well, we are!" shouted Ned.

"We're not, son," said his dad. "We did what we had to do. And we *harmed* him. He would have already risen by now if we hadn't. We've got to finish the job we started, son, for everyone's sake."

Lucy went over to Ned and took his hand. "We're all innocent, Ned – not just your josser friends. We're all fighting the Darkness, and what you thought you saw just now is only a taste of what will happen to everyone if we don't win this fight. You know I'm right."

"I don't know, I…" Ned was at a loss for words.

"You have to believe me or your powers won't work," said Lucy, looking into his eyes. "It's the guilt that's holding you back, Ned."

Ned sighed and looked out of the window at the street that only moments ago had been teeming with nightmongers.

"Now, want to try again?" asked Lucy.

Ned looked back at her in shock. Half the street had already been destroyed and his old neighbours would be utterly bewildered once they stepped outside and saw all the damage.

But Lucy was smiling, broad and bright, and he couldn't help but join her.

"Go on then."

His friend closed her eyes as Ned turned to the window once more. A moment later, a huge nightmonger appeared, climbing up a nearby tree, heading towards their window. Ned raised his ring hand and with just the smallest notion it fired, a burst of energy shot out of his Engine and the beast was turned to fire then ash, all in less than a second. It was a gruesome spectacle but had proved beyond doubt what they were all anxious to know.

"I think it's safe to say you're cured!" said Lucy.

The room erupted, Ned's parents hugging each other, the Ringmaster and Mr Fox slapping each other on the back, before they all crowded round Ned.

"Well, you had me going, Lucy!" said a bemused but beaming George.

"Hang on, you mean you weren't in on it?" asked Ned.

"Absolutely not, old bean," said the ape. "You know full well I would've tried to stop them if I'd known."

"Which is exactly why we didn't tell you!" said Olivia Armstrong, throwing a fake punch at George, who fake-growled back at her.

They were interrupted by a loud shout coming up from the street. The room grew quiet, and they went over together to peer out of the window.

Faces were pressed up against every living-room window on the street, and the Johnstons' door had been flung open. Mrs Johnston was standing in the middle of the road brandishing a large wooden rolling pin and staring up at their window.

"I've called the police and they're on their way! If I were you, I'd clear off immediately."

"Don't worry, Ned," whispered Mr Fox. "The BBB will have this cleared up in a jiffy."

Mrs Johnston blinked up at the window – was that the face of a giant gorilla staring back at her expectantly?

George waved down at her.

"What on earth…?" she said, then did the only sensible thing she could, and fainted.

Lucy couldn't help but laugh and Ned found a smile forming on his lips.

"Lucy Beaumont, I cannot believe you tricked me!"

"You're welcome," grinned Lucy. "It's good to have you back, Ned."

CHAPTER 55

Ready?

Before returning to the Nest with the others, Ned asked if he could have a minute alone. His parents hadn't been happy about leaving him there, but he'd been quite adamant – the Hidden and its world of shadows could wait. Ned wanted a moment in the real world, or at least the world he'd left behind.

Half the street was outside now, along with the fire brigade, an ambulance crew and a local news team. There were expressions of shock and excitement on all his old neighbours' faces. Their road had been torn to shreds, a water pipe burst and apparently Mrs Johnston, who was being fanned by Mr Johnston, had seen a giant ape and a group of weirdos in the old empty house opposite. It didn't matter – Ned would be long gone before anyone came over to investigate.

Children often see adventure where adults see distress. A toddler four doors down was playing in the new "fountain" made by the burst pipe, and another one was trying to build a snowman from a block of ice that had turned to slush. No one, however, could have been more excited than Gummy and Arch. Their faces lit up as they examined the wreckage of their street. There would be at least a dozen conspiracy theories from each of them before the night was out and not a single one would come anywhere near the truth because they didn't even know who Ned was any more – he'd seen to that months ago.

Ned looked down at his ring and allowed himself a small smile – just by his finger, a globe of liquid glass hovered in the air changing shape playfully, and all at his command. It felt good to be "back", as Lucy had put it, and he'd enjoy the feeling while it lasted.

"You ready, Gorrn?"

The floor rippled oozily. "Arr."

"Me too."

CHAPTER 56

The Forest Darkens

Tial and Aman had hunted in this part of the forest for their whole lives. Their father and father's father had proudly watched its borders and until recently so had the young bucks. They were not yet full stag-men, but their numbers were dwindling and food was scarce. Everyone had to hunt.

Ahead Aman stopped, stooping low to the ground on his haunches, hand closed to a fist – "stop".

Tial notched an arrow to his bow and sniffed at the air. He knew every pine tree by the river, every oak and yew. They had, until the metal ones came, always spoken to him, not in words but in their own way, through the rustling of their leaves and the yawn of their bark.

Aman flattened his hand again, like a sheet to the ground – "slow".

They moved side by side, deeper into the forest and away from the river.

"What did you see?" whispered Tial.

"Not see, brother. Smell."

Tial drew in through his nostrils again. Nothing. Aman was always more heightened in his senses, though Tial faster of hoof and bow. The herd had once been powerful shamans, humans that took the form of their animals so they could run with them in the forests and green places of the world. They had forgotten how to change themselves back long ago, but magic still coursed through their veins.

"Magic?"

Aman shook his head.

"Different."

Tial stopped by a yew tree, pushing the fingers of his still human hand into the earth by its roots. Cold and soft – too soft. It had started not long after the metal ones had come, not long after the fortress had been built in the heart of their forest. That land was protected by the wolf-pack and the weirs had grown more bold because of it. A sickness was spreading and even the herd's old magic could not hold it. Tial took the tip of his arrow and stabbed it into the yew tree's bark. Black sap seeped from the wound, pouring like rotten blood down the shaft of the arrow. A smell of iron and sulphur filled the air.

"Sickness. The sickness has spread even to here, brother!"

Ahead, something moved amongst the gloom of the trees. Not a weir or Darkling, but something else. The brothers stood now, ready for fight or flight. Their father had taught them well – always watch and listen. Too big or too many a beast and you must run – these days there was only running. Wordlessly, Tial and Aman paced backwards, but the gloom had started to thicken, to grow darker. Tial looked to the yew tree. From the small hole his arrowhead had made and from the ground where its roots tried to feed, a blackness started to grow. Oily and slick, reeking now of sulphur, the sickness flowed, till the tree in its entirety became an oozing, tarry mess of decay and illness. They had seen it before, where the wolf-pack roamed, but never so quick or sudden.

"Run!" spat Aman from deep in his chest.

And the two brothers flew, breaking now at a gallop of hoof on ground. Behind them the forest roared, with its darkening leaves and branches. It was the roar of a dying thing, a thing that is becoming something else.

Over boulders, then crashing through the waters, the two brothers sped, behind them a rushing wall of black and angry branches. Vines had come alive and snared at their legs, with great thorns gouging at their skin.

"Tial!" shouted Aman.

And as Tial turned, he saw that his brother had been struck by a flailing branch. His arms and ribs were broken, the strength knocked from his chest. All around him, knotted roots laden with thorns the size of daggers grew up from the ground.

"Aman!" Tial leapt to his brother, drawing his flint knife from his side. He struck at the roots, again and again, till their thorns broke his skin and bruised the bones of his fingers.

"Get away, go to the mountain. Warn them – we've lost the forest…" cried Aman.

"Quiet, brother, all will be well."

But Aman's eyes grew wide, looking beyond his brother at something behind him. Tial turned to follow his gaze.

A great cage of razor-sharp thorns had grown up around them, trees bent forward to crush and skewer. There were no Demons, no Darklings or metal monsters. The Darkening King had found a new way to feed, and the forest was now his to control.

CHAPTER 57

Really Real

When Ned left his quarters the next day, the Nest's corridors were completely empty. He could still see the telltale signs of the gor-balin attack: musket shot in the walls, the black streaks of fire damage and doors that had been smashed in the fight.

He looked to his hand and the ring on his finger. His powers were his again and there was no one else around, so just to prove it he blinked for a moment and the walls on either side of him warped and buckled languidly, as though he was on the inside of some great jellyfish of his own making. He blinked again and they turned from ice to metal to rock, then back again. It felt different from before, playful even. He'd never had so much control over his gifts; they'd never flowed with quite the same ease. Maybe the break he'd had from it all was a good thing? He still couldn't believe what they'd all put him through to get there but he really was back now and more in control than ever.

"Not bad, eh, Gorrn?"

His familiar merely bobbed its head to one side with a disinterested "Whatever".

Then the thought hit Ned – the horror of last night, even if it wasn't real, was just a taste of what lay ahead. Now that his ring was working, he'd have to face the Darkening King and so would Lucy. He picked up the pace of his steps, heading to Lucy's room, but when he got there he found it empty.

"What's going on?"

His shadow oozed with a quiet "Roo?", which in this case meant, "Don't know."

"Master Armstrong, sir?"

It was Mr Badger. They had never spoken before and Ned was, until that moment, quite sure that Mr Badger didn't really like him, or anyone else.

"Mr Badger, good morning. Where is everyone?"

"Follow me."

The burly agent turned on his heel and headed for the nearest lift, Ned following behind. They were now in one of the smaller service lifts, with no view into the Nest's inner atrium, just drab fibreglass walls and a grey-haired agent for company. Mr Badger pushed the button and folded his arms. There was a stomach-churning lurch as the lift kicked in.

"Where are we going, Mr Badger?"

"Up, sir."

"I guessed that much, but where?"

"There's been a development, this time in the forest. And your mouse thing would like to see you."

Ned was quite sure that it was in fact the eccentric scientist part of Whiskers and not his beloved old dog-mouse that wanted to talk. In the floors above, engines were being fuelled, weapons readied. If the Tinker or Faisal had called him, they had to have a plan. Either they'd cracked the code that would turn Barbarossa's metal men, or else there'd been some breakthrough with the Heart Stone beyond what the Tinker had already told them.

When they arrived, the surrounding labs outside the Tinker's own were a mirror of what Ned had seen just days before. Lab staff both from the BBB and the Hidden were close to breaking point with frantic last-minute research. The Heart Stone and the Central Intelligence's code were now the only two projects any of them were allowed to work on, and they had thrown themselves at the tasks single-mindedly without pause for breath, food or sleep. But as Mr Badger led Ned through the workshops to the Tinker, the workers did pause. They looked up from their monitors and printouts and, bleary-eyed, they nodded; one or two even saluted him, and an elderly minutian got up from his stool and shook Ned by the hand.

"We've all heard, Master Ned – about your gifts coming back. We're behind you, sir, one and all."

The little scientist looked quite overcome and went back to his desk and his printouts, leaving Ned with the once-more dawning realisation that the return of his powers meant a face-to-face confrontation with the Darkening King. He had been brave about it before, he realised now, because he'd lost his powers. The idea of them actually seeing the creature hadn't been real – not really, not then. It was at the precise moment when he walked into the Tinker's lab and saw only Lucy that everything – their role in what lay before them, the creature they would have to battle – became frighteningly real.

CHAPTER 58

Artificial Intelligence

"Ned?!" said Lucy. "Ned, are you in there?"

Lucy was smiling, but she looked nervous, Ned realised, as he focused on the room again.

"Yeah, sorry. I had a bit of a, um, moment outside. How's my frenemy today? Tricked anyone? Scared them out of their minds?"

"Not yet, but it's still early!" replied Lucy brightly.

"Ahem? When you two have quite finished."

Ned looked down to see that it wasn't the Tinker, but Whiskers talking, in a decidedly tinny and high-pitched voice. Try as he might, Ned still couldn't get used to him speaking.

"Congratulations on your returning powers, Master Ned," said a grinning Tinker.

"Thank you, Tinks," said Ned. "It's a start at least. Where's Bene?"

"He's with your parents and the others. They're reaching out to the Hidden, asking them to fight."

"So we're going then? It's really happening?" said Ned.

"In the morning, from what I understand."

Ned took a minute to let it sink in. He looked at Lucy, who shrugged. He supposed they'd known this moment always had to come. At least now he had something to take into battle.

"And on that note, I need to ask you a favour, Ned."

"A favour? Of course, anything, Tinks."

"I, that is, we —" the Faisal part of Ned's mouse bobbed its head in solidarity — "still believe that taking out the Central Intelligence is the only thing that will turn the tide. There are vast amounts of Guardian-class tickers in the taiga now. If we can turn them against Barba, there's a chance of getting you to the Darkening King, or at least to Sar-adin. Our issue is the code. We've run every test imaginable, but the definition of artificial intelligence is that it's intelligent – it can think for itself, and change accordingly, should it come under attack."

"So what can we do, Tinks?" asked Lucy.

"We hit it back with artificial intelligence," said the

Tinker, who was now beaming, as though he'd just told them the secret to eternal life.

As far as Ned could tell, there was one glaring issue with this idea. "Erm, but I thought the Central Intelligence was unique – or am I missing something?"

The scientist part of Whiskers sat upright, his two eyes blinking like flashlights.

"Actually, Master Armstrong, you're missing *me*. I, like the Central Intelligence, am both sentient and made up entirely from code. We were made in different ways, thank the Cogs, but if I can get close enough, if I can connect to his circuitry and I'm quick enough, I can take it over – at least in principle."

Lucy shot a look to Ned. She knew how much the mouse meant to him and what the Tinker's favour would entail.

"You want to put the future of our entire alliance in the hands of my pet mouse?"

"That's about it, Master Ned, yes," blushed the Tinker.

Ned's blood was starting to boil. He wasn't sure whether he was more angry about it having to be Whiskers, or that he and Lucy would die if the little wind-up rodent failed.

"I take it you'll be sending top agents with him?"

"The best," replied the Tinker, whose face was now going from a deep fuchsia to an unsightly purple.

Ned calmed, but only slightly. "So, let me get this right. While I was away on a desperate mission to save my parents – with Lucy's help, of course."

Lucy smiled appreciatively.

"You hijacked my childhood pet and stuffed your great-uncle into his mind – or circuits, whatever. And now..." Ned had to pause. "Now you want to break into the Central Intelligence's stronghold in Gearnish and use my mouse, again, to take him – *it* – over? In, err, *principle*?"

The Tinker beamed up at him proudly, and so did Ned's mouse.

"Yes, sir, I think you have it exactly."

Ned leant in to the table. "Whiskers? You in there?"

The furred ticker did a sort of twitch, then blinked its eyes repeatedly, before sticking its tongue out and wagging its minuscule tail. Faisal had relinquished control and handed it back to Ned's pet.

"We're in a bit of a bind, aren't we, pal?"

Whiskers nodded.

"You don't have to do this, you know. You've got a soul in there somewhere, so if you do, do this, you have to do it because you want to."

The Debussy Mark Twelve cocked its head to one side and started to flash his eyes with Morse code. A long dash and two dots: a "D"… Little by little, the small rodent blinked out his message.

"D O N ' T - B E - D A F T - I ' M - O N L Y - D O I N G - I T - F O R - Y O U - A N D - L U C Y."

Ned's chest suddenly felt tight – his pet mouse and eternal sidekick was going to risk everything to help him and Lucy on their mission.

But Whiskers hadn't finished.

"D O N ' T - M E S S - T H I S - U P."

CHAPTER 59

Time's Up

It was the morning of the battle – no time for doubts or regrets. In one hour they would take off for the Siberian taiga, with no knowing how many, if any, would return.

The Nest's laboratory was home to some of the greatest minds in existence, but for all their gadgets and testing, the Heart Stone was still largely a mystery. They knew only what Tiamat and then the Tinker had told them: that the Source, Ned and Lucy's rings and the Heart Stone were all linked; that they somehow drew on the same magic. They wanted more time to run their tests, but time had simply run out.

George had been helping Monsieur Couteau and Grandpa Tortellini and their teams with last-minute training in the central courtyard. The kindly ape had been using his extensive knowledge of Darklings and Demons to point out some of their weaknesses, so that they might be used in the coming battle. By the time he'd finished, the agents' faces had turned as white as sheets, with the point he was trying to put across now fully understood and one that they would be taking with them to Siberia: Darklings and their Demon masters had no weaknesses, not when it came to the art of war.

When the training session was over, George noticed Lucy in the corner with Ned. They had been watching, and as the session had ended, Lucy had started to cry uncontrollably.

"Dear girl," said George, running to her, "this isn't like you. Please calm down!"

And in that George was right. Since being reunited with Ned, Lucy had seemed so in control, so in charge of her gifts and what lay ahead, that Ned had felt slightly jealous.

Lucy looked beyond the ape's shoulder to the agents he'd been briefing. She closed her eyes and drew in her breath slowly, visibly calming as she did so.

"Do you know what it's like being a Farseer, George?"

There wasn't much George hadn't read about, though the world of Farseers was well known for its secrecy.

"A little, Lucy – but only because of what you and Kitty before you have shared with me."

"I wish I only knew a little, but I don't. I know what all of those agents are feeling, especially since you finished your talk. I know how scared they are, despite their training. I know what the troops and citizens of St Albertsburg felt when they saw their city being destroyed. And I know you, George – I know everything about you."

As she said it, the anger and worry drifted from her face to be replaced with a single tear, warm and wet, rolling down her cheek.

"I know how you long to meet another George or Georgia, someone like you. I know how hard it's been to fit in, even with the Hidden. I know you love bananas because they make you feel like 'you'. I know you love books because they don't judge, because they share their knowledge freely."

George couldn't speak.

"I know you'd do anything for Ned, and me, and I know that not just because I'm a Farseer, but because I've seen you do it. I know you'd do anything for anyone you love because you don't have a family and because of that, you're the kindest, most selfless creature in the world.

But I don't just see it, do I, George? I *feel* it – every bruise, every heartbreak, from you to all of them, and if Ned and I fail, I know what it will mean to all of you, what it will feel like, *because I'll feel it too.*"

George was a creature of strong words and even stronger feelings. But Lucy had drawn the words out of him and left him speechless and silent, so he did the only thing he could. He pulled his two wards into his chest for a rib-cracking hug. For a moment, the three of them stood there swaying silently, till Lucy finally spoke.

"I'm sorry, George, I didn't mean to upset you. Are you all right?"

"I think I may need a banana."

***

In the central courtyard, not far from where the three friends stood, was a single camera and its blinking green light. It was put there along with countless others in the Nest to ensure the base's security. The network had not been able to detect the gor-balins until they were already in the ventilation system. It did, however, serve a second purpose and one that it was currently taking care of admirably. In a different room, on a different floor, Mr Spider's bulbous eyes watched the feed on his monitor. Mr Spider liked to keep records of everything and would be sharing his findings with Mr Bear and Mr Owl. The more he saw and the more he shared, the more obvious it was that Mission X was necessary. A shame really, but no matter which way you looked at it, the human race at least would go on. Bear and Owl would see to it, and so would their bomb.

CHAPTER 60

The Un-Hidden

Ned sat on the deck of the *Gabriella*, watching the world go by beneath him. Despite the gravity of their mission, it was always exciting to be flying through the sky in Benissimo and the Circus of Marvels' great flagship. This high up it was hard to imagine the troubles of the world below – or the battle to come.

They had been flying all day and the sun was now low in the sky. It was bitterly cold and they sped across the Siberian countryside, cresting the forest, with great looming trees ahead and behind them. Their staging ground was to be one of the taiga's largest natural clearings and the closest spot they could land on next to the fortress.

Flying with them were some of the Circus of Marvels' most loyal and bravest troops. Scraggs the cook had come with his gnomes, and Monsieur Couteau had accompanied Grandpa Tortellini along with his rabble of grandsons. Rocky and Abi the Beard were cooped up in their own cabin, enjoying what might be a last supper and going through their preferred list of weapons. Even the Glimmerman had gone with them, though what the portly gentleman would do in the coming fight was anyone's guess.

On a normal voyage and on a normal mission, there would have been excitement, a rousing speech from their Ringmaster to muster what was left of the troupe, but Benissimo had barely spoken a word in days and neither had Mr Fox. Their call to arms had been answered by no more than a few aged fighters still loyal to Benissimo. The Hidden, battered and bruised as they were, limped across the sky in a flotilla of airships. Not a man or woman aboard the *Gabriella* really believed they would or could win the fight, but they had climbed aboard nonetheless. That was the way with Benissimo's troupe, and that was the way with the Armstrongs.

"They still might come," said Ned, as his parents came out to join him on the deck. But he didn't say it with much hope.

Ned's mum put an arm round her son. She had barely

smiled once since Oak Tree Lane, and the certainty of what lay ahead was weighing down on them all.

"The Hidden are hiding, like always."

"Livvy, we used to hide ourselves, remember?" sighed Terry. "Don't judge them too harshly."

Ned's mum winced at the memory of it, but then managed a smile for her son.

"Well, we're not hiding any more, are we, boys?"

Ned felt in his pocket for the Tinker's perometer. It had been vibrating solidly since they'd left the Nest. He pulled at its clasp and opened it. Its single needle was pointing in perfect alignment with the *Gabriella*'s course, as it had been since Dover.

"Useful thing, Tinks's perometer," said Ned. "Did you know the name comes from '*periculum*', which is Latin for 'danger'?"

"Yes, darling," said his mum distractedly.

"When George gave it to me, he said that if it pointed solidly I was to go the other way. There is no other way now, is there?"

His parents didn't answer, because they didn't need to. There would be no hiding from the Darkening King for any of them.

Ned closed the clasp again and was putting the device

away, when there was a mighty boom from one of the *Gabriella*'s cannons. A second later and her engines slowed dramatically, as the great flagship prepared to come in for landing.

Just then, George came bounding up to them from the *Gabriella*'s bow.

"George, what is it?" yelped Ned.

Lucy's beaming face appeared a moment after. "Come and see – quickly, come on!" she screeched.

Breathlessly, Ned and his parents followed them round to the front of the ship as the *Gabriella* came in to land. They touched down at a vast and rocky clearing, the taiga's limitless dark trees stretching for miles in all directions.

But they were not alone.

A very confused Ned stepped out on to the airship's walkway to the single most glorious gathering of the Hidden he had ever seen.

"Just look at them all!" said George, with a ridiculous, beaming grin that ran from ear to ear.

Ned watched in awe as the sun started to set over the forest. They had come in their tens of thousands. Giants, gnomes, dryads and dwarves. Witches from the far north, with their flowing black locks, stood deep in conversation with a group of elderly Farseers. There were feathered swan-men from Eastern Europe and hundreds of trolls from Norway, Russia and beyond. Each of the burly trolls was more ugly than the next, and Ned spotted Rocky rushing towards them, half laughing and half fighting with one of his reunited cousins.

Ned's parents and George were immediately swamped by Mr Fox and the BBB's higher-ups, who were desperately trying to make sense of it all, while Ned and Lucy, brimming with excitement, walked into the bustling crowds.

They came across a great contingent of blue-skinned Apsaras water nymphs. Ned had never seen one before and marvelled at their blue-green skin and peacock-feathered hair. So far from the ocean, they had to constantly douse themselves in salt water and with them, along with their sea spray, they had brought the Jala-Turga from India – powerful, jaguar-like men and seasoned fighters to the last. As Ned stared, he saw countless others that he had no name for. Some were slender and covered in a layer of unmelting frost; others looked as though they were made of glass, their bodies almost completely transparent. There were at least a hundred Kirin. The rare creatures had the bodies of tigers though they were covered in tiny pearlescent scales with small, dragon-like faces and antlers at the tops of their heads. Further along there was an almighty scream as a series of quickly erected tents was crushed by an unwitting colossus.

"Arooora!"

Ned looked up to see, towering above them all, not one but six colossi – great monolithic creatures that dwarfed even giants with their size, their heads barely visible silhouettes against the sky. And that's when Ned noticed – the sky itself was full to bursting with every imaginable form of transport. Airships in their hundreds were flying in and out, either dropping off allies for the fight, or going back to their homelands for more. Ned could see the Viceroy's owls and their experienced riders marshalling them all amidst a soaring blur of wild griffins, a herd of flying Pegasus and a pair of giant eagles that were even larger than the owls. It was only when he heard the unmistakable cry that he was able to pick out an old friend.

"Aark!"

High above them, Finn's two-headed hawk was surveying the forest.

"Lucy, look! Finn must be up there somewhere."

There were heavy freighters with vast balloons, sleeker

single-masted sloops with powerful propellers and other steel-plated airships that bristled with harpoons and cannon. No two from region to region were the same other than their obvious intent – they had all come to stand with Benissimo's alliance and face Barbarossa and his Darkening King.

"Isn't it brilliant, Ned? Just look at them – the great un-Hidden! Abigail reckons this is the biggest gathering they've ever had!"

Ned's skin tightened when he saw an entire platoon of heavily armed tin-skins. The last time he'd seen one had been on Atticus Fife's command, and he'd barely escaped with his life.

Ned and Lucy circled round and headed back for the *Gabriella*. The air was heavy with woodsmoke and the constant barking of orders as the Hidden's army, in all its splendour, set up camp. Amidst the chaos and wonder, Ned saw Benissimo. The Ringmaster was deep in conversation with Mr Fox by a red and white striped tent.

Ned looked at the Ringmaster, more than ever the anchor in their storm, and for maybe the first time since stepping into Mavis's Ye Olde Tea Shoppe, Ned felt hope.

But like all things behind the Veil, it was not to last for long.

CHAPTER 61

Wild Horses

As they approached Benissimo and Mr Fox, the enormous figure of Mavis came into view, a set of freshly brewed teapots at her fingers. Scurrying through her legs were the other Mavii doppelgängers and there was a fast-growing queue of folk falling in line for her teas.

"Ha-har!" she roared, her giant pearl necklace swinging about her neck like a mace. "Come on, you lot, try my Fight-tea – it'll put hairs on your chests, all right!"

There was a tap on Ned's shoulder. He turned round to find one of the Mavii standing behind him, with a tray of china and cucumber sandwiches.

"I told you, didn't I? You've more friends than you know!" she smiled.

"Number Six?"

"At your service. And we've brought more than tea.

Half our patrons have answered the call, or at least they did when Mavis told them to, and you won't find a tougher bunch from here to Timbuktu."

As far as the eye could see, there were tents and makeshift housing spilling out away from the forest with hundreds more popping up by the minute. Coming out of one of the larger tents, Ned saw the distinctive sight of Longhorn's Rodeo, one of the Twelve's most gifted circuses, and beside them the Jade Dragons from China.

"Bene, I thought Longhorn was with the Twelve?!"

"The Twelve are finished, pup – as of last night. My brother's smart, cunning even, but he didn't think things through. After his attacks, there was a backlash. St Albertsburg was the last straw, and it didn't take the fair-folk long to realise that Fife must be working for my brother. Six of the Twelve's circuses have already joined, with more on the way."

But as he said it, Ned noticed that Benissimo was not his usual self. There was a something behind his eyes, and when he saw Ned staring he looked away.

Mr Fox reached into his breast pocket for his packet of soft mints. "It's been a logistical nightmare. We've had to tell the press that there's been a system crash at every major airport. The entire continent's airspace has been shut down to let this lot in."

Benissimo clapped Mr Fox on the back. "Do you know, Mr Fox, I have no idea what anything you've just said means, but I'm beginning to rather like you."

But there was a tremor to the Ringmaster's voice, despite his attempt at bravado.

A sudden cheer rose up from the staging grounds. Ever competitive, Longhorn's Rodeo had challenged the Jade Dragons to a race, and a stream of horse-riding circus folk had darted towards the trees that barred their way to Barbarossa's fortress, to see who could get there first. Ten horsemen galloped ahead, the Longhorns like thieving rustlers from an old western in red, white and blue; the Jade Dragons with flowing green scarves about their heads. The fair-folk laughed even as their tents were flattened and their cauldrons knocked from their fires. Two of the best riders jumped their horses over a pile of supply crates and careered ahead and into the lead, and the crowd cheered them on. The Hidden weren't hiding any more, no matter how deep the forest or how deadly Barba's minions. Every one of the assembled had stopped what they were doing to watch, cheering at the riders' bravery as they bolted for the forest.

For a second, Ned saw, or at least thought he saw, something move in its wooded darkness, but a blink later and it was still again.

Horns were blown and drums beaten and a mighty cheer erupted from the entire crowd. The horsemen were almost there now, speeding closer and closer, moments from the forest's edge.

And that was when both Ned and Lucy heard it.

"*YeSsSs.*"

"NO!" screamed Lucy. "Turn back!"

But her voice was a single raindrop in a deluge of others, and as the winning riders stopped triumphantly by the forest's edge, its branches reached out to ensnare them, great knotted sinews of slick, sickened wood erupting from the trees. What had been a great rousing cheer from the crowd turned to a choral scream. The poor brave men on their mounts could only look back in terror as they were clutched in the forest's embrace, vines about their arms and necks. In a heartbeat, every rider and horse was no more, swallowed whole by the forest and the master that it served.

All along the wall of trees, a thousand thousand Darkling eyes blinked open and bright, as if the forest had been lit up with stars.

The voice of the Darkening King boomed across the taiga, till the earth shook and every man, woman and beast heard its call.

"*ComMeEe*."

CHAPTER 62

The Night Before the Darkness

The mood in the camp had turned to silent terror. Ned hadn't spoken to Lucy about the voice. There was no need. Every one of the gathered fair-folk had heard it and they all knew what it meant.

Ned and Lucy said their goodnights to his parents and headed towards their tent. They'd been given separate bunks under the same canvas. George, Rocky and Abi the Beard would be outside keeping a watchful eye for intruders, and beyond them were the Tortellini brothers, Monsieur Couteau and a combined force from the Longhorns and the Dragons.

There was no snow now in their part of Siberia, but heavy rains, and the constant pounding of feet had turned their encampment into a muddy, rock-strewn mire.

Everywhere they looked they saw the same thing – men and women, magic or otherwise, huddled around fires, trying to stay warm. Some were singing, others arm in arm, a few telling stories in hushed whispers to pass the time or to ease their listeners' troubled hearts. Those that hadn't seen it with their own eyes had all heard about the riders and the forest, had all glared at the wood knowing what it had become.

Ned and Lucy's tent was at the encampment's rear and high up on a hill to give George and the others a clear view of anyone approaching from the fortress. A little way up its steep slope they slowed in the mud and Ned spotted a man huddled under a decidedly battered top hat. He had a thick blanket wrapped round his shoulders and was sitting on a box of munitions, staring at the campsite below.

"Lucy, look…"

"Bene's been sitting there all evening. Hasn't spoken a word to anyone," frowned Lucy.

As far as the eye could see, there were tents and fires with terrified men, women and creatures bunched around their flames. They had all come because Benissimo had begged them to. He should have been out there amongst them, rousing their spirits, thanking them even, or at least sitting at a table with Mr Fox and the Viceroy, who'd been shut away for hours going over last-minute plans.

"I don't know what he thinks he's doing!" said Lucy.

But Ned knew only too well. Benissimo had known since the beginning what was coming and had sworn Ned to secrecy about the brothers' curse, how they were linked to the Darkening King. He wouldn't betray his trust, but he could still let Lucy know at least a part of it, the only part that really mattered.

"You know, I don't get to say this often, but for a Farseer you're being a bit blind."

Lucy scowled. "I should probably punch you for that, but I'm too tired."

Gorrn shifted in the mud uneasily.

"Oh, Lucy, don't you get it? He's saying goodbye."

"To who?"

"To all of them. To the Hidden, to us, to everyone he's spent a lifetime trying to protect."

And even in the thin orange light that came up from the campfires, Lucy could see the sadness on the Ringmaster's face.

"Some of them will make it – *we* might even make it, Ned!"

But she still hadn't understood what he was trying to say.

"*If* we get into the fortress, and it's a big if, what do you think will happen?"

Lucy looked confused. "Well, we have to find and kill the Darkening King…"

Ned sighed. "And who do you think is going to try and stop us?"

Lucy looked to Benissimo and she realised what he was trying to say. "Barbarossa! His brother, the curse… Of course! I've been so focused on the stone and your powers coming back that I forgot."

"Some of the Hidden will make it, and some of Fox's men too, but Bene won't, Lucy. He's not coming back. If we succeed, he dies."

Ned's throat and mouth dried up and he could feel his eyes welling. When he looked at Benissimo, under his drenched top hat, he didn't see a Ringmaster but the loneliest man alive, completely and resolutely determined to save his people no matter the cost – even if he had to pay with his life.

"There's got to be another way, Ned! We could capture Barbarossa, lock him up – anything but that! I'm going over there right now."

Ned put a hand on her shoulder. "There's no other way, Lucy, we both know it and so does Bene. If you really care about him, let him have his goodbye in peace."

Against everything she knew or thought she knew, Lucy followed Ned up the hill in silence, passing by the most selfless man that either of them had ever known, and headed sadly back up to their tent.

As they stepped inside, it came as a surprise to both of them that there was another man sitting within its canvas walls. He was eating a fresh golden-green apple, savouring its sweetness and the crunch of its flesh. On his head sat a bowler hat with three black feathers, and resting in his lap was a meat cleaver.

"Hello, Ned," said Barbarossa. "Hello, Lucy. I hope you don't mind me dropping in unannounced?"

CHAPTER 63

Barbarossa

Everything happened at once. Lucy turned to scream, only to come face to face with Sar-adin. The Demon was in his human form and had been waiting to one side of the entrance. She looked at him, confusion burning on her face, but before she could open her mouth he struck a blow to her head with his cudgel and she fell to the ground.

Fury raged through Ned and he raised his arm, a surge of pure power tearing through his nerves, and from the shimmering air he produced a set of circular spinning blades. Each one was the size of a small plate, their edges perfectly serrated for cutting, and ready to fly at the butcher.

"Arr!" snarled Gorrn.

To Ned's side his familiar rose up angrily, his surface billowing and ready to strike.

Sar-adin stepped between them and his master, as

Barbarossa watched, still eating his apple as though nothing of any interest had happened.

The Demon now faced Ned and, with his back to the butcher, he raised the cudgel till it was level with his own cruel face. But instead of bringing it down on Ned, he placed a finger to his lips and his eyes narrowed. The message was clear: "Say nothing." Ned breathed a sigh of relief – the Demon was still on their side.

Quickly he took in the scene. Lucy was still breathing and Sar-adin had clearly held back from using his full strength. Behind the bloated evil that was Barbarossa, Ned could see a large cut in the rear of the tent, which explained how they had gained entrance, but not how the butcher hoped to leave.

"You're mad. All I have to do is scream and they'll come running, all of them," Ned seethed.

"Mad? I've been called worse, dear boy, and by my own brother."

His voice boomed like a deep bass drum. Ned hated him, hated him for always addressing him as though they were friends, for the smug smile etched on his face, and for even attempting to conceal his malice.

Gorrn was shaking, waiting only for Ned's command to fly at the butcher or his Demon.

"I can assure you of two things. I am not mad, and no one is coming. No matter how loud you shout, they won't hear you. Sar-adin has cast a silencing spell. We will hear *them*, they won't hear *us*. And in any case, most of them, like Lucy, are unconscious with a mouth full of mud. Be a good boy and lower your toys."

Sar-adin walked behind Ned to cover the entrance. Ned thought desperately – he could make a break for it, but that would leave Lucy with the butcher. Why had Barba taken the risk of coming, if not to kill them both? He let the blades fall. If Barba tried anything he could always make more.

"Stand down, Gorrn."

"Unt!" his familiar refused, its starry eyes flicking between Lucy and Barbarossa.

"I said, *stand down*."

Reluctantly his loyal blob oozed back to the ground and slid into Ned's shadow.

"Very wise, dear boy, very wise," gloated the butcher.

"What do you want, Barba?"

Barbarossa took a last bite of his apple and tossed the core aside.

"What I've always wanted. You wouldn't be killed by

my clowns – a terrible shame, and to think Mr Fox could be capable of such violence?"

And there it was – Sar-adin had lied to Barbarossa! The butcher, smug and cruel as he was, had a chink in his armour, even now.

"You look surprised. Yes, I know all about your poor Mr Fox. How he became an agent, the girl that was taken from him before he joined the BBB... I know it all."

Ned remembered his mother's training – *breathe*. Everything hung in the balance, Barbarossa couldn't find out about Sar-adin, no matter how much Ned wanted to shout it loud to wipe the smug look from the monster's face.

"After much thought, I've realised that you've done me a favour by making it this far. You've brought all my enemies to one place. St Albertsburg, the attack on your Nest, even the riders this morning... they were all meant to break your collective spirit."

"It hasn't worked!"

"No, not yet, but if you were to fall in the battle tomorrow, the Hidden would surrender."

"Why not just kill me now?"

"If they find you dead in your tent, they will not fight, and I will waste years hunting them down one by one.

But if they see you fall in the thick of battle, I shall have them, all of them, surrendering at my feet."

Ned felt a rage brewing inside him and his Amplification-Engine started to hum.

"And what on earth, Barba, would make me do that?"

Barbarossa grinned. "Because you can't possibly win. The forest is mine. It was a simple matter to circle around you and approach the encampment from the rear. I have Gearnish's metal men, I have the Darklings, the Demons, and by the end of tomorrow, I shall have the Darkening King."

Ned stared at him, defiance bubbling in the pores of his skin. *They* had the Heart Stone, and Ned's Engine, and Sar-adin, and the Central Intelligence's metal men if the Tinker was right. No matter what armies the butcher had, they *could* still win – the butcher was wrong. Ned allowed himself a small smile.

Barbarossa's eyes narrowed and his great bearded mouth pursed. "A smile? Ha! Sar-adin, the boy thinks he can beat me! Because you have the Heart Stone? The Fey have had the Heart Stone for thousands of years, and no one has ever mastered it, not even Tiamat before them. You will try and you will fail."

Ned didn't answer.

"Help me tomorrow. Pretend to fall, and walk away. In return, I will let those that you love *live*. The Circus of Marvels, your parents, dear old George, I will spare them all."

And almost on cue there was an oafish rustling outside the tent.

"Your stoopid nanas," said the voice of Rocky. "You need meat before fight, monkey."

"Keep your voice down – they're trying to sleep. And anyway, meat dulls the mind, old bean. You of all people are a prime example of a fruit-deficient diet."

Rocky laughed and thumped the great ape on the arm. "Da, George. You know, if I die tomorrow, I will miss your ugly mug."

Barbarossa looked at Ned with almost genuine pity.

"How sweet, your two protectors, enjoying a little banter. I don't need to kill them, Ned. I need to *rule* – and we both know I will, whether you pretend to fall or not."

"Never."

"Think on it, boy. Why waste the lives of the people you love, if the outcome is the same?"

Ned couldn't read him. If the butcher was right and they were going to lose either way, then he might as well stop him here and now, before the beast rose.

"I'll fight you now!" he said. "I could shred this tent with a blink – George and Rocky would see! They'd be on you in a second."

"My Demons have them surrounded. They would be crushed. If you care about your friends at all, you'll do nothing."

Ned's blood boiled. Barba had him right where he wanted him and he knew it.

As the butcher went to the tear in the tent that he and the Demon had made, he looked to Ned one last time and smiled. It was ugly and gloating, and it made Ned's stomach turn.

"Sar-adin, our friend needs rest," he said and promptly disappeared out of the back of the tent.

Sar-adin was close behind him and Ned could feel his breath at his back.

"Eastern tower," whispered the Demon, barely loud enough for Ned to hear, then his cudgel fell hard on the back of Ned's skull.

Ned's eyes filled with stars and the tent spun into darkness.

CHAPTER 64

"Good Luck"

Ned woke with a fresh bruise throbbing on the back of his head and his mother shaking his arm. Outside their tent he heard shouts and orders as the Hidden army readied for battle.

"Ned? NED?"

"Hi, Mum."

"Never mind that, what happened?"

Lucy was standing next to his dad and had clearly told them everything up to the point where she'd been bludgeoned by the Demon. Ned cast his mind back to Barbarossa's gloating face and shuddered.

"We talked. H-he asked me to walk away. He said that if I did, if I let everyone think I'd fallen, that he'd spare you and Dad, the circus, all of them."

His mum looked furious and spotted Gorrn skulking under his bed.

"And where were you in all this, blob?"

"Roo?"

His mother tutted.

"And what about Sar-adin, hitting Lucy like that? To think we believed him!"

"He had to do it, and he lied to Barba about the clowns and what happened to them. Barba doesn't know what Sar-adin said to us, I'm sure of it, and the Demon passed on another message – he just whispered, 'eastern tower'."

Ned's mum frowned, seemingly unsure as to whether they could trust the Demon, but Lucy was adamant.

"It was only a second, but even in that time I could sense that Sar-adin was worried, not about being caught by George and the others, but about Barba finding out."

Ned's parents looked at each other, and nodded.

"Good. Well, I hope you told Barbarossa where to go!"

"Of course I did," said Ned. "He's adamant that we can't win. But we can – we *can* win, right?"

He was asking all of them, Lucy included, but her eyes dropped to the ground. Even as a Farseer she had no answer.

His mum sat down on the edge of his bed, her face lined with worry, and just then he noticed that Whiskers was perched on her shoulder. The Debussy Mark Twelve looked at him intently, its tail wagging gently at its back. At least Faisal had been decent enough to let him have one last moment with his old pet before the coming battle. The newly acquired scientist part of Whiskers was nowhere to be seen.

"Hello, boy."

Whiskers blinked.

"What are you doing with him, Mum? I thought he was heading for Gearnish?"

Ned's parents shot each other a look.

"He is, darling, and me and your dad – well, we're going with him."

"*What?*"

"Now, Ned, before you get fired up, hear us out. We're the best people for the job and you know it…" started Ned's dad.

"Hear you out?! I've *been* there – I've seen that thing. Lucy, tell them – send someone else! Anyone – *please!*"

But Lucy said nothing and his father's face stayed resolute.

"I'm your dad, and an *Engineer* – it should be up to

me to fight what's coming. But it's not, and if you and Lucy have to face this monster, we'll be damned if we don't do everything we can to give you a fighting chance. Taking down the Central Intelligence, turning Barba's ticker army against him, is as good as it gets."

No matter the reason, Ned hated that he was always the last to know.

"When did you decide?"

"At the Nest, the night you got your powers back," answered his mum.

Terry Armstrong got down on his haunches. "Ned, none of us wants what's coming, but if we're going to do this, then we all have to play our part, no matter what we have to face."

Just then Mr Badger appeared by the entrance to their tent.

"Mr and Mrs Armstrong, I'm sorry, but the Tinker's ready – we need to leave."

The grey block that was Mr Badger couldn't have known how his words sounded. To Ned they were like the ringing of church bells, only sad and heavy and grim. But he held himself together for his parents and Lucy's sake, and they did so in kind for him.

"You're going with them, Mr Badger?" asked Ned.

"I'll be stepping through the mirror but on different business. Mr Fox has a message for his superiors that I need to deliver in person."

Mr Badger waited outside as the three Armstrongs and Lucy Beaumont said their goodbyes by the tent's entrance. One by one they whispered, "Good luck," Gorrn and Whiskers adding an "Arr" and a "Scree" for good measure.

Ned gave his parents one last hug. Had the world not been waiting, he would have stayed in their arms forever.

But the world was waiting, and so was the Darkening King.

CHAPTER 65

Mr Rook

Mr Rook's preflight routine was always the same. He would walk the runway long after the Engineers had given the OK and cleared the area. Just Rook and his wings, alone on the tarmac – that was how he liked it. He was afforded this odd luxury because he was the best pilot in the BBB. He was a good ten years older than the next in line and still beat all of them in every flight test and in every plane. No other pilot could claim to have a one hundred per cent success rate on all of their 200 missions because no other pilot was Mr Rook. His training and the consequent wiping of his memories had been so thorough that he did not know who his parents were, where he'd been born or even the country in which he'd taken his first gulps of air. The only thing he knew with absolute certainty, and which had been confirmed by his superiors, was that he was the best pilot in the world.

Mr Rook knew nothing else.

He spent a while admiring the silhouette of his HO-9. Despite its deadly cargo, it was a feat of engineering elegance. Its nose was as sharp as a razor, its body and wings more graceful and lithe than a hawk's. They needed to be. The HO-9 was the first of its kind, developed by the BBB to be completely undetectable. Radar only reached so far, and the HO-9 flew higher, riding the thermals like a bird of prey at the very edge of the earth's atmosphere. Part glider, part jet, but all stealth.

He climbed the ladder and lowered himself into the cockpit. To any normal man it would have looked like an indecipherable mess of dials, switches and levers, but Rook knew them all so well he could have worked them blindfolded. There was only one light that he needed to see. Currently it was red. Were it to turn green, he would launch the laser-guided bomb and a thirty-mile radius in the wilds of Siberia would be instantly turned to ash. Nothing would survive the blast.

In their wisdom, the highly trained psychologists that advised his higher-ups had decided to have the colour of the light give the command. Were it to come via radio, another HO-9 pilot might ask questions, might even hesitate at the last minute. But Rook knew that Fox, Bear and Owl had to be in agreement for the light to turn green. In any case, it was not his job to ask questions, only to launch the bomb.

Besides, Mr Rook knew nothing else.

CHAPTER 66

The Wall of Wood

Ned and Lucy pounded through the mud. A line of armed fair-folk stretched out beyond the horizon. Above them but further back was the Hidden's great armada of airships, those salvaged from the onslaught at St Albertsburg and those valiant others that had answered Benissimo's call. Troops in the line that were brave enough to look away from the forest spotted their breathless Engineer and Medic racing to meet Benissimo.

"Good luck, Lady Beaumont."

"Gods be with you, Master Armstrong!"

On and on, from giant to dwarf, from satyr-horned acrobat to leafy-skinned dryad, the Hidden saluted, with arms, swords and muskets.

"For the Hidden!"

"For us all!"

And the more they cheered, the more they turned, clapped and whistled, the more Ned prayed that Barbarossa was wrong – that they could, and would, win.

At the centre of the line stood Benissimo, Mr Fox and the Viceroy in a last-minute briefing of the Hidden's generals. The Ringmaster turned to Ned and Lucy. His eyes were lit up like fires and his moustache was in full twitch. Gone was the sodden figure huddled under a blanket. Today Benissimo was the eye of the storm, ready to fight, and most assuredly ready to die.

"Pup, Lady B," he grinned, with a doff of his beaten old hat. "Today we travel in style!"

And through the crowds, Ned heard a familiar trumpeting. In a burst of leathery grey skin came the Circus of Marvels' winged elephant.

"Alice!" smiled Ned.

Alice licked him affectionately and pressed her head to his shoulder. The dear old creature was painted from head to toe in red and yellow war paint, and her wings were safely tucked away under a leather harness. As happy as Ned was to see her, he could think of a number of better-suited creatures with which to ride into battle.

"Bene? Isn't she a bit –" Ned continued in a whisper, ever mindful of the old girl's feelings – "*old?*"

Benissimo had to stifle a laugh, but equally mindful of Alice's feelings, leant in close to Ned and Lucy.

"Alice has seen more fights than our Viceroy and Mr Fox put together. There's no finer beast to ride in on, of that you can be sure."

Lucy grinned and patted Alice's trunk. "It's an honour, Alice."

"Besides, if your intel is right and we're to reach the eastern tower, we'll be needing wings." As Bene said it, he lifted a small leather bag up from the ground. "Which one of you wants to carry it?"

They didn't need to be told what it was.

"I'll take it," said Lucy, and she stowed the Heart Stone over her shoulder as though it was a backpack for school.

"Well done, child, that's the spirit."

Ned thought back to the dragon, and the stag-men that had led them to him. The sight of King Antlor now would give the troops a wonderful lift, but he hadn't seen him as yet.

"Bene, where is Antlor and the herd?"

"The fortress lies between us and their mountain, but Fox still has King Antlor's horn – we just have to pray they hear it when the time comes, and that they can fight their way through that sickened mire in time."

Ned peered at the wood ahead of them. Its bark was dripping with oily darkness. Antlor and his herd had been its keepers and he had no doubt now that what they had once watched over had turned on them. If any had survived, would they even come?

"Now," said Benissimo, moving on, "Tom here will attack from a different angle with his owls and airships – that should take their air defence's eyes off us, so long as they don't realise Alice is a flyer till the last minute."

Now Ned understood why Alice's wings were bound.

The Viceroy saluted an assent. His face was mostly healed now and he looked glorious in his golden armour, beaked helmet under one arm and lance in the other.

"Master Armstrong, Miss Beaumont – let's give these devils a good kicking, shall we?"

Ned's chest swelled. Just days ago, the Viceroy had come to the Nest a broken man with a broken people. But today, like Benissimo, he was the man they all needed, and Ned would be the boy.

"I think we're about ready to try, sir," smiled back Ned.

Together with Lucy, Ned followed Benissimo's lead and climbed up aboard Alice's back, Ned patting her gently as they did so.

"Hello, girl. I'm glad it's you," he said as they took their seats across her harness.

There was a faint sound of humming coming from ground level.

"Mr Fox?"

The agent smiled back up at him. He had an assault rifle in his arms, a pistol at his waist and a layer of Kevlar armour adorned with radio, munitions and grenades. At his back, carefully tied down, was the Stag King's horn.

"Are you nervous for us or them?"

Mr Fox stopped humming and took the safety off his rifle. "Just me, Ned. I hate violence in any form but I appear to want to do some."

"Good luck, Mr Fox," said Ned.

Mr Fox looked up to both Ned and Lucy.

"Good luck to you both, and do try to stay alive – the world wouldn't be nearly as interesting without you two in it."

There was some shuffling from behind Mr Fox and his men in grey when, pushing through the crowds, came Rocky, his wife Abigail and the Tortellini brothers. Scraggs the cook came next, his gnomes armed with a vicious array of kitchen knives, followed by master swordsman Monsieur Couteau. Man by man, and woman by woman, the Circus of Marvels' troupe – from the leopard- and feather-skinned dancing girls, to the three emperor monkeys, Julius, Caligula and Nero – formed a party around Alice. Atop her back and to Ned's rear, Gorrn shuffled with a quiet but resolute "Arr".

Finally, there was George.

"Geo—" began Lucy.

Benissimo stopped her with a raised palm.

"I wouldn't do that if I were you. George is someone else right now."

And the Ringmaster was right. The great ape's fur was slick with sweat, every animal instinct fired and ready. He walked on all fours, his great knuckles gouging the mud, and took his place in front of their mount. George would be leading the charge and his two wards – there was no question of it – and pity the devil or tin man that stood in his way.

There was a low grunt and the ape paced forward, Alice following in his wake. As she did so, a deep bass drum sounded out from behind their lines.

Brum, brum, brum.

Behind Benissimo, Lucy put her hand on Ned's.

"Are you OK, Lucy?" he whispered.

She looked at the forest ahead of them. It stood, dark

and brooding, like a wall of wood, and within it an army of Darklings and Demons lay in wait. Beyond them, metal men with gears for hearts were ready to cause harm.

"Not really, but I don't think it's me you should be asking."

Ned looked now at the Ringmaster's back, quite possibly for the last time. Heart Stone or not, Benissimo would not return and they both knew it.

Brum, brum, brum.

"Bene?"

"Yes, pup?"

"I know what you're going to do, and I..."

But there was nothing he could say. His and Lucy's welling eyes were already speaking volumes as Benissimo turned to them both.

"Now, now, you two, there'll be plenty of time for that after."

Ned pushed away the lump in his throat.

"It's been an adventure, Benissimo – every bit of it."

Brum, brum, brum.

George's pace quickened, and Alice followed in kind, while to their left and right the great line moved with them.

"Indeed it has, pup — and it's been an honour to walk its path with you both."

Brum—

The drum silenced.

George suddenly reared up on his hind legs, his back arched and his arms raised high in the air. He roared and bellowed, beating at his chest defiantly, then brought down his fists in a pounding strike that was heard all down the line.

"Go on, George! You show 'em!" yelled Abi the Beard.

The forest had no answer for George's show of strength, and Ned glowed at the sight of it. George the Mighty broke into a gallop, Alice's body heaved and Benissimo pulled himself up, eyeing his allies on either side.

"Odin and Zeus protect you all," he screamed. "CHARGE!"

The earth shook with pounding feet, the air trembled, and the army of fair-folk and grey-suits at their sides and back roared in return.

CHAPTER 67

The Central Intelligence

The Tinker, Whiskers and Ned's parents used the Glimmerman's skeleton key to gain access to the city of Gearnish. Like the many glittering rectangles of his mirrored jacket, it could open portals, but with one extraordinary advantage – the skeleton key could open *any* portal mirror, and they had used it to access the exact same mirror that Ned and Lucy had used to escape the city only months before. Stepping through now, none of their party of four could have been prepared for what they found.

Everywhere they looked, black rubber-encased cables covered walls, filled rooms, at times blocking whole corridors. Some were as thick as a man's waist, others as thin as a strand of hair. They lay over the once-bustling factory like a nest of snakes, seemingly without end.

"What are these things? What's it trying to build?" said Olivia Armstrong, eyes straining at a particularly thick set of cables that led out through a window and into the city beyond.

It was Faisal who answered. The tiny body of the Debussy Mark Twelve stopped, eyes like flashlights following her gaze. "Itself."

"Mouse, apparently you're very clever," said Olivia Armstrong, "but that's hardly an answer."

The little frame of Ned's beloved old mouse looked up to Olivia Armstrong.

"These cables go out to the rest of the city. It's spreading its reach. If it hasn't already, it will eventually *become* Gearnish."

Terry and Olivia Armstrong both stopped dead in their tracks.

"Why? It's been controlling the factories for years. Why does it want to *be* it?"

The Debussy Mark Twelve's vocal cords strained and clicked. "Cloud computing. It's a josser term, but it does apply. By linking computers over a network, a single machine becomes a hive mind, its power only limited by the number of connections that it makes."

As Faisal explained, Olivia followed the lines of cable

back from the window. They seemed to be converging at a single point, out through a large doorway ahead.

"That's how it stole the Twelve's ticker spies. That's how it controls the Guardians. They're all connected to its code and, looking at this lot, I'd say its power has expanded at an alarming rate."

Terry Armstrong got down on one knee. "Faisal, Tinks – you're telling us that this creature's code is becoming part of an entire city?"

"Actually," said the Tinker, "I'd say the city is becoming part of *it*."

Terry gave the Tinker an eye roll and the diminutive minutian quietened. "Our son, my wife's ward of twelve years, every man, woman, beast and wonder of the fair-folk, as well as the agents of the BBB, are all about to charge into a forest, relying on us to take over this thing with a… a *mouse*, a *thing* that has grown considerably in size!" As he said it, Terry's voice was shaking with both anger at the two scientists and utter terror at the thought of what would undoubtedly become of his son and Lucy should they fail.

But before he could answer, his wife spoke. Though not one for drama or effect, her voice wavered. "I know where it is."

Her arm pointed directly ahead.

Tock, tock, tock.

The sound they now heard was not from some wind-up toy, or even an actual ticker. It was too deep, too slow and pensive, to be anything but the Central Intelligence itself. As they followed its sound, the smell of oil and grease, pig iron and steel filled their noses. Steam gushed from grates and pipes, and the heat steadily rose.

"I don't understand – where are his Guardians? We haven't seen any since we stepped through."

"I have a theory, ma'am," said the Tinker. "If he's connected to the whole city now, well… these aren't corridors and passages, machines and cables – they're *him*. We're just germs – no more important or threatening than a common cold."

A few feet ahead of them, the Debussy Mark Twelve stopped, its tiny torch-like eyes flashing at the next doorway.

Tock, tock, tock.

"Great-uncle? Great-uncle, what have you…"

As their small party walked into the next chamber, the Tinker's voice fell away. What they found there was not what Ned or Lucy had described. The Central Intelligence filled the entire factory. It was hundreds of feet high and wide, a great monstrosity of machine-designed building. All over its vast structure, an army of crablike tickers walked and welded in a never-ending endeavour to build on to the already dizzyingly complex structure. Though now hundreds of times larger than Ned or Lucy had described it, it still bore at the top of its spidery torso the grotesque and ill-fitting attempt at a human face, now vast from its own making. Its eyes were shut as though quite without life but for the constant *tock*, *tock*, *tock* of its metal heart.

Olivia Armstrong's face turned white as she stepped to her husband's side.

"What was it Tinks said?" asked Terry.

"I think he said we… we were germs."

Terry Armstrong could not pull his eyes away. As an Engineer he had a love of all machines, however evil. Whatever the Central Intelligence was, it was a feat of construction the likes of which he had never seen.

"It's… it's sort of beautiful, in its own ugly way."

"Yes, darling, I'm sure it is. Now, how do we kill it?"

Terry looked down at the Debussy Mark Twelve.

"I need to get in its head," croaked the mouse.

"Just like that?"

"Well, it does appear to be asleep."

The room glowed suddenly. Through vents along the creature's casing, orange fires burned and its great metal eyes opened.

"Not asleep, Faisal. I've been – tzsk – *thinking*. So many *things* – bzdtz – to think upon."

Its voice was a grinding of metal on metal. As the Central Intelligence spoke, the heat from its inner furnaces washed over them in a stifling wave.

The Debussy Mark Twelve looked up, a tiny speck under the gaze of a metal leviathan.

"You know my name?"

Vents blew another gust of broiling air, and the Tinker and Armstrongs recoiled.

"You are my – bzdtz – creator, yes?"

"I designed your code. I did not make you."

The machine-mind quietened, its great iron-lidded eyes closed in thought. As it did so, small spider-like tickers drew up from the metal grating, their sharp limbs reflected by the machine-mind's orange glow. They approached as a small army of sentinels, each and every one focused on the mouse.

The Debussy Mark Twelve now controlled by Faisal quickly turned to the Armstrongs and Tinks, its tiny eyes flashing with Morse code.

"D - I - V - E - R - S - I - O - N," spelled out Ned's dad.

Terry and Olivia looked at each other, trying to think of the best course of action.

"The cables!" whispered a crazed and sweat-drenched Tinker, screwdriver in hand. "They're feeding it. *We cut the cables.*"

The factory's walls shook and once again the machine-mind stirred, eyes looming on the mouse.

"PROBLEM – dztsk – kill creator? PROBLEM – ethic – grdzt. YES – brrdt – NO. BUILD MORE – drtz – FIND ANSWER."

It wasn't so much addressing Faisal now but talking out loud, struggling with the moral dilemma of what it should do.

"LIVE – brt – DIE. YES – grttz – NO, one or zero?"

The Tinker finally understood. "By the gears, it's gone mad! That's what it's been doing in here. It thinks that by growing it will solve its problem."

Terry looked at the frenzied machine as it struggled and steamed. "The problem of whether or not it should kill your great-uncle?"

"Oh no, Mr A. The problem of *why* it's right or wrong. But life can't be figured out with ones and zeros. It's trying to solve it with maths, with raw computing power, when what it really needs is a—"

"SOUL! CREATOR – brdzt – made no soul. *KILL CREATOR.*"

CHAPTER 68

Charging into Darkness

George raced ahead of them, at his heels the Circus of Marvels' bravest and best. Ned's breath was stuck in his chest, as though he was strapped to some roller coaster, some great galloping frenzied wave of the Hidden and the BBB. Faster and faster they sped till the wall of trees loomed tall and dark.

"Brace!" roared Benissimo.

In a blur of breaking branches and frenzied limbs, Benissimo's army leapt at the forest. Lucy gripped Ned's hand so tightly he thought it might break, and all as one, their giants, their dwarves, the men of the BBB, crashed into the undergrowth, waiting for the counter-attack. Gorrn reared up behind Ned and Lucy, his surface rippling and ready, as Ned closed his eyes, and to their front and sides he produced ice-heavy corkscrews of spinning daggers, ready to fire, expecting the clash at any moment.

But when Ned opened his eyes again, there was nothing but darkness. There were no screams, no clashes of sword against flesh or bark, just an ominous stillness to the air, mixed with the dank smell of rotting mushrooms, iron and peat. George slowed, and little by little their great charge came to a confused and clumsy halt, the only sound the snapping of twigs and the heavy breathing of Alice beneath them. Under the trees' canopy, it was so dark that Ned could barely see even their closest allies.

A voice called out in a whisper. It was Mr Fox. "Bene, what's going on? Where are they?!"

"Lights!" ordered Benissimo.

One by one their forces turned on torches, some of the magic casters even summoning balls of light to their aid. A great shimmer of yellow spread in a broken line to their left and right. It was eerie and cold. Ned could see the air from his heaving chest come out of his lips in great puffs of cloudy breath. But there was little else, just the tall sentries of black, sickly trees standing quiet and still.

"Unt?" asked Ned's familiar.

"Quiet, Gorrn. Something's wrong," whispered Ned.

Benissimo's whip coiled nervously in his hand and the Ringmaster lowered his cutlass.

"Have you noticed, Fox? The forest is darker than on our last visit. No light to speak of at all."

Ned felt Lucy shuddering beside him, her eyes closed in thought.

"Lucy, what is it?"

"They're everywhere."

"Who are, child?" asked the Ringmaster.

"Demons and Darklings – and the forest, it's... it's trying to hide them."

Ned looked up and saw only black, till he squinted his eyes.

"Mr Fox, can I borrow your light, please," asked Ned.

The agent reached up and Ned took his torch, then shone it directly above them. At first he could only see a pitch-black darkness, but through the halo of light from Mr Fox's torch, he picked out lines against the wood. The further they were from the forest's edge the more the lines converged. Every branch and twig was woven together like the insides of a giant bird's nest, criss-crossing back and forth from one tree to the next to form a solid ceiling, high enough above their heads for even their giants not to have to stoop.

Finally he understood. "Demons hate direct sunlight, Bene. It's not just hiding them – it's protecting them from the sun."

"Blood and thunder…" mouthed the Ringmaster.

Mr Fox called up again in a whisper. "Your orders, Mr B?"

"Orders?" Ned could hear the smile in the Ringmaster's voice. "You're taking orders from me, Mr Fox?"

There was a noticeable silence.

"Yes, you old goat, and you don't need to sound so happy about it. Now, what do you want us to do?"

"Use those clever night-vision goggles of yours and scout up ahead with your men. The rest of you, *slow*."

Ned could feel the forest watching them as they walked. He had never known such suffocating dread. Pace after pace they moved, ever mindful of the vines and branches that surrounded them. Ahead he could see the large silhouette of George leading the way; on the ground beside him, Abi the Beard and Rocky in his troll form, moving like ice-clearing juggernauts. His mind drifted back to the horse riders and their smiling faces as the taiga turned on them. Any moment now it could do the same to them, and yet it held back and kept on holding back – what was it waiting for?

Suddenly there was a snap of branches, first one, then another, powerful and loud.

"B-Bene," stammered Lucy, "they're coming."

Above their heads there was more snapping, and the clear sound of limbs on wood. Like drums in some foul orchestra, the thick trunks of the taiga reverberated with the footfall of creatures making ready to pounce. Louder and louder the forest awakened, behind them and above. Finally there was a great rushing as countless birds filled the air from their web of woven branches. But they did not attack. They flew in a dizzying wave of beak and metal-boned wing, startling Benissimo's great line like a tidal wave.

And just as suddenly – they were gone.

"Bene?"

"Pup?"

"They didn't attack. I think they were just getting out of the way."

"Dear Gods of Old – MOVE!" ordered Benissimo.

And what had once been a glorious charge became a desperate stampede to escape. The Hidden and the BBB's great line broke at a pace, the forest roaring at their rear.

"Go, Alice, GO!" urged Lucy.

Confusion and terror gripped the line as they stumbled

and fell over rotting trunks and branches too dark to see even by torchlight. What had started with the snapping of a twig became a great surge of bellowing rage. The forest had awoken and let out its dogs of war.

On and on they ran, poor Alice's panting rasped and strained, when up ahead Ned saw the unmistakable figures of Mr Fox and his men. For once the agent looked startled, as the fair-folk's line came at him like a stampede of frightened cattle.

"THEY'RE BEHIND US – RUN, FOX! RUN!"

As one they passed through a river, sodden and soaked, spurred on by the waking wood and the invisible jaws at their heels. Whoever fell was left to the forest and Ned turned to see one of the dryads being swallowed whole by angry branches, all about her the glow of yellow eyes and the lashing of Darkling limbs. Through bogs, up and over hills they ran, till Alice reared from the cuts at her legs. Then, just ahead, they saw it – light, piercing the woven canopy.

"Go on, girl, just a little while longer!" commanded Benissimo.

And as suddenly as their fumbling line had started, it came to a stop. Ned winced as he adjusted his eyes to the sky. Grey and heavy with cloud as it was, its light now felt blinding. Miraculously they were out of the forest, or at least in a clearing. It was miles wide, thick with mud and perfectly circular, and at its centre was a great metal tooth.

Barbarossa's iron fortress dwarfed them all. Ned, Benissimo and the rest of the fair-folk stared at it in dumbstruck horror. The fortress walls rose hundreds of feet into the air. Like the butcher's fleet of *Daedeli*, it had not been built for beauty. The scar of metal sat like a cruel and ugly jailer, its single purpose to protect what lay within. There were few windows along its walls. In their place were jagged metal shards like spears and loaded cannon ready to fire.

It wasn't just the fortress that had silenced them, but the sight of the Guardians at its base – row upon row, formed in a great protective circle. There were thousands of them, gleaming with burnished metal, their eyes glowing and red. As he watched, Ned's world shrank around him. These creatures, every one, had come from Gearnish, and his parents were there now! How could he have been so stupid? How could he have let them go?

"Odin's beard!" spat Benissimo. "The forest was herding us like sheep. They aim to crush us between two lines!"

What came next was louder than any roaring giant, louder even than a horde and its forest, or the ticking and whirring of a thousand gears.

"*YyEEsSSsS!*"

Hearing its call, the Guardians broke into a run and, as they closed in on the petrified alliance, the forest behind it came alive with renewed vigour. From in front and behind came the ticking and whirling of metal hearts, the snarling of hateful teeth.

CHAPTER 69

Tick, Tock

No sooner had the words left its metal lips than Terry and Olivia Armstrong sprang into action. Olivia turned and drew her rapier, lashing at the nearest cable. Terry in kind drew great spikes of metal from the ground in a blur of bursting atoms and launched them at a wall of its coiled, snake-like limbs. The Tinker, bright red and shaking with both excitement and fear, ran headlong, screwdriver at the ready, and stabbed at a knot of wires.

"KILL – crdtz – KILL!"

Crabbish, spidery metal arms unfolded from behind the machine-mind. They were the size of crane arms and pointed like blades at their ends. It wasn't until the rest of the factory came alive that they understood what the Tinker had meant – the entire factory, every bolt, every pipe and steaming vent, was the Central Intelligence, and it now rose up in fury to destroy both Faisal and his companions.

A great drilling spike struck down at Olivia, but her keen reflexes fired and she cartwheeled away. Two more went to strike at Terry, and he pulled more metal from the factory floor in a shield of spitting atoms.

Crash!

Metal struck metal and he was flung to the ground, Olivia rushing to his side.

"Get up, you lump, get up!"

Tick, tick, tick, tick.

They both turned in horror to see six large Guardians coming out from openings in the walls and rushing towards the Tinker.

The tiny minutian dropped his only weapon in terror, his screwdriver clunking to the floor, and just stood there dumbstruck, waiting for their inevitable strike.

"Here, you monsters, HERE!" yelled Olivia.

And the monsters turned. More and more of the Central Intelligence's Guardians poured from walls, rudely awakened with eyes gleeful and red for slicing.

Terry fired a blast of frozen air at the tickers, and they all stopped, their arms and mechanisms locked in place.

"That's it, you brilliant man, that's it!" yelped Olivia.

But even as she said it, another ten knocked the frozen tickers to one side and descended on the Armstrongs. Olivia lunged, stabbing and thrusting with her sword, only to have it bounce from their casing like a toy.

Terry and Olivia Armstrong now stood back to back, surrounded by Guardians. Above them the crablike arms of the Central Intelligence were poised to crush and skewer, with one of its horrid extensions pinning the Tinker to its factory wall. On the ground and writhing like snakes, the machine-mind's smaller cables coiled about their ankles.

"Livvy?"

"Yes, my darling?"

"I love you."

Olivia turned to her husband, their son and her old ward Lucy's very existence hanging in the balance, the same existence they had spent over a decade trying to protect.

"I love you more, always have," she said. "NOW WHERE IN THIS FLAMING, METAL HELLHOLE IS THAT MOUSE?!"

CHAPTER 70

Into the Fray

Ned watched in horror as the Guardians charged. His friends in the Circus of Marvels formed a circle round Alice and her passengers, Gorrn still behind him rearing his head to and fro, not knowing which danger to watch for or from where, and all down the line Benissimo's captains barked.

"HOLD FAST!"

From giant to gnome to grey-clad agent, the Hidden and the BBB looked their fate dead in the eye and held. But bravery, like ice, is only firm without fire.

Behind them the forest erupted with the stench of sulphur and, daylight or not, its Demons charged. Some were alight with flames, others charged like bulls with great dark horns and rows of knife-sharp teeth. Some ran on all fours; some flew with stretched and leathery wings. Ned saw past their great axes and spears, beyond their armour and their rippling scale-hard skin, to their faces. In each and every one he saw glee, the glee of unbound evil no longer hiding in their pits, but raging to fight, and burn, and kill.

The ground shook with metal and claw, as closer and closer the two fronts charged. For a moment Ned's breath left him and his eyes widened, as everything, all the shouting, all the clamouring and barking of orders, became a shapeless noise.

Crash!

The air shook with the painful screaming of fair-folk. Even as the Demon horde laid waste to the first line, a second wave approached. Weirs and Darklings roared and ran. The wolf-pack and the bear-clan, like Antlor's herd, had once watched over the forest, keeping Darklings at bay, but now they ran together, claws hungry for flesh and bone. Everywhere Ned looked, the Hidden fell. Through the chaos and its violence Ned heard a single voice.

"Ned! *Ned! NED!*"

Ned turned and Lucy took his face in her hands. Her eyes were bright and wild, her shoulders heaving.

"Ned, they're not supposed to protect us, they never were – we're supposed to protect them!"

Benissimo turned on her angrily. "Don't be a fool, child! We wait for the Viceroy. When their air defences are focused elsewhere, we head for the eastern tower."

"No, Bene, we don't. We make a stand!"

Ned had never heard her speak with more conviction. Her voice was shaking, but not from fear – Lucy wanted to fight.

"Nothing is more important than your mission, child – nothing!"

Stunned and listless, Ned looked to the ground. Scraggs had fallen, with four of his gnomes dragging him away from the fight. George was leading a valiant defence with the BBB, their electrical batons swinging and stabbing at the Guardians, holding them back for precious seconds, but the machines' unending numbers would not be held for long.

"*They're* more important, Bene," said Ned quietly. "What's the point of beating your brother and the Darkening King if the fair-folk die? What's the point of any of it?"

Benissimo's face became soft and his brow stilled. For just a hint of a moment, Ned saw the man behind the top hat and whip. The man huddled in the rain knowing his end was near.

"We have until the Viceroy's first volley of cannon. Make it count!"

As one, all three leapt from Alice's back. Gorrn protested with a quiet "Unt" but a second later had caught up with Ned's shadow. Benissimo marshalled Monsieur Couteau and Rocky, while Ned looked to his furred protector.

"Lucy, your powers won't work on the Guardians," said Ned. "Go with Bene and help push back those Demons. I'll go to George."

But there was no answer.

"Lucy?!"

The brave Medic and Farseer had already run ahead of Benissimo. Two Demons loomed up to her. One as large as a troll with legs as thick as tree trunks, a great spiked club in its hands; the other sleeker and more lithe, its face bright with red scales, broad black lips and even blacker teeth.

Lucy did not flinch, but calmly held up her hand. Her powers as a Medic could make her heal the cells of almost any wound because she chose to use her Amplification-Engine for good, just as her mother had and the other Medics before her. Today, here and now, Lucy made a different choice.

Foom!

Her hand tore forward and the Demons howled, bracing in pain and anguish. There were no wounds or cuts across their skin. The harm she'd done them was inside, deep in their bellies and chests. Again she struck, over and over, at more of the gnashing monsters, and again they fell where they stood.

Ned turned and ran to George. He was back to back with one of the grey-suits, a pair of Guardians closing and fast.

"Ned?! What are you doing? Go back to Alice this instant!"

Saying nothing, Ned raised his hand just as Lucy had before him and a surge of power tore through his arm. As they ran, the Guardians fell quite literally apart, a hand here, a leg there, till a string of lifeless bolts and armoured casing was strewn on the ground.

"George, I've waited a really long time to say this," smiled Ned. "Get behind me."

And quietly and quickly, the great ape and the grey-suit at his back did as they were told. Ned pushed onwards, cutting a line through the Guardians like a knife through butter. One by one they fell, as Ned's will and his ring fired. He reached into their inner workings and pushed and pulled at them, throwing them to the ground like a puppeteer discarding his dolls.

Gorrn hung back in his shadow, eyes in quiet awe, and across the line the fair-folk cheered. Redoubling their efforts, a great surge of Demons and Darklings rushed on Lucy, only to fall in screaming pain. On Ned's side of the battle, a deluge of armoured machines charged and were cut down by Ned's Engine, till their parts piled up like a scrapheap.

"Good Lord, old bean! Why didn't you do this before?" stammered George, his animal rage now turned to wonder.

"Didn't know I could!" beamed back Ned.

For a moment, on either side the fighting mellowed as both fronts looked to the centre in awe. By an elderly elephant, a boy and a girl were single-handedly waging war.

And that was when it started. A vast tree came hurtling through the sky. It landed like a bomb amongst the Guardians.

"Arooraa!"

Towering over them all were the fair-folk's six colossi. They were wading through an angry wood, its black branches snagging at their legs like spears, but the colossi did not flinch. They were tearing their way through the forest, trunk by trunk, to join the fight, and as they did so they hurled the felled and broken trees over the canopy and their gathered allies, deep into the amassing metal foes.

Somewhere in the chaos, a man with no past paused, and looked across the battlefield searching for someone's eye.

He found it, and Benissimo nodded back.

Mr Fox stared at the fair-folk fighting beside him, prayed that they might have a future and took the aged horn from his back. And he blew. When he did, the sound that came from the Stag King's horn filled the air not with a rallying blast but with the sound of stamping hooves.

A cheer echoed through the ranks, and on the other side of the fortress's clearing the trees parted. Running at full gallop came the herd, King Antlor at the centre of at least two hundred of his rushing warriors. They charged, crashing into the Guardians at the fortress's back in a stampede of bone and metal.

"Aark!"

Ned paused to look up. High above Antlor's herd he saw Arrk and Finn, the circus's Irish tracker. They had circled the taiga for miles to flank Barbarossa and draw his air defences away. Behind the hawk and the winged warrior, the sky was full. Giant owls, griffins and huge eagles filled the air, and behind them – the Viceroy's fleet.

BOOM!

The air burst with cannon fire, striking at the far side of the fortress and below to the gathered Guardians. Benissimo's great army cheered once more, surging forward to their front and rear, when the air began to shake. Those not fighting could only strain their necks as Barbarossa's *Daedali* appeared through some giant glamour of invisibility. There were more than a hundred of the looming black machines and they had been waiting for the Viceroy and his owls to reveal their strength. From their bows and walkways poured wyverns, a great black swarm of leathery-skinned death. Below them the fortress's ground-to-air flak cannons erupted and the sky screamed.

Everywhere, from the earth to the clouds, the two brothers' armies were fighting and perishing. Ned's stomach was turning and his ears rang till he thought they might burst, when there was a leathery prodding at his shoulder in the form of Alice's trunk. On her back were Benissimo and Lucy.

"Quickly, pup, we go now!" ordered Benissimo.

Ned looked to his left and right – despite their best efforts, their bravery and the Viceroy's fleet, the fair-folk were losing. The forest's hordes vomited more and more of its Demons and Darklings, and for every felled Guardian, three more took its place. Ned's heart physically shook, not just for the brave men and women he was being asked to leave, but for his parents. Whatever had become of them, one thing was abundantly clear – they had not turned the Central Intelligence or his army, and without that precious help, all would be lost.

"We can't leave them, Bene. They'll be slaughtered!"

He turned, firing up his ring, when Alice's powerful trunk reached round his waist and hoisted him on to her back.

Lucy was busy with their mount's leather harness, working the straps frantically to unleash her wings.

From down below, a bruised and battered George looked up to Ned, his face even now managing a smile.

"Don't worry, old bean. They've got me, haven't they?"

Behind him the ground shook as a fresh row of Guardians marched.

"Run, George, get out of here!"

"Run? My dear old chum, there's nowhere else to go."

"Ready, Bene – she's ready!" screamed Lucy.

"Alice, old girl, give us everything you've got."

With a great trumpeting, Alice surged forward, her white wings unfolded and she launched herself into the air and over George's head.

The last thing Ned saw was Mr Fox and a handful of agents. They were hurriedly forming a circle, as if discussing something of the utmost importance. Mr Spider was there. He had a small device in his hand and was whispering in Mr Fox's ear.

CHAPTER 71

Mr Spider and Mr Fox

Mr Fox did not like Darklings, nor did he like Demons, but what he especially hated was Mr Spider, for insisting he take the call. At every side their forces were surrounded. With George's help his agents formed a protective wall round Mr Fox so that he could see the video call feed of Mr Bear on the tablet. Mr Bear was sitting in his grey-walled office, thousands of miles away and had followed the entire battle from the safety of his desk.

"Fox?" barked Mr Bear. Even over the fighting and shouting and gunfire, his voice came clear enough through the tablet's speakers.

"I'm here."

"Spider tells us you are losing."

"It may look like that, sir, but I assure you that everything is in hand."

"IN HAND, MAN? The Armstrongs have clearly failed in Gearnish, and you are completely outnumbered on the battlefield. In what possible way could things be in hand?"

Mr Bear leant back in his chair, allowing Fox to see that Mr Owl was also at his desk. Standing behind them both was Mr Badger, as ever a block of emotionless muscle, watching but inert. He had arrived there via mirror with two more of Fox's grey-suits before the fighting had started.

"The children, sir – they're heading for the fortress."

On-screen Mr Bear's face reddened. "Too little too late, Mr Fox. I see you've called the Chinooks. Have your men withdraw and I will give Mr Rook and his HO-9 the order to drop the bomb."

Mr Fox began to hum, then stopped. "No."

Bear looked at Owl then back to the screen.

"No? Fox, you have to get out of there and you have to give me the launch code. It needs all three of us to give the green light."

"No," said Fox.

And beside him Mr Spider began, rather oddly, to lick his lips. Back on the tablet Mr Bear turned purple.

"Fine, have it your way. Spider, relieve Fox of his command."

Mr Spider was about to say something. He was about to tell both Bear and Owl how happy he was to do his duty for the BBB; he was about to tell them that he would not let them down; he was about to say a lot of things. But when he leant forward, Mr Fox took the butt of his handgun and bashed it rather forcibly on the back of his head. Mr Spider fell face-first into the mud, where he lay, without saying a word.

George, who was now watching, raised an eyebrow and grinned. Over the trees' canopy came the fast-moving silhouettes of the BBB's Chinooks.

"Fox, your time amongst the Hidden has cracked your mind! The Chinooks are there – for pity's sake, man, get aboard and give us the codes!"

"That would be rude. You see, Benissimo was not the only one to put out a call. Several days ago I sent every recording, every photo and dossier we have on the Hidden and their kind to both NATO and the combined representatives of the rest of the world's armed forces."

Mr Bear's eyes widened, as did Mr Owl's. Behind Mr Fox they could see soldiers rappelling from the helicopters and into the fight – soldiers from American Navy SEALs to the Russian Spetsnaz, the British SAS and countless others. There was a loud crashing of tank tread on bark, as, further off, powerful tanks finally broke through the taiga's wooded wall.

"You've gone mad – the world's not ready. They can't know about the Hidden – they can't know about any of it!"

"But they *do*, and they appear to want to save the Hidden as much as the Hidden appear to want to save them. Mr Badger?"

The rock behind both Bear and Owl smiled. "Yes, sir?"

"Arrest them."

Within seconds, Mr Badger and his grey-suits had both Owl and Bear in handcuffs.

"You can't do this!" yelled Mr Bear.

"It looks rather like I have."

"On what grounds?"

"Intended murder."

"You fool! I am trying to save lives."

"No, Mr Bear, you are trying to wipe out everything that you do not understand. You are hereby arrested for intended crimes against life in all its forms. George, why don't you wave goodbye?"

A confused but elated George leant in so that his toothy face filled the screen.

"This is George – now he really *is* trying to save lives, yours included, Mr Bear."

The last thing they saw on the tablet's screen was the beaming smile of Mr Badger as he led the two men away.

"Do you know, Mr Fox," began George, "I'm beginning to think that some of you jossers aren't so bad after all."

CHAPTER 72

Tricks and Traps

Every Demon now rallied to the call and the battlements of the fortress clamoured with feet scaled and clawed. Now was their time – their time to be free. No more would they lie in hiding, in the dark hot places beneath the crust of the world. The fair-folk and the humans, every animal and plant would cower to their king.

Or so they thought. Sar-adin remembered things differently. It was true, they had walked the earth when their king walked with them, but as slaves, not masters. They were tools to do his bidding and he ended their lives just as freely as the lives he ordered them to take. The Darkening King fought and burned and killed for himself, and for power, and in the end there would be nothing left alive. Sar-adin knew it just as surely as he knew that Barbarossa had lost his mind. And in that fervour, in the pounding of feet and scale, the rushing to the butcher's call to kill or be killed, Sar-adin would find his moment and his end. There would be no forgiveness, no place to hide, but even his kind, cruel as they were, needed saving.

He had done as Barbarossa had asked and left him to his dinner and guests, to gloat over the battle. Now, quickly and quietly, he made his way through the hallways of the fortress and the eastern tower. The hallway was empty and the door unguarded, just as Sar-adin knew it would be. But when he turned the key he found that it was already unlocked, and on the cold hard stone outside two of his kind were waiting.

"Traitor!" seethed the largest.

He had fought with one of them more than a century ago. He did not recognise the other. Barbarossa had known! How like him to plan and counter-plan. When had he realised? Surely not before sending him with the clowns? And then it dawned on him – the flies that had gone with them, the machine-mind's spies, must have seen more than he knew, seen what he'd done to the clowns, and now the butcher knew Ned's exact route to the fortress.

"Everything I have done, I have done for our kind,"

said Sar-adin, no remorse or sadness in his voice, only the certainty of what was to come.

The largest Demon drew his dagger, slowly and with purpose. If Sar-adin could not best them, the Engineer and Medic would walk into Barba's trap and everything would be undone.

"If you kill me, you kill us all. Our king will feed on the folk and humans and when he is done, who do you think he will feed on next?"

Both of the Demon's eyes glowered with rage, and they closed the gap between them.

"Not you, traitor – our blades will feed on you first."

Sar-adin moved quickly, his arms pouring with flames even as he drew his weapon. How many times had he been ordered to take lives in the name of evil? Too many to count, he realised, and it was then that the blade struck deep into his belly.

CHAPTER 73

Whiskers and the Scientist

There are few advantages that a mouse has over a factory-sized machine, apart from perhaps its size. Past its cranes for arms and its great oil-slicked jaws ran the Debussy Mark Twelve as it had never run before. Inside the Debussy's tiny frame, red-hot cogs screamed like Catherine wheels till steam poured from its eyes and ears. Even as a young man, the minutian scientist that was Faisal had never been one for sport and he'd sensibly made the decision to leave the running of its legs to Whiskers' more experienced control. Whiskers ducked under pistons and vaulted through the gaps in its clattering gears. They were inside the machine-mind now, the terrible grinding of its metal brain closing on all sides.

"Faster, Whiskers, faster!" screeched Faisal.

Behind them the machine-mind's spidery sentinels ran

on needle-sharp legs. They lunged, over and over, three of the creatures ripping at Whiskers' fur. Finally they came to an opening of sorts. Within it burned a furnace, bright and hot, and within the furnace was a block of metal alloy too hard to melt.

"STOP – crdzt."

The voice rang out all about them with the clicking and hammering of gears. The Central Intelligence's spiders stopped and so did the mouse.

"Leave – drrtz – my mind."

Faisal regained control of his invention and peered at the furnace in front of him.

"Krddz – *please*." This time when the machine spoke, it was almost in a whisper.

"Don't be frightened. I'm here to help you," squeaked the mouse. Behind its back its tail wagged, and then it jumped headlong, right into the fire.

CHAPTER 74

The Eastern Tower

Up Alice soared, her wings beating wildly, till they were over the battlefield in clouds of burning smoke. Above, below, to their left and right, the air exploded with the firing of shells.

"Hold on!" roared Benissimo, and Ned clutched at the elephant's harness till the bones in his fingers throbbed.

Two wyverns had spotted Alice and were tearing towards her when, from nowhere, one of the Viceroy's armoured owls flew at their sides. In a burst of leathery wing and feather, owl and wyvern fell from the air, still fighting and clawing even as they struck the ground. The second wyvern screeched, launching a torrent of spittle-heavy fire. Alice dropped fast but not without a painful scorching at the tips of her wing. The wyvern was joined now by three others and they pursued her with venom as she desperately tried to reach the eastern tower.

"ZEUS'S BEARD! LUCY, NED – *DO* SOMETHING!" roared Benissimo.

They both turned, the air rushing by so fast that they were nearly thrown from the elephant's back, when all of a sudden, the wyverns stopped, hovering in mid-air like dragonflies.

Down below, from all across the battlefield, the fairfolk cheered. Ned looked down to see tanks and soldiers joining the ranks of Antlor's stag-men and on the other side, the colossi, having broken through the forest, laying waste to Darklings with the heels of their feet. But that in and of itself was not the reason for their howls of joy. Ned could see George and Mr Fox rushing forward with Rocky the troll and Monsieur Couteau and a full squad of the BBB at their backs – and the Guardians didn't try to stop them. On the contrary, they parted to let them by!

"Ned?"

Ned couldn't answer.

"THEY'VE DONE IT, NED! THEY'VE DONE IT!" yelled Lucy.

"Barking dogs," he whispered.

"Barking dogs indeed, pup. I knew they'd do it!"

Almost as one, Barbarossa's metal army stopped their ceaseless surge as new directives were fed into their code. Above and below, the flow of fighting changed – wyverns now dived in straight lines to aid their Darkling kin and their Demon masters. Owls unfettered from their tearing claws descended on the *Daedali*'s crews while the Viceroy's guns turned to the forest's edge and pointed at the horde within its branches. Ned watched George, pounding on all fours, his great muscles heaving him towards the fortress. His parents, his tiny mouse and the Tinker had beaten the Central Intelligence!

"They're *alive*!" he exclaimed. "They're blooming well ALIVE!"

Behind him, within the shadows of Alice's harness, came a satisfied "Arr", but beneath them all poor Alice was rapidly losing control from the burns on her wing, and try as she might, she couldn't steady her path.

"Come on, girl! Hold it together!" yelled Benissimo.

She approached the top of the eastern tower like a burst balloon, skidding along its short metal roof and collapsing in a heap of weary grey limbs. Dazed and confused, her passengers clambered down from her back, Lucy quickly using her Amplification-Engine to tend to Alice's wounds.

"There's no time for that," spat Benissimo, his whip curled and cutlass drawn.

"Oh, go to hell!" seethed Lucy, her eyes misting even as she worked her ring. "You'll be fine, Alice – I'll have you fixed up and good as new in no time."

The great elephant's eyes were mournful and red, and her trunk hanging limp to the ground.

The Ringmaster fumed. "Don't you understand, Lucy? Our troupe, all of them, will die if this monster rises!"

"He's right, child," said a voice behind them. "There's no time for any of us."

Ned spun round to see Sar-adin approaching. On the ground by his feet were two felled Demons, their faces cruel and wicked even in death. Ned studied the Demon – in his belly was a blade, no doubt put there by one of the Demons at his feet.

"My master is expecting you."

And with that, Sar-adin, murderer and Demon, fell to the ground and breathed his last breath.

Ned raised his eyes to see a door in the wall waiting and open, and just as he saw it, the tower was shaken by the booming of a voice.

"*NeDdD.*"

CHAPTER 75

Together

With the Heart Stone still at her back, Lucy ran with Benissimo and Ned into the fortress, Gorrn trailing behind. The entire structure was a mixture of angular metal and black marble, its corridors cold and quiet. Down a spiral staircase and through corridor after corridor they ran, till Lucy paused, her face suddenly as white as snow. The fortress shook once more then along the floor ink-like fluid started to rise up the walls.

"I don't understand. I can feel its hatred as though it were mine, but I can't get a fix on where it's coming from."

The fortress shook so hard this time that Ned stumbled.

"Please, child, focus!" urged Benissimo.

As Ned looked at the liquid, it changed form, as though it somehow sensed him. And then Ned realised. He pulled the perometer from his pocket and it spun this way and that, from one strand of fluid to the next. The forest surrounding the fortress had had the same oily slickness at its branches and boughs. But it wasn't, as he'd thought, an illness at all. The Darkening King had reached into the wood to feed and the oily liquid it had used to do so was the Darkening King unformed.

"It can't be!" he murmured. "It's in the walls, in the forest... It's—"

"*EveRryWhHere.*"

Ahead of them two metal doors swung open. The perometer's needle spun one last time and then stuck, like an arrow pointing to the opened doors. Finally its glass casing cracked and the Tinker's device shattered in Ned's hand.

As suddenly as it had started, the fortress's shaking stopped.

Lucy, still ashen-faced, peered ahead through the open doors. "We've got time."

Benissimo turned to them both. "Ned, Lucy – I wish I could do this without you. I wish I'd had the strength to break the curse before you were even born, but I didn't and I'm sorry – for us all."

Ned looked at the Ringmaster. There were a thousand

things he wanted to say, and a thousand ways to say them. But in the end he took Lucy's hand and Benissimo's and simply said, "Together."

Accompanied by a sometimes brave familiar, an Engineer and a Medic walked hand in hand with a Ringmaster, to face a butcher and his king.

CHAPTER 76

Barba and the King

Beyond the doors lay a large chamber. On one side was a vast window that arched at its top, looking out over the battlefield. A burning hearth faced a grey granite table that had been carefully prepared with a banquet of roasted meats, wine and fruit. Two men were seated there. Atticus Fife, the tin-skin and would-be leader of the Twelve, and a man who Ned had never seen before. He was dressed from head to toe in gold. Their faces were planted unceremoniously in their plates because, like Sar-adin before them, Barbarossa's guests were now entirely dead.

In front of the window was a circular opening in the floor the size of a swimming pool. Ned could see that it ran all the way down to the base of Barbarossa's fortress. Up its sides, reaching to the top, more strands of oozing darkness flowed.

Standing in front of it was the pirate-butcher himself. Even as his Guardians turned outside, he smiled as only a madman could.

"You came alone? But I prepared a little welcoming committee! Never mind, at least you're here now. Tell me, are you hungry? I sent the staff away so I could enjoy this in peace. There's a wonderful view and it would be such a shame to let Sar-adin's hard work go to waste, especially as he's become such a good friend of yours."

So Barba had known! That at least explained the Demons at Sar-adin's feet outside and the dagger in his belly. Ned could see the knuckles in Benissimo's hand turn white and his whip was wagging now, like the tail of a lion before a lunge.

"Stop this! Stop this madness before it's too late!"

Barbarossa's eyes were wild and dark, his bowler hat was missing and his clothes torn.

"Madness? You're as bad as these two. Atticus, aren't you going to say anything to our guests? My brother and the children have had an exhausting journey."

Ned realised that Benissimo was right – Barbarossa had quite clearly lost his mind.

"He's dead, you fool, and no doubt by your own hand!"

Barbarossa looked at his brother and squinted, then back to the battlefield.

"Dead? Dead, dead, dead. Oh yes, that's right, though Fife put up quite the fight before I finished him. We had a difference of opinion if I recall rightly – it's been quite a day. You see, dear brother, everyone *wants* something. The Shar there wanted wealth – he saw this whole operation as a business opportunity. As for Fife, well… he thought he might walk away from it all with Europe – imagine that? I suppose in hindsight that is what they were promised, but in the end, you see, we couldn't escape one rather important issue."

As he spoke, Lucy took the bag from her shoulder and Benissimo edged forward. By the hole in the ground Ned could see more of the ink-like fluid seeping up and over its edge.

"Which is?" asked Benissimo.

"I WANT IT ALL!"

Benissimo looked to the window. Outside, two of the *Daedali* were burning and one was crashing to the ground. The Central Intelligence's Guardians had initially been designed to fight Demons and they were doing so now to great effect as the fair-folk charged the fortress.

"The Guardians have turned, your Demons are losing

and your ships have been knocked from the sky," tried Benissimo, hoping even now that his brother might see sense.

"Look again, *fratello*."

Ned saw it first. Along the ground at the forest's edge and on their side of the fortress the same oily darkness was spreading, creeping through the mud and up metal ramparts. Benissimo, the Viceroy and Mr Fox's forces were too engaged in the battle to see, for what little good it would have done them.

Bene recoiled in horror. "You're going to kill them all?!"

"I don't want to really, but our friend has a terrible hunger," Barbarossa said, and looked to his hole in the floor and the darkness forming at its edges.

"Now, Lucy, NOW!" barked Benissimo, and his arm ripped forward, striking at Barbarossa with his whip.

The butcher took the lashing with an ugly grin and launched himself at his brother. In a second they were on the floor and rolling, arms flailing and eyes locked.

Lucy almost tore the bag apart as she pulled out the Heart Stone.

"Lucy, the Source back in Annapurna," said Ned, thinking fast, "it's connected, literally, to magic, to everything. If the Tinker's right and it was designed to work like the Heart Stone, then we have to connect to it, the way we did before."

The Darkening King's inky fluid bubbled up from the chamber's hole and began to flow more freely now, on to the ground and towards Ned and Lucy.

"Well, whatever we do – we have to do it now!"

Ned got down on his knees next to Lucy. Even as he took her hand and they placed their other hands on the stone's cool surface, he could feel the Amplification-Engine at his finger stir. Beneath the skin its tiny tendrils came alive, connecting to his every nerve, and in there, in that brief moment, he felt Lucy with him. The stone warmed, either from Ned and Lucy's touch or with a power all of its own.

"I think it's working," gasped Lucy.

Around them the oozing darkness rose, till Ned heard his familiar quaking behind him.

"Unt!" it whimpered. "Unt, unt, unt."

"NOT NOW, GORRN!"

"*ChHillLdDrrENn.*"

Ned could feel a building power, not in the stone itself, but connected to it. Like the Source, it was a conduit for magic itself, and like the Darkening King it had a voice, but a voice without words. How could Ned speak to it? He tried in the same way he used his ring – to bring it under his control, to tell it what he wanted it to do…

"Ned? Ned, we're losing it – the connection's fading!"

From the great hole a gush of black fluid tore upwards, striking at Ned and Lucy, while the Heart Stone was sent skittering across the ground. To his right, Lucy lay howling in pain.

As soon as the creature touched his skin, Ned felt all the light and joy of the world being drawn out of him; his every happy thought, of his mum and dad, of dear old Gummy and Arch, of Lucy and George, suddenly distant and dark. There was nothing but an empty void, an endless darkness, and it called his name.

"*NnEedD.*"

CHAPTER 77

The End of Everything

The room was split. To one side the two brothers fought; on the other Ned stood watching as Lucy desperately searched for the Heart Stone. Between them all was the Darkening King.

Ned's mouth hung open. Every hair on his neck and arms prickled and his mouth ran dry. He'd thought he knew what fear was, what the face of terror looked like. He'd thought he had faced it before, but in front of him, here and now, the end of everything was becoming all too real, grotesque and black and seemingly without end.

The Darkening King rose higher, not as a single creature but as a dripping half-formed thing. Its surface billowed and bubbled, rearing up then falling away again as it clung to its first moments of new life.

On his feet now, Barbarossa took his dear Bessy and

hurled the cleaver at his brother with all his might. Benissimo ducked and it struck the pillar behind him, lodging noisily in its stone. Benissimo returned in kind with a flame-tipped lashing of his whip, and again the butcher took the lashing and grinned. The pupils of his eyes were so large now that there was almost no white in them at all and his mouth was locked in a smile full of hunger and hate.

"You know, I tried to turn the boy. I came to his tent last night, but he wouldn't listen. No one controls the Heart Stone, Bene – not the Fey, nor Tiamat before them. Do you see now? Do you understand how futile all this is?"

The Ringmaster breathed, his chest heaving, eyes and arms burning to fight. "And what if he had fallen? Dear old Barba would have let them all live?"

"The Darkening King needed a battle to rise, just enough killing to bring him back. If Ned had listened and your army had knelt, I could have stopped it before it came to *this*."

Bene's arm pointed to the battlefield and the encroaching darkness outside. "How can you not see it? We're the Darkening King's pawns, *both of us*. Hundreds of years we've fought and it's all led to this, to that horror behind you. It's going to feed on them and it's going to feed on everything till there's nothing left."

The butcher stopped and turned to see that the Darkening King almost filled the arched window behind him.

"You're wrong. A Demon's word is binding. He will give me the world." But even as he said it, Benissimo could hear the cracking in his brother's voice.

"Sar-adin betrayed you – he was bound by his word, wasn't he? Our father made a deal with the Darkening King, without even knowing, but he didn't get what he wanted, did he? What are you really going to rule, Barba, when this monster kills everything? It will just be you and I and bones, till the end of time."

As Benissimo pleaded, Barbarossa looked slow and listless, as though waking from a dream. He turned to the beast, watching it grow and grow, and seemed to finally understand.

"Kills *everything*?"

"We have to stop it."

"Our curse – our lifeblood – is his. It cannot be stopped, unless…"

Barbarossa's eyes grew wide. He knew now what Benissimo already understood. To end the Darkening King they would both have to die, here and now.

"*StToP!*"

The room shook and the Darkening King lashed out. This time it struck both brothers to the floor violently.

"The Heart Stone, Lucy, FIND IT!" yelled Ned.

"*STtTopP!*"

As it bellowed, the great wall of blackness formed and reformed. First a row of gnashing teeth, then clawed limbs and horned heads. As he watched the beast desperately trying to find its form, Ned realised something as incredible as it was unlikely – the Darkening King was scared.

"Stop?" Ned screamed. "And what will happen to them? What will happen to the BBB, to the fair-folk, *to the rest of the world?*"

"*THheYy aRre FfoOoD.*"

The beast filled one half of the room now. All round it great arms rose up like snakes ready to pounce, and within its centre two eyes of burning black light peered down on him.

"You're wrong," said Ned. "They're living, breathing men, women and wonders, who care and feel, and they're dying in their thousands to stop you, because everything you are is wrong!"

"*THhEy'Re wWeEakK.*"

"*They're innocent!*"

As the words came out of him, a rage in Ned's chest burned bright and true. He didn't care about fear, he didn't care how old or evil the beast in front of them was, and of its own accord his ring fired. He struck at the creature, using slabs of stone flooring, ripping pillars from their bases and hurling them with abandon. Atoms fired and fizzed, blasted and crackled, as Ned filled the air with his rage. The more he struck, the more the beast changed, morphing from one shape to another, striking at the ground with black spears for claws.

From the corner of his eye, Ned saw a streak of light. Benissimo's whip tore through the air, and next to it, Barbarossa's cleaver struck out, both aiming at the creature, deep at its core.

"*EnNouGhH!*"

A hundred arms poured out of the beast like a swarm of giant insects. Again the two brothers were knocked to the ground. One of its claws was about to hit Ned, when Gorrn tore up from the ground, defiantly blocking its path.

"UNT!"

And a second later, Gorrn was no more.

"Gorrn?!"

The beast now filled the room entirely. Two great arms

and legs clearly formed, the rest of its hideous body still snarling and twisting to find its final shape. All daylight from the window was blocked, the room now lit only by the flickering fire from the butcher's hearth. In its folds of black upon black Ned could see two great eyes, glowing and cruel.

"DdieE!" boomed the monster and its blackness closed all around them. Ned held his breath, all light and hope extinguished... and then Lucy took his hand.

"Stop," she said quietly, her eyes shut tight, and the beast recoiled.

For a second everything was still.

"Take it," said Lucy, and put the Heart Stone in Ned's hand.

"What did you do?"

"I'm still doing it."

A tear was rolling down Lucy's cheek and her hands were shaking. Ned watched in horror, as did both Bene and Barbarossa from the other side of the room.

"Y-you're in its mind, Lucy! It will kill you!"

"You're going to have to do this bit without me, Ned."

Benissimo took Barbarossa's arm and together they faced the source of their curse and power, each knowing what they must do. The strangest thing of all, beyond the united brothers, was that Benissimo was smiling as truly and calmly as the old goat knew how.

Ned looked at the Heart Stone. What could he say? What words could he use? How could you control a thing so powerful? Perhaps that was the point – perhaps he couldn't control it. When Ned worked his ring, he controlled it with his will, but the Heart Stone couldn't be forced, it had to agree, and for that to happen, it would need to be asked a question.

And then he heard the voice of Tiamat in his head, when he'd asked him for help: "DO NOT ASK ME – *ASK THE HEART STONE.*"

And quite suddenly Ned Armstrong knew exactly what he had to do.

The room shook and Lucy wavered. Ned took one last look at his friend, at Benissimo and Barbarossa, and then closed his eyes.

In the depths of his mind he felt the Heart Stone's wordless voice again, and his ring finger thrummed with power. From his lips poured four letters, and as he said them, Benissimo and Barbarossa lunged at the beast.

"Help?" asked Ned in barely a whisper.

And his ring fired.

CHAPTER 78

Light and Dark

Seeing, Telling and Feeling. These were the foundations of an Engineer's powers. How they split and reformed atoms to their will. What coursed now through Ned's mind and body had no beginning or end. It was pure power, a surge of blinding energy amplified not only by his ring but by the Heart Stone and the magic it drew upon, and as it did so, the rock in his palm grew hot, breaking away like particles of flowing dust till the Heart Stone was no more. Energy, light and sparking, burning atoms poured out of Ned, from his hands and eyes and mouth.

"NoOoOoo!"

He looked for just long enough to see the monster screaming with a hundred misshapen mouths, its form across the walls, the ceiling and floors retreating, shrinking

444

and cowering till in a final violent shockwave of light and dark, there was nothing left of it at all.

The room became blurred and strange. Ned was barely aware of Lucy bending over him, tears pouring readily down her cheeks. She was shaking him, her hands frantic across his face, but her words were distant and soft. The walls around them were crumbling, the great window shattered, and where Benissimo and his brother had lunged, there was only an empty hole, dark and quiet and empty.

The last thing Ned saw was a heavily panting Alice. The old girl had come running and was trumpeting wildly, her trunk now tight round his waist.

CHAPTER 79

Presents

Ned did not see how the Demons and their Darklings fled. How, one by one, Barba's remaining *Daedali* raised their white flags. He didn't see the faces of the fair-folk or their new allies rejoicing. And long after the fires had smouldered their last and King Antlor had reclaimed the forest, he did not see Lucy watching over him with George.

Almost two days later, the very first things Ned Armstrong *did* see were the faces of his mum and dad.

"Mum, Dad?"

No sooner had he opened his mouth than they pulled him in a human tug-of-war, each of them hugging the arm or shoulder nearest, till the Armstrongs were sitting at the edge of his bed, in quiet, well-earned joy.

"Lucy and George, are they—"

"They're fine, son. It's over — *it's over*!"

And though he knew his dad was right, that it really *was* over, he couldn't hope to truly believe it.

"Are you sure? Please tell me you're sure."

He looked up to his mother's eyes and she smiled. "Barbarossa's gone, darling, and so has his monster."

And what had started on a birthday with the scratching of nails at his sitting-room's patio doors had finally come to an end. But just as he was beginning to believe it, his parents turned quiet.

"Are you two all right?"

"Bene would have loved this," his dad finally managed.

Ned thought back to the fortress and the look on Benissimo's face. "Be happy for him — he got what he wanted in the end and he was smiling. I think he was relieved. Barba went willingly. It'll never make up for what he did, but Bene found peace in it, I'm sure."

Benissimo had given his life for them all and he had done so asking for nothing in return. Despite Ned's words and the truth of them, he knew that he had lost one of the greatest and most noble men he would ever meet and that he and the world that the Ringmaster had saved would be poorer without him.

He looked around his once bare quarters in the Nest.

Every part of it, from the walls to the desk to its polished concrete floors, was covered in the strangest assortment of objects he'd ever seen. Marble busts, oil paintings and letters. Flowers, pastries, locks of hair and rare silks. The largest pile by far was of actual gold and next to it stood piles and piles of cash in almost every currency.

"What's been going on?!"

His dad laughed. "You, my boy, are really rather famous. When Fox contacted the jossers, they sent their tanks and troops, but they also sent word to just about every news outlet on the planet. Everyone knows what's happened, what you and Lucy did, and they've been sending gifts from both sides of the Veil for the past twenty-four hours."

Ned saw a particularly strange object lying on his desk. "Is that what I think it is?"

"The Stag King's great horn. Apparently if you blow it he'll come to you, no matter where you are – he and the herd will hear it."

"They're actually pretty scary – I think I'll leave it where it is, thanks."

"There's more. We've heard from Lemnus. Seems his people have forgiven him for ridding them of the Heart Stone. Turns out they're grateful too, and want you to visit them in Dublin, which by the way, we absolutely forbid."

"So the Heart Stone – they don't want it back?"

"It's gone, Ned – whatever you did unmade it. No one's getting it now."

Ned thought of the dragon in the cave. How desperate and full of anger it had been.

"What about Tiamat?"

"According to Antlor's herd, the dragon let out a cry when the Heart Stone was destroyed. Whether it was a source of Tiamat's power or its actual heart, we'll never know. The dragon is solid rock now, a part of the mountain it lived in."

Before he could ask what had happened to his parents and the Tinker, or how they beat the Central Intelligence, his door slid open.

"Hello, old bean," smiled George.

There was a crack by the great ape's side and Lucy jostled him out of the way.

"Now you look here, young lady, I got to the door first!"

"Button it, monkey. Ned, you are never going to believe what's happening in Gearnish."

CHAPTER 80

Mr Fox

Mr Fox quit his job with the BBB shortly after his return to Dover. He realised an hour or so later that he had nowhere to go, no family to return to and no place to call home. Having been a man who handled stress rather well – in fact, better than nearly every operative the BBB had ever had – he took to the realisation well enough.

Unfortunately, despite having saved Siberia from a nuclear bomb and playing a key part in preventing the end of the world in general, there were issues with his decision. Mr Fox had no name, no proof of identification, no dental records or public records with his name on them of any kind. Because of this, he had no way to open a bank account, which wasn't as bad as it sounded, as he had no money to put in one anyway. So when the prime minister tracked him down and offered him a job ("on behalf of the entire world"), he was happy to accept. It turned out that there were other ways to save people that did not involve violence.

Within a week, he became one of the most famous people in the world, not because he was magical or special, but because those who were, trusted him. Needless to say, there were a lot of emails – several hundred million, in fact – and had it not been for the diligence of his team, led by Mr Badger, the one he really cared about might never have found him.

Her name was Elizabeth and she had loved him, apparently with all of her heart. But the Darkling that had snatched her had dropped her in its escape and she had sustained a bump to the head that for a while had lost her her memories.

Months later, just as they were slowly returning, Mr Fox had joined the BBB to have his own removed. Better to live without knowing anything about her than to live without her. Elizabeth had searched for him year after year so was rather shaken to find out not only that the world she lived in was one filled with magic but that the love of her life had been a part of keeping it whole.

Mr Fox looked in the mirror. He was wearing a dark blue suit. He could get away from grey, but suits would take months to get out of his system. Tonight he would re-meet Elizabeth for the very first time and unsurprisingly she knew his real name. Mr Fox was not one to flap, not even when facing down a twelve-foot ogre. But today and now, as the butterflies formed in his tummy, Mr Fox realised that he was pleasingly and giddily terrified.

CHAPTER 81

George and the Jungle

Ned, George and Lucy stepped through the mirror and into the beating heat of the Amazonian jungle. George was unnaturally quiet, especially for him, and both Ned and Lucy knew he was suffering from a terrible bout of nerves.

"George, you really don't have anything to worry about. Stop being so silly."

"Easy for you to say, madam. You aren't about to be reunited with your missing species."

Of the many things to have taken place since the discovery of the Hidden and their subsequent reintegration with the rest of the world, Mr Fox's discovery of George's fellow gorillas had been, at least to Ned and his friends, the best. Using the Tinker's surveillance network, which had been greatly expanded with the cooperation of several global powers and independent corporations, a city hidden deep in the rainforest had been spotted from satellites high up over the earth's atmosphere. On contact, the gorilla citizens living there had asked to be left alone but had expressed great excitement at the thought of meeting George, and two of its more elderly apes believed that they not only knew how he had come away from the city as a baby, but exactly who he was.

"If they really are your parents, George, you have nothing to fear. I should know, eh?" said Ned. "And besides, you'll have so much to talk about. You do know they have six varieties of banana here, right?"

"Actually, old bean, I do. There's Prata, da Terra, Maca and Caturra, Danica and my personal favourite – Ouro. Ouro means 'gold' by the way, and—"

"Hush, George, they're waiting," said Lucy.

The great ape leant down low and hugged his two wards.

"I shall miss you, you know."

"We'll see you soon, George. I promise," said Ned.

And with that, George stepped towards the jungle. Ahead of him there was a loud grunting of joy in the leaves and bushes. George turned back to them and smiled that great big toothy smile of his, and then he ran – ran to meet his past and future with every bound.

CHAPTER 82

Toys

The factory of the Central Intelligence was as hot or hotter than the Brazilian rainforest, though much improved since their last visit. Now freed, minutians walked and worked busily, and gone were the thundering pistons of its great and terrible machine. It still controlled a great part of the city's more complex workings, but the day-to-day running of its production lines had been happily handed back to its citizens. Gearnish no longer made weapons, or Guardians; no longer made anything capable of causing harm. That lesson had been learnt and at a high enough price. Today and for evermore, the city of Gearnish made the very thing that had brought it its fame and fortune in the first place.

"Toys, master and miss – toys, toys, toys! We've orders all over the world now, thanks to Mr Fox and his whistle-blowing. The jossers'll pay a fortune for our wind-up marvels, and if it weren't for my great-uncle Faisal here, we'd be well behind schedule."

Ned turned to the newly cast face of the Central Intelligence. It had a rather fatherly sort of look and, aside from the numerous cables protruding from its head, reminded him of the mild-mannered Cogsworth he had met in Amsterdam.

"Master Ned," steamed the great machine, "I'm afraid Whiskers' body was melted down to ashes before I could do anything, but, like me, his soul was transferred to the machine-mind instantly. In any case, he's been rebuilt from top to bottom and we've added a few enhancements I think you're going to like."

Ned didn't want any enhancements – he just wanted his old dog-mouse again, and by his side.

The newly formed Debussy Mark Twelve came running out to meet him, tail wagging, and ran through Ned's legs and right up into Lucy's arms.

"Err, thanks, I think," grinned Ned. "It's good to see you, boy."

CHAPTER 83

Everywhere

A last push through cool glass and they stepped into Ned's old bedroom at Number 222 Oak Tree Lane. On Ned's request it had still not been touched.

"I can't believe you were ever this messy, Ned."

"Yeah, it's pretty bad. I think it's going to be a project for when I get back."

Outside they heard the flapping of Terry and Olivia Armstrong.

"Livvy! Livvy, I can't find my shoes – we're going to be late for work."

"Well, where were they the last time you saw them?"

"On my blasted feet!"

Ned and Lucy stepped out on to the upstairs landing. It was hard to believe that the world owed Ned's parents such a great debt; that they, along with Ned and Lucy, had played such a key role in saving it. What Ned and Lucy saw now was chaos, and the black fumes of burning toast coming up from the kitchen.

"Ned? Lucy!" said Terry Armstrong. "Good Lord, I'd almost forgotten. Have you seen my shoes?"

Lucy blinked her eyes shut and smiled. "Bathroom, under a pink towel."

"Thank you, dear. Livvy, they're here!"

Ned's mum came out of the master bedroom wearing a smart grey suit. She had rarely looked more elegant in her life.

"Darlings, how were George and the Tinker?"

"Great, thanks. George calmed down once we got there. And look what Faisal made us!"

Ned's mum looked at Lucy's shoulder, where Whiskers sat, wagging its tail like a dog about to play fetch.

"Whiskers, welcome back! I must say, I'm very happy to see you out of that machine and back to your old self. Ned, Lucy, are you sure about this?"

"Yes, Olivia."

"Quite sure, Mum. Do you have it?"

"Terry, go and get them the jacket, would you?"

Ned's dad walked to his bedroom and began rifling through the closet.

"Are you two going to be OK, Mum?"

"Well, it won't feel quite right without you, but at least we'll be busy. It really was very kind of Mr Fox to give us both jobs."

"You and the rest of the troupe. Poor man needs all the help he can get. What was the title the UN gave him again?"

"Chief liaison and president of josser–Hidden affairs. It's going to take years to integrate them properly, but if anyone can speak for them both and fairly, it's Fox. Besides which, no one else would step forward to deal with what was left of Barba's Demons or their Darklings."

"Self-imposed exile… do you really think they'll stick to it?"

"If they know what's good for them. Fox explained the effects of thermonuclear weaponry in detail to them and how he stopped the bomb from being dropped. They've agreed to stick to their side of the Veil permanently in return for being left alone."

Ned's dad returned with the jacket Ned had asked for. Of the many gifts he and Lucy had been given, it was without doubt the best. The Glimmerman's jacket had countless rectangular mirrors all over it and would open just about every mirror-portal in the world.

Ned put it on, and he and Lucy walked back into his room. His parents hugged them both, his mum looking slightly teary as she did so.

"Take as many weeks as you need. We'll be right here when you're ready, and Gummy and Arch could do with a couple more friends."

"*Are* you ready, Ned?" grinned Lucy.

"No, not even a bit."

"Don't worry – you've got me. How about you, Whiskers?"

"Scree."

Finally Lucy looked to a spot just by Ned's neck and shoulder. "Gorrn?"

There came a tiny "Arr" and what was left of his old familiar peered nervously from behind Ned's neck. Gorrn's surviving shadow was barely the size of a finger and would be little use for fighting or biting. It didn't matter – the Engineer and Medic weren't really planning on either.

"Son?"

"Yes, Dad?"

"Where will you go?"

"Everywhere, Dad. I think we're going to go everywhere."

And with that, Ned Armstrong and Lucy Beaumont, with their mouse and shadow, stepped through the mirror and were gone.

THE END

ACKNOWLEDGEMENTS

As this book ends, it's hard to know where to begin. Following Ned on his journey has been both a privilege and a joy and I could not have done it without the incredible team at HarperCollins. As I have come to discover, they are some of the most patient, hard-working and humorous people I have ever met, whether in person or through the impassioned and precise comments of a Word document.

And so to Nick Lake, Sam Stewart, Lily Morgan and Madeleine Stevens – thank you so much for everything you have done for me and the pages of this book – and to Manuel Šumberac for his brilliant cover illustrations and Elisabetta Barbazza for her inspired cover designs. I could not be more grateful for what you do or the way in which you do it.

I would also like to thank my agent, Paul Moreton, again, because I'm allowed to, and because he continues to be marvellous.

I thanked my friends and family in *The Gold Thief* – that does not make their continued support any less important, so thank you again.

Lastly to the four souls that share a house with me – you make me laugh and cry, but mostly laugh. You have done nothing but hinder every word of this book, but only because you're such exhaustingly good fun. I am as always beyond lucky that you're mine.